EVERYONE IS TALKING ABOUT

EVERYTHING YOU NEED TO SURVIVE THE APOCALYPSE

"*Everything You Need to Survive the Apocalypse* is funny, heart-wrenching, and true. An amazing debut."
>—Morgan Matson, author of *Amy & Roger's Epic Detour*

"Smart, honest, and thought-provoking, *Everything You Need to Survive the Apocalypse* is like nothing I've read before. What an amazing debut!"
>—Lisa Schroeder, author of *I Heart You, You Haunt Me*
>and *The Day Before*

"Curious, funny, and heartfelt."
>—Albert Borris, author of *Crash Into Me*

"A moving tale of the things that bring us together and the things that tear us apart. Klauss navigates the fragile landscape of faith, friendship, and love with wit and insight."
>—Carolee Dean, author of *Take Me There*

"Razor-sharp, hilarious, and so smart. *Everything You Need to Survive the Apocalypse* is the book you were afraid to let yourself want."
>—Hannah Moskowitz, author of *Invincible Summer* and *Break*

"A funny, thought-provoking look at the friends you lose and the friends you keep, the girls you get and the girls who get away, and the big questions you ask, even when they don't have answers."

—Leila Sales, author of *Mostly Good Girls* and *Past Perfect*

"High school only feels like the end of the world. What do you need to survive? Good friends, faith it will all work out, belief in yourself, and a sense of humor. *Everything You Need to Survive the Apocalypse* delivers on all fronts. I would recommend this book in your survival kit instead of bottled water and extra batteries."

—Eileen Cook, author of *The Education of Hailey Kendrick* and *Getting Revenge on Lauren Wood*

"Struggles with faith, family, friendship, and first love aren't the end of the world, but sometimes they feel like it to fifteen-year-old Phillip Flowers. Author Lucas Klauss skillfully and honestly portrays the complexities of teenage life, as Phillip discovers that the only thing scarier than, say, a universe-imploding supercollider accident is having to pick up the pieces and find the answers—or at least the questions—when life goes on."

—Michael Northrop, author of *Gentlemen* and *Trapped*

"A powerful, thoughtful story about the wonders of first love and a young man's quest to find a truth he can believe and live for. Lucas Klauss has written with courage about love and faith."

—Francisco X. Stork, author of *Marcelo in the Real World*

EVERYTHING YOU NEED TO SURVIVE THE APOCALYPSE

LUCAS KLAUSS

SIMON PULSE
New York   London   Toronto   Sydney   New Delhi

SIMON PULSE

An imprint of Simon & Schuster Children's Publishing Division
1230 Avenue of the Americas, New York, NY 10020
First Simon Pulse hardcover edition January 2012
Copyright © 2012 by Lucas Klauss
All rights reserved, including the right of reproduction in whole or in part in any form.
SIMON PULSE and colophon are registered trademarks of Simon & Schuster, Inc.
For information about special discounts for bulk purchases, please contact
Simon & Schuster Special Sales at 1-866-506-1949 or business@simonandschuster.com.
The Simon & Schuster Speakers Bureau can bring authors to your live event.
For more information or to book an event contact the Simon & Schuster Speakers Bureau
at 1-866-248-3049 or visit our website at www.simonspeakers.com.
Designed by Karina Granda
The text of this book was set in Adobe Caslon.
Manufactured in the United States of America
2 4 6 8 10 9 7 5 3 1
Library of Congress Cataloging-in-Publication Data
Klauss, Lucas.
Everything you need to survive the apocalypse / Lucas Klauss.
p. cm.
Summary: A fifteen-year-old high school student becomes involved with an evangelical
Christian girl in spite of his father's adamant atheism and his own confusion about life.
ISBN 978-1-4424-2388-6 (hardcover : alk. paper)
[1. Evangelicalism—Fiction. 2. Christianity—Fiction. 3. Grief—Fiction.
4. Interpersonal relations—Fiction.] I. Title.
PZ7.K67822Ev 2012 [Fic]—dc23
2011031392
ISBN 978-1-4424-2390-9 (eBook)

For Mom and Dad

ONE

Ow.

Ow.

Ow.

Pain cuts through my foot each time it hits the pavement. I hobble and curse, and then I stumble onto a nearby lawn. The muggy air feels like gauze against my face.

Asher and Mark stop running too. We all catch our breath.

"What happened?" Asher says, planting his hands on his hips and doing that thing where he shows his top row of teeth as he inhales. The front two are perfect and white like crunchy gum.

With my butt perched on the curb, I lean back on my hands. The grass feels soft but prickly and it smells as much like chemicals as gas.

"I bent my foot," I say. "On the curb."

"What?" Mark says, cocking his head sideways.

"He stepped on the curb," Asher says. "And his foot bent."

He demonstrates with his own foot, twisting it sideways.

Mark starts to jog in place. He's lanky and looks kind of like a giraffe when he runs. "Dude, get up," he says. "If Ferret sees us just standing around, he's gonna—"

"Yeah, I know." Ferret, otherwise known as Randy Farragut, is the thirty-year-old assistant coach of boys' cross-country. During practice he rides his bike along the course to make sure everyone is running as fast and as far as he thinks they should.

And he despises the three of us.

Partially because we sometimes don't run as fast and as far as he thinks we should. Partially because we obviously don't care. Partially because everybody started calling him Ferret this summer and he decided that we were responsible. And we kind of *were*, but . . .

Anyway, it's mostly because he's a dick.

And even if he does believe that I injured myself, which he won't, he'll still bust Asher and Mark for standing around.

Which means sprints. A lot of sprints.

And a lot of public mockery when girls' cross-country catches up to us in a couple of minutes.

"Try to get up," Asher says. "Maybe it's okay now." He wipes the sweat around his sports goggles with his ratty Atlanta Cup tournament T-shirt, from when we still played soccer.

I push up from the grass, take a step, and grimace from the pain. I sit back down.

"Just go," I say.

"You sure?" Asher says.

Mark kicks the toe of his sneaker against the asphalt and glances behind us again.

I shake my head. "Save yourselves."

They laugh at me, and I think: This is why we're friends. Because if either of them were in my position, I'd leave them, too.

Mark points behind me. "Hide behind that mailbox."

In a yard off the nearby cul-de-sac, I see it. As big around as a column and made of brick, it's more like a mail *fortress*. It's perfectly sized to conceal a crouching coward, but—

"Just rest for a minute and take the shortcut," Mark says. "We'll meet you." He looks back again, his eyes a little panicked. The Slow Freshmen—the only group of boys slower than us—are about to catch up. "Come on, dude."

"Okay, okay. Go."

Asher and Mark take off, and I push myself up again. I press my weight onto my good leg and limp to the cul-de-sac, flexing my hands and cringing as I go. I plop down onto a patch of shady grass behind the mailbox and shift myself so I can't be seen from the main road. I gasp.

And then I hang my head and say, "Dammit."

Because now I'm trapped. My ankle already really hurt, and I just made it worse. There's no way I can meet up with Asher and Mark before Ferret sees them. And when he sees them and doesn't see me, he'll come hunting for me, the lame gazelle at the watering hole. Or whatever ferrets hunt.

I'll be embarrassingly easy to find. But, to Ferret, the fact that I'm even trying to hide will be proof that I'm faking, that I really am as lazy as he keeps saying. Even though he's the one who rides around on his Schwinn while the rest of us suffer.

He'll insult me. He'll humiliate me. He might even suspend me from the team.

And I'll try to defend myself, but not hard enough. I'll just take what he dishes out and call him Ferret behind his back. Because that's what I do.

I hear a group of girls run by, their sharp breathing and the clap of their shoes against the pavement. I imagine Ferret barking at them to come see Phillip the Gutless Wonder.

I can't stay here. After the girls pass, I'll stagger away, no matter how much it hurts. I'll limp through people's yards and sneak back to the locker room and never come back.

I mean, I might come back if—

Footsteps.

I hear footsteps.

One set of footsteps. On this street. Coming closer.

I didn't hear Ferret's bike, but I wasn't really paying attention.

No no no.

My body tenses up. A cold drop of sweat dangles from my eyebrow. I want to swat it, but only my heart moves, like a dragonfly hovering in my chest.

The footsteps move softly. Closer.

I look up.

Standing, towering over me, green eyes catching the light.

There's this girl.

TWO

I've never seen her before. I would have remembered.

Her cheeks are round and faintly freckled. Her hair is a deep, dark brown, and her curls strain against the blue stretchy band that lays them flat against her head. She wears black baggy soccer shorts and a gray tank top over a purple sports bra.

Her boobs are amazing.

And her legs. They're toned. And her body is lean, but not angular and tiny, like how hot girls are supposed to look. She's unconventionally hot.

That's how I'll describe her to Asher and Mark. They'll know exactly what I mean.

"Hi," her mouth says.

I mean *she* says. She's talking to me. And looking confused and a little weirded out.

My mouth has to say something.

Say something.

"Hi," I say. "I'm just . . ." I wave toward the street, trying to figure out how to explain this. I look back at her. Her eyes pin me to the ground.

I should just tell her. "Okay, so I bent my ankle over there. Running. And it really hurt. So I couldn't run anymore. And then I came over here to . . . rest. And kind of to hide, I guess. But obviously that didn't really work, so . . ."

She looks at me like I'm a barely amusing child. "Hide?"

Awesome. She already thinks I'm an idiot. "Well," I say, "mostly hiding from Ferret. I mean, Coach Farragut, but—"

She laughs. "Is that what you guys call him?"

"Yeah," I say. "Actually, I came up with it."

Mark would claim he did, but he totally didn't.

And even if he did, he's not here right now. That laugh was for *me*.

"That's mean," she says. She's still smiling, though.

"Well, *he's* kind of mean."

She looks off toward the road, her smile fading, and she shrugs.

What does that mean? Did I offend her? Should I apologize? I try to figure out the right thing to say, but the silence stretches on, and she's still looking away from me.

Shit. This happens every time I try to talk to a girl. I make things awkward, and then I panic and make things more awkward.

And then I slink away. "I should probably get back before—"

"He's coming." She points at the road.

"What?" I say, twisting back to see, but the rise of the yard blocks my view.

"Ferret." Her lip curls up just a little as she says it.

She still thinks it's funny.

She still thinks *I'm* funny.

She needs to leave. Now. Because it's about to get really not funny.

"Um," I say, "he's probably going to yell at me, so . . ."

She looks at the mailbox, silent. Her lips hang open just a fraction of an inch. She stares at the box, like she's trying to see into it.

"What's your name?" she says.

"Phillip."

"I'm Rebekah. Like in the Bible."

It must be obvious that I'm trying to figure out what she means, because she attempts to explain.

"With a *k* and an *h*."

I nod to pretend I know what she's talking about. And then I hear the whirr of rubber against the blacktop.

"Hi, Mr. Farragut," Rebekah says, waving toward the street.

I look at her amazing boobs again. It's only fair. I'm about to be fatally humiliated.

"Ms. Joseph," Ferret says, in his sleaziest Georgia drawl. "I keep on telling you to call me Randy."

He doesn't coach the girls. How does she know him?

Ferret skids into view, brakes with a squeal, and glares down at me, face tight with disgust. "Flowers," he says. Never my first name. Always Flowers.

"Coach," I say, nodding, wishing I'd called him Randy.

"What's goin' on here?" he says, squinting against the sun. He swoops his leg over like he's dismounting a motorcycle and leans the bike against the mailbox. "Lounging around as usual, Flowers?"

He smiles a little Ferret smile.

I grab a fistful of grass in my hand, trying to think of something to say that won't sound obnoxious or whiny.

But she does it for me. "Phillip hurt his ankle," Rebekah says. "So I told him he could rest in my yard."

Her yard. I was cowering behind *her* mailbox.

"I didn't realize you two knew each other," Ferret says. His tan skin shines like leather. "Anyway, your friends told me about your ankle too. Funny how you got all the way over here, Flowers."

"I wanted some shade. I kind of stumbled over."

"Sounds to me like another one of your funny stories, Flowers. Looks like you even tricked a nice young lady."

"He didn't trick me," Rebekah says.

Ferret raps his fingers along the hard cushion of his bike seat. "Ms. Joseph, I know you wouldn't lie. But Flowers is known to exaggerate the truth—poorly—and I would hate it if he made you an accomplice. I don't know what you were doing, but I saw y'all from over there." He points to the road. "And it seemed to me like you were just having a nice little chat."

"We were," she says, her voice sharp.

Ferret's eyebrows rise. "Really? What about?"

She hesitates for a second. "Phillip was just saying he might want to come to Wednesday nights."

Ferret guffaws.

I stare at her, expecting some clue as to what that means, but she's just looking at Ferret and fiddling with her ponytail.

He points at me. "I thought you were Catholic or something, Flowers."

I shake my head and wipe a creeping bead of sweat from my face. "Nope."

I have no idea why he thinks I'm Catholic or what that has to do with Wednesday nights or what the hell is going on right now.

Rebekah crosses her arms over her chest. "What if he *was* Catholic?"

Ferret's grin disintegrates, and he ducks his head to pretend to inspect the rubber on his handlebar. For a second he's speechless. "No, you're right, you're right," he says, nodding at Rebekah. "We welcome everyone, no exceptions." He pauses, and the grin crawls back onto his face. "Even you, Flowers."

I rip a fistful of grass.

Silence settles between the three of us. I hear the hum of a distant lawn mower. And the rhythmic steps of runners passing us by. Ferret and Rebekah turn their heads.

"You gonna let those girls pass you by, Ms. Joseph?" Ferret says.

"No," she says.

"Better get back out there, then."

"I will. Once I get some ice for Phillip."

Ice? Why is this girl being so nice to me? Did I accidentally woo her?

Ferret bites his bottom lip and nods his head slowly, as if he has the power to give her permission. "Alright," he says finally. "Flowers, I'll pretend I believe you this time. I have no idea how you plan on getting back to school with your ankle so busted up, but I'll let your friends know where you're at so they don't leave you." He mounts his bike, twisting his hands around the handlebars like he's revving the engine. He squints at me. "And I do look forward to seeing you Wednesday night. You too, Ms. Joseph."

And with that, he plants his foot on the pedal and charges off.

The sound of his tires fades, and then it's just me, her, the noise of the lawn mower, and my throbbing ankle.

I look up at her. I have a million questions.

Rebekah looks at her black sports watch. "Hold on," she says, and she sprints past me. I watch her run up the driveway, into the garage, and then into the house. The door slams.

Okay now.

I breathe. Deeply.

I test my ankle. Ow.

Okay. Okay. Okay. What is going on?

Apparently I'm going somewhere on Wednesday night. Ferret will be there. Rebekah will be there. And I didn't want to admit it at first, but it sounds like—

Like a church thing.

The door slams again. I turn back to see her walking out of the garage carrying a bulging brown plastic grocery bag and a wooden crutch.

"My aunt broke her leg last year," Rebekah says. "So she still has this." She stands over me, holding up the crutch. Then she squats down and plops the bag of ice in my hands.

We sit there for a moment, barely looking at each other.

"I don't exaggerate the truth," I say.

"What?"

"Ferret said that I 'exaggerate the truth,' but I don't. He just confuses bad excuses with lies."

She smiles. "Put the ice on your foot."

"Oh. Right." I put it on my foot. It's so cold I suck air through my teeth.

"You don't have to go on Wednesday if you don't want to. I'm sorry."

"No, I—"

"Because that wasn't fair." She lays the crutch on the grass next to me. It lies just off parallel to the sheer edge of the driveway. "I shouldn't have put you in that position. I just felt like he would go easier on you."

"Yeah."

She moves the crutch like she's trying to get it exactly parallel with the cement line. The thin beams of wood trample the grass as she shifts them back and forth. Her hands, small and surprisingly delicate, are so close to mine.

This never happens when I try to talk to a girl.

"You really shouldn't worry about it," she says. "It's not—"

"I'll go," I say.

For a moment she's still. Then she lets go of the crutch and jumps to her feet. "Good. It's Wednesday night at seven thirty at Wesley Road Faith Church. Okay?"

"Wednesday, seven thirty, Wesley Road Faith Church."

"Okay." She jogs toward the street. Her baggy soccer shorts make a sound like rustling paper. "I've gotta catch up with everybody. I'll see you. Bring friends if you want!" She runs, and disappears in front of the mailbox.

"Thanks," I call out.

And now it's just me, and the purr of the lawn mower, and the crutch, and the bag of ice, and my throbbing ankle.

And the hot, thrilling air in my lungs.

I'll go.

THREE

"One of you guys has to go with me."

As soon as I say this, Mark suddenly becomes very interested in his chicken sandwich, and Asher looks somewhere across the lunchroom like he didn't hear me.

I drop my pizza slice, and it lands with an oily slap. "Dudes," I say.

Dude is bond.

Dude should make one of these a-holes have to come with me to church.

"I don't know, dude," Mark says. "Like, youth group?"

"I guess," I say. "It's just some people."

"And some girl," Asher says. He brings a forkful of pale corn to his mouth. "Since when were you such a ladies' man?"

"Shut up. I didn't even do anything."

Asher leans back. "She just sounds a little—"

"Weird?" Mark says, and they laugh.

"What?" I say, my face heating up. "How is she weird?"

Asher shrugs and looks to Mark for words.

Mark is always happy to provide words. He gesticulates with his chicken sandwich. "Well, this girl that you've never seen before comes up to you out of nowhere and then tricks you into going to church? And she's supposedly hot?"

"*Unconventionally* hot. And she didn't *trick* me into going."

Mark points at me with the sandwich. "She told Ferret you were going to be there. She may be unconventionally hot, but she tricked you, dude. Because she wants to *convert* you." He takes a bite. "Not that you don't need it."

"Shut up," I say.

I look up at the blue and yellow banner hanging across the lunchroom that reads WELCOME BACK TO BAXTER HIGH, BOBCATS! and I have this urge to pitch my apple through it. I'm not angry because Asher and Mark are making fun of me—we do that all the time. I just really needed one of them to help me.

Because I can't be alone with this girl again. Coming up with a funny animal nickname for your coach only gets you so far. This time I'll have to have a real conversation with her, and I have no idea how to do that. I spend most of my time reading fantasy novels, playing computer games, and worrying about ways that human civilization will probably come to a fiery and terrible end.

I'm pretty sure girls don't like talking about those things. So I need someone to help me not talk about them. To say other things. To just be there.

Plus, there's no way I can tell Dad I'm going to church. Just no way. So I don't have a ride, and I need one of these people I'm tentatively calling my friends to provide one.

But I drop it for the rest of lunch, and we talk about other stuff, and they forget about it, and I pretend to forget about it. Finally the bell rings. The room erupts in a huge squeaking of metal chair legs and a great crushing of plastic trash.

One of these guys has to go with me. I decide to hone in on Asher. Yes, he's technically Hindu, but I'm vaguely atheist, and he's much more easily guilted than Mark, who's allegedly Catholic but actually a devout Mark-ist.

Asher scoops up his tray and heads for the trash. I follow, limping slightly, and catch his eye. "So you wanna help me out? Wednesday night?"

He sighs. "Yeah. I'm going. We were just messing with you, anyway." We toss our trash in the bin.

"Right, I know." I take my phone out, pretend to check the time. "So your dad can drive us or—"

"Yeah."

"Awesome."

Mark pushes through us, his bobbly head leading the way. "See ya later, turds."

Asher and I roll our eyes, flick him off behind his back, and turn separate ways to go to class.

FOUR

"Who is Margaret Thatcher?" Dad says.

Swoop-swish. He circles one of the $200 squares on the hand-drawn grid we use to keep score.

On TV one of the contestants buzzes in, and Alex confirms that "Who is Margaret Thatcher?" is the right question. But Dad never waits for Alex. He disdains Alex, as well as most of the people who appear on this show.

"I knew that," my brother says. Chris lies back in his usual spot on the big gray recliner, the cushions swallowing his skinny frame.

"Then why didn't you say it?" Dad asks. He combs the tuft of hair at his temple with the pen. His smile is a taunt.

"Didn't want to," Chris says, flicking his sock lint in a high arc toward Dad.

I need to get the next question. We did this all summer, and I could usually answer a few right away. But today I haven't gotten one yet, and Dad's closing in on me, even though he always starts off with negative $5,000 to help us out. It's just kind of hard to concentrate on the game right now—at this time tomorrow I'm supposed to be at church already.

Alex reads: "'In one of *his* finest hours, this prime minister . . .'"

I'm watching the screen, but from the corner of my eye I see Dad mouth something to Chris.

"Who is Churchill?" Chris says warily.

"Yep," Dad says. He leans over the table, circles the $400 space, and writes Chris's initials.

"Bullshit!" I say. "I saw that."

For a second Dad keeps a straight face, tapping the pen against the paper. But then his features melt into a smile and he leans back on the couch. "Okay," he says, laughing. "Four hundred dollars for Phillip."

"Daaaad," Chris says, rolling his eyes and pulling the lever on the side of the recliner so that he lies nearly flat.

Those are the rules. If Dad tries to help one of us and the other calls it, it's Bullshit, and the Bullshit Caller gets the points instead. Dad hasn't tried that in a while. He's a terrible liar.

And so am I, which might be a problem.

"You're right, you're right," Dad says. "You knew that one without me." He scratches his head with the pen, leaving a contrail of red on his shiny peach scalp. Meanwhile, the show's gone to commercials. Dad hits the mute button and starts adding up the scores so far.

This would be a good time to lie to him. He's focused on something else, and I'll have an excuse for not looking him in the eye.

I remind myself that he's making me do this. Even if he doesn't know it.

Because my dad isn't just an atheist—he's an atheist enthusiast.

16

He goes to see authors of atheist books when they come to Atlanta. He's helped pay for pro-atheism ad campaigns in New York and Los Angeles. He has a T-shirt with a design that's just the word "God" in a red circle with a red slash across it.

He never wears it in public, but still, he would freak if I told him I was going to church. I know from experience, actually.

But I have to go. I told her I would.

So I have to lie. Now.

Lie to him now.

"Hey, Dad," Chris says, popping up from his prone position, the gears of the chair complaining. His Flowers-brown hair flips into his eyes. "You know soccer practice starts next Tuesday, right?"

Dad's pen stops mid-zero. He looks up, the thought-creases creeping up his forehead. "Oh, right. Yeah." He nods. "Is that *three* days a week now?" He draws perfect cubes in the margins of the score sheet. He's an engineer, and when I was younger and used to draw, he gave me tips on how to make precise lines and shapes.

"Tuesday, Wednesday, Thursday," Chris says, pride creeping into his voice.

"Wow, that's a lot of work," Dad says. He's quickly drawn a small army of cubes. "I guess we won't be able to do this a whole lot anymore. Us three. It'll be just me and Phillip facing off most nights." He punches my thigh and smiles weakly.

This hurts.

"Uh, actually . . ." I say.

Dad looks at me quickly and then starts drawing more cubes. "Yeah?"

"I have, uh, this thing on Wednesday. Like, a study group. With Asher." My chest feels tight.

He leans back on the couch, dropping the pen onto the score sheet. It rolls in a small circle until it clinks against a coaster. "A study group already? The semester's barely begun."

"Chemistry looks pretty hard. And you know I'm not good with, like . . . science."

"Yes, you are. You just don't give yourself enough credit."

"Well, also it's that Dr. Baker wanted us to have study groups."

I just know he's going to call me on this. I'm *sweating*.

But he doesn't notice.

"Okay," he says. "We can work it out with Chris's practice. I'll drive you."

"No! Actually, Asher's dad is picking me up."

He looks at me, confused. Finally he smiles, just barely.

"Yeah," he says. "Of course."

He goes back to drawing cubes. When the commercials end, Chris has to tell him to turn the sound back on.

FIVE

Okay. My mom is dead.
    It was a long time ago.
    Everyone has their shit.
    I'm fine with mine.
    That's all.

SIX

"You two were planning to attend this meeting, correct? Or just observe from here?"

Mr. Venkataraman, Asher's dad, eyes me in the rearview mirror. He and Asher and I are sitting in the Venkatara-van (a name Asher still refuses to find funny), in the parking lot in front of Wesley Road Faith Church. The church is squat, flat, and brown, like an enormous toad. Above the big glass front doors, the word FAITH is spelled out in large white letters.

And the big lawn to the side of the church is alive with *them*.

There are so many of them. They play basketball on a half-court. They play volleyball, ten to a team, with a crisp, white net and chunky sand. They sit on benches in front of another brown building labeled YOUTH CENTER, with their legs folded under them, and they braid each other's hair.

"Do you see anybody we know?" I ask.

"Maybe," Asher says. "I mean, there's Corey Nash."

"People we *know*."

"Oh. Well, then. No."

"I don't see Rebekah, either."

"Oh, my, my, my," Mr. V says, grinning. "Who is Rebekah?"

"Dad, come on," Asher says.

"What? I'm allowed to drive you here and back but I'm not allowed to know who Rebekah is?"

"She's just a girl," I say.

"Then what are you waiting for?" Mr. V says. "Go tell her she looks pretty."

"Dad," Asher says, "that's not how it works."

Mr. V throws his hands up. "You boys think you know everything."

"*I* don't," I say.

"Then this one does," Mr. V says, reaching over and attempting a noogie on Asher. "He gets it from me!"

Asher ducks and tries to block the noogie, but Mr. V is unfazed. He clicks off his seat belt and reaches over with both arms. "Dad! Come on!" Asher says. He climbs out of the van and slams the door.

So I guess we're going to church now.

"Thanks, Mr. V," I say.

"No problem. Tell her she's pretty," he says.

I slide open the door. Asher and I look at each other and then at everybody else and then back at each other. Then we, the atheist and the Hindu, walk across the warm asphalt toward the church, listening to the bright sounds of the Christians.

"Do you see her anywhere?" Asher says.

"Not yet," I say. We've walked into the middle of the crowd. All around us people talk, laugh, chase each other, and even dance. But none of them are her.

Asher squints at his watch. "It's about to start. I don't want to go in there if we don't know anyone." He adjusts the arms of his glasses around his ears.

I haven't seen Rebekah at school, and I haven't been at practice since Monday, but I know I remember what she looks like. I scan the crowd again—and make accidental eye contact with a slightly older girl, probably a senior. Her hair is shoulder length and quiet blond, and she wears a bright red T-shirt that says THIRD ANNUAL YOUTH IN CHRIST CONFERENCE: WHAT WOULD JESUS THINK?

She smiles and starts walking toward us, her eyes locked on mine.

She's coming to reap our souls.

I shove my hands in my pockets and look elsewhere, but she smiles and weaves her way back into my vision.

"Phillip," Asher whispers urgently.

But it's too late. She's here.

"You look like you're lost," she says. Her round cheeks are flush with cheer.

"Sort of," I say, desperately searching the lawn. "We're waiting for somebody. I mean, we're supposed to meet them. Someone."

I'm so sure she's going to say, "I think you mean Jesus."

But she doesn't. "Who are you meeting?" she asks, still smiling.

Asher looks off across the parking lot like he's considering a quick escape.

"Rebekah?" I say.

And then somehow she becomes even happier. "Oh, Rebekah Joseph?"

"Do you know her?"

"Yeah! Rebekah's great! I love her. We've been so happy to have her join us."

"So, is she here, or . . . ?"

"Yeah, she's inside, I bet. She's always helping out before everything gets started. I'm Amanda, by the way." She thrusts her hand toward me, and I shake it and introduce myself.

She leaves her hand out by Asher, who is forced to draw his eyes back from the promise of the horizon. "Asher," he says.

"Oh," Amanda says. "Asher. I *love* that name."

"Um, thanks," Asher says, seemingly unable to set his glasses just right.

I notice that suddenly people all around us are walking into the youth center, like they've been called by a whistle only Christians can hear.

It's starting. Amanda's going to ask us to come in with her. This is going to be so awkward.

Where *is* she?

"Hey!" comes a voice from the doors of the youth center, and I know it. I know it before I see her jogging down the stairs, her hair bouncing against her neck.

"Rebekah!" cheers Amanda.

I glance at Asher. He's stopped touching his glasses. The corners of his lips threaten to smile.

Rebekah stops suddenly by Amanda's side, sticks a brown leather Bible under her arm, and plucks her thumbs through the belt loops of her jeans. Her hair falls casually into place, draping along her shoulders. She's wearing a dark blue polo shirt.

I love it when girls wear polo shirts.

Rebekah squeezes Amanda around the waist and makes a cute little noise like "eep." She looks around the circle and says to Amanda, "Making friends, as usual."

"Yeah, I was just meeting Phillip and Asher. They're great."

How does she know that?

"Tim said you had a couple songs to lead," Rebekah says.

Amanda's mouth forms an O. "You're right. I should go, then." She turns and blankets us with her smile. "It was so nice meeting you. I'll see you later."

Amanda bounds up the concrete steps into the center, and now it's just us. My stomach tightens.

"Hey," Rebekah says to me.

"Hey."

She looks down at my foot and scrunches her forehead. "So, where's my crutch?"

Damn. The crutch. "Oh, I, uh—"

Rebekah has this lazy smile, like her lips move in slow motion. "Well, you obviously don't need it anymore. So that's good."

She was joking. Calm down.

"Yeah," I say. "I mean, I still walk like a grandpa."

Asher laughs and Rebekah gives me this look of amused pity. Then she points at Asher. "Aren't you . . . ?"

"In Latin?" he says.

"Yeah. You're Ms. Nevins's favorite."

Asher grins and shakes his head, but of course it's true. "You're the one who saved Phillip from . . ." He trails off.

"Ferret?" she says, laughing.

She still thinks it's funny.

"Yeah," he says, surprised that she knows the name.

24

Unbelievably, I haven't screwed this up yet. But someone else could.

I look around. "Is he, you know, *here*?"

"Yeah," she says. "But he's inside somewhere. I don't think you'll see him." She pauses and smiles. "Unless you want to."

"No, that's okay," Asher says.

A little piece of me kind of wants to see him, so he can see I actually showed up, that I'm actually talking to this girl he probably sleazes over all the time. That I actually won.

But it's Ferret. So, actually, no.

From the open doors of the center, the sound of heartily strummed acoustic guitars wafts toward us.

"We should probably go inside," Rebekah says. She turns toward the center and then twists back. "If you think you can get up those steps, Grandpa."

The stairs are each maybe three inches high.

She's taunting me. Again.

"I'll *beat* you up those steps, young lady," I say, but my voice falters on the last part and I only fake like I'm about to run.

Rebekah takes off.

I look at Asher and he raises his eyebrows and points. "Go!"

I speed-hobble after her and finish in second place.

Rebekah did not explain that singing was required.

> *"Lord, I don't know what I should bring with me*
> *Or what I should leave behind . . ."*

Asher isn't even trying.

But no one expects him to—he's brown. So in this thoroughly

white town, that means he's sometimes not even expected to speak English.

I'm standing right next to Rebekah. She has a great voice—quiet but cutting—and she doesn't have to read the words off the projector screen at the front of the room. She sings with her eyes closed and her leather Bible tucked tightly under her arm. Her voice drifts over the three guitars and the dim sound of the crowd.

> *"Lord, I know, I know, I know,*
> *I've got a long way to go . . ."*

I don't sing. So I don't sing.

But I want to look like I'm trying. So I speak the words. Melodically. Sort of.

I wonder what Rebekah's expecting from me. Did she invite me here because she wants me to convert tonight? No. I mean, probably not. But if not, I still feel like I'm supposed to be interested. This place is obviously her life.

> *"But I can always keep my stride,*
> *Because you're right by my side . . ."*

She's singing not only as if God actually exists but as if He can hear her specifically. How can some godless jackass like me expect to . . . Well, I don't really know what I expect.

At the front of the room, the guitar players strum furiously, each one bobbing his head, and everyone's voices rise together.

"I know, I know, I know,
Lord, I've got a long way to go."

The guitars and the voices slowly sink, like a sheet that's been tossed in the air.

And then a stout thirtyish guy with a thick brown beard walks onto the carpeted platform up front. He wears green cargo shorts and yellow flip-flops, which snap quietly as he walks up to the microphone. Everyone sits down on the floor.

"That's Tim," Rebekah whispers to us, pointing toward the front and smiling as she crouches down.

"Oh," I say, nodding. Whoever Tim is, that's him.

I look at Asher again. He leans back on his hands and shrugs. He looks like he's tubing down a lazy river.

"How's everybody?" Tim says.

Rebekah hollers along with everyone else, and I clap a few times just so I don't look weird. She glances at me, smiles, and opens her Bible.

"Sounds good," Tim says. He exhales through his nose into the microphone. "I know I usually make a lot of dumb jokes up top here, but if you don't mind, I want to get just a little bit serious tonight. I wanted to talk about your life. The life you choose."

Oh, come on. "The life you choose"?

"I want you to close your eyes," Tim says, "and think about a time you had to make a really important decision."

I check my watch. It's only 7:44.

We've got a long way to go.

♥ ♥ ♥

"So, what'd you think?" Rebekah says.

I shove my red, carpet-dented hands into my pockets. We stand at the back of the room. Tim's "message" is over, and everybody's laughing and talking. The fluorescent lights leave a hazy glow in the air. "It was good."

Asher looks across the room, like he's seeing through the wall and into the sky.

Rebekah nudges him. "So, what'd *you* think?" Rebekah says.

He pauses. "About? Oh!" he says, shaking his head. "It was, uh . . ." He looks off again. "It was overwhelming." He smiles. "In a good way."

"In a good way. Alright."

He asks where the bathroom is, and I stop myself from joking about how overwhelmed he must be. Rebekah tells him where to go, and he walks off through the crowd.

I'm alone with her again.

Asher, you bastard.

Rebekah and I look at each other. This is when I'm supposed to do something, say something, make her laugh.

But I don't know how.

"So," she says, "you didn't like it."

"What?"

She shrugs. "It's okay if you didn't like it."

I feel a little queasy. "No, I mean, I liked it."

Her smile fades and she locks on to me with those green eyes. "Phillip. Tell me for real."

I try to hold her gaze, but it's too steady.

Dammit.

I *didn't* like it.

It was so corny. I felt like I was listening to one of those motivational speakers they force everyone to endure in the gym once a semester. Except in this speech there was way more God stuff, all of which sounded ridiculous and made up. It was actually kind of sad, like listening to a grown man who still believes in Santa Claus talk about all the presents the elves are making for him.

There. I said it. To me. But I can't say that out loud. She wouldn't understand.

"I don't know if . . ." I say. "I don't know if it's my thing. Kind of."

She tucks her Bible under her arm. "What *is* your thing?"

She doesn't want to know what my thing is. She's just being nice.

"Books?" I shrug.

"What books?"

Embarrassing books. I can't tell her what I read. But I have to say something. "Fantasy novels, I guess? Sometimes. But other stuff too, though."

"Fantasy novels. Like with dragons?"

I'd be sure that anyone else asking that question would be making fun of me, but she looks serious.

"Some of them."

"What else?" She crosses her arms, hugging her Bible to her chest.

I look off toward the front of the room. Where the hell is Asher?

"What was the last book you read that wasn't fantasy?"

No. I cannot tell her that. That's even more embarrassing. No one, especially not her, needs to know about my stupid obsession. Not even Asher and Mark know.

"Come on," she says, tilting her head. "It can't be *that* bad."

It can be.

But I can't say no to her.

"It's basically this book about our country, and sort of the whole world, I guess?" I say, every word making me cringe inside. "There are a lot of pretty bad things happening. Like with global warming and oil and nuclear weapons."

Rebekah's eyebrows perk up, and she thrusts her Bible toward me. I flinch. "Revelation," she says.

"Revelation?"

"The last book of the Bible. You should read it."

"I thought it was 'Revelations.'"

"No, it's just one big revelation."

I look down at the book. I edge it toward her. "This is yours, though."

"Just give it back when you're done."

She pokes the corner of the Bible at my stomach and aims to poke again. I reach to block it, and now it's in my hand.

She smiles. Tricky.

Over her shoulder I see Asher coming back.

So I take the book. I grip it by the spine, then tuck it under my arm, then cross my arms and press it against my chest. But the weight of it is uneasy, no matter how I hold it.

SEVEN

Huh-CHOO.

"God, do you have to sneeze so loud?" Chris says, picking up another bag of dirt.

"Yes. That's how I sneeze."

"Not all the time." He lifts the bag, shaking a little under the weight.

Dad walks back from deeper in the basement, stepping over a crowd of water jugs on the concrete floor. The sweat on his scalp shines in the hazy light from the window. "I didn't remember that you reacted this way to the dust," he says.

"Neither did I," I say.

When Dad told me he needed us to help him with some chores this weekend, I was more than fine with it. I still felt bad for lying to him, and I'd just slipped Rebekah's Bible under my mattress when he knocked on my door to tell me. Plus, with a doctor's note basically giving me permission to skip practice all week (suck it, Ferret), I was pretty sure my ankle would be okay by the weekend.

But I didn't realize he was going to wake us up at eight thirty on Saturday morning to haul boxes and carry soil in the unfinished half of the basement. So now I'm a lot less than fine with it.

I'm tired. My ankle still kind of hurts. I'm sneezing my face off. And I haven't been down here in . . . I don't know. A long time.

"Why are we doing this?" I ask.

Dad picks up his clipboard, and dust kicks up from the windowsill. The motes swirl in the light. "Just to get an idea of what's down here."

"A lot of crap," Chris says as he walks past me with the soil bag. He flops it onto the pile and throws his hair back.

"A fairly accurate description," Dad says. "But I'd like to get a little more accurate."

"Come *on*," Chris whines to me as he walks back to the scattered pile on the floor.

I ignore him. "For what, though?" I ask Dad.

He looks up from his clipboard and jiggles his pen. "I don't know. Maybe sell some of it online."

"*Sell* some of it?" A sneeze rises through my chest.

Huh-CHOO.

Dad taps his pen against the clipboard while I wipe my nose on my shirt. I look at him for an answer.

"Like that generator way back there." By the back wall a crumpled blue tarp covers a large, lumpy hulk. In the dark, I remember, it looks a lot like a monster, crouching. "We could probably get some good money for that."

"Can we split it?" Chris says, struggling with another bag.

32

"Sure. Ninety-nine percent for me, one percent for you guys."

"*Dad.*"

He laughs and puts the clipboard back on the windowsill. "Okay, okay. Just joking."

I look off toward the back wall, into the rest of this clutter. Boxes and piles of stuff. I remember it.

Dad turns to me. "Phillip. You okay? Need a break? I didn't know the dust would be so bad."

"No. I'm fine."

I just didn't realize. That all this stuff wouldn't be here forever, or that we wouldn't use it. That it's a lot of crap that can be sold online to people all over the world.

Chris walks up to me and shoves a bag of soil into my chest. We stare at each other for a couple of seconds, then I pick up the bag. I turn to drop it onto the pile, which is almost as tall as Chris now.

"Why do we even have soil, anyway?" Chris says. "Like, why would we even need that?"

Dad reaches for the clipboard again and stares at it while he scratches his head with the pen. "I don't know. The situation was a little crazy. At the time."

I watch him concentrate on the paper in front of him, and I wish he would say more. So I could understand why he thinks this is okay.

But it *is* a fairly accurate description. So maybe not.

EIGHT

I slump up the stairs. After we finally finished with the soil, leaving three white, careful stacks that looked like beekeeper's hives, Dad told us our work for the day was done. I want to shut my door and step out of my shoes and collapse into my bed.

But something's picking at me.

So I shut my door and step out of my shoes, and then I open my closet and flip on the light.

On the shelves along the wall: my stacks. Jumbled and worn. Pages curled and stained. Spines creased and cracked.

Nuclear Catastrophe by Benjamin Vinnis. The tiny radioactive warning sign on the spine glows a dulled yellow.

Sweatbox: Global Warming in the 21st Century by Patricia Laurentis. It lies open on the shelf, still at Chapter 5, I think.

The Long Crisis by Gerald Onhart. It stands on top of a pile of other books, leaning against the wall like a drunk.

And my favorite: *It'll All Be Over Soon: Or, How I Learned to*

Stop Worrying and Love the End of the World by Paul Getz. The cover is black and the main title is in big white block letters. The subtitle is printed in small font in the bottom right corner next to a tiny picture of a mushroom cloud blooming into a heart.

It's a funny book.

I grab it and flip through, the familiar pages spilling over my fingers. Next to it I find my old drawings: the mushroom cloud heart, detonating in rows of a dozen each, covering the page. My name written in big, ornamental medieval-style lettering, just like Getz uses in his book. I haven't looked at these in forever.

I put them back, facedown, and pick up a stack of printouts from websites and clippings from magazines. Big headlines and scary graphics.

Glaciers are melting. Oil is disappearing. Species are dying. Plagues are spreading. Bombs are blowing the fuck up.

Good.

I'm not crazy. Dad is.

We can't just sell all that stuff. We can't just run away from it. We can't just pretend like nothing bad's going to happen.

Lots of bad things are going to happen. All around the world. Soon.

A few minutes later I stick some pages back into a pile and turn off the light and close the closet door. Strips of daylight fall across my floor. I close the shades.

I fall into bed and go back to sleep. Eventually.

NINE

"Check this shit out," Mark says, twitching the blue chalk against the tip of his cue stick.

Asher looks up from the corner. "I can't wait," he says. He leans forward on the poker table, resting his beer on a coaster.

It's Saturday night, and we're in Mark's basement, which is much nicer than mine and almost entirely finished—except for the water heater closet, where we hide the beer. Even though Mark's parents never check on us.

I wait on the other side of the pool table for Mark to break.

"Exactly what is this shit you want me to check out?" I say. I sip from my warm, sour beer. I feel it slide all the way down.

God, we need to make some cooler friends—with better alcohol.

Mark lines up the shot. He slides the stick back and forth over his thumb and leans down to eye the cue ball like he's about to assassinate it.

Then he does it. Without even looking up.

"My parents are getting me a BMW." He fires his stick at the cue ball. The other balls explode in different directions. Two solids drop in two pockets. He stands up straight and smiles.

"What?" Asher and I say at the same time. I throw my cue stick to the floor and smack the edge of the table. Asher's mouth drops open.

Mark just nods.

"How do you know?" I say.

"I found, like, a brochure on my dad's desk with some cars circled. My parents' cars are both pretty new, my sister is, you know, ten years old, and it's my birthday in a week and a half, so . . ."

He shrugs. And we just stand there. Thinking.

One of us has a car. A BMW. In a week and a half.

This will change our lives.

"Dude," I say. "That's fucking awesome."

We all laugh. We talk about all the awesome things that we can now accomplish with *our* car, from the most awesome (more easily procuring alcohol, maybe actually getting some girls to hang out with us) to the pretty awesome (being able to drive to the QuikTrip whenever we want taquitos).

"And if I can find a parking spot near school," Mark says, "Asher's dad won't have to pick us up after practice."

"Pretty awesome," I say. I actually don't mind that, and I don't think Mr. V does either, but anything involving this car seems awesome right now.

"Actually, that reminds me," Mark says, grabbing his cue stick and pointing it at me. "You're gonna be at practice on Monday, right?" He sets up his next shot.

Instinctively I flex my foot. A dull pain crackles through it.

"Maybe."

Mark looks up at me. "Come on, dude. We can't handle Ferret on our own." It almost sounds like a compliment, but his eyes are expectant. Like he just gave me a car, so I have to give *him* something now.

I look at Asher. He shrugs and looks at his beer.

A-holes.

"Fine," I say.

"Good," Mark says. He takes the shot and misses.

TEN

"Welcome to Blood Hill, gentlemen." In front of us Ferret sits on his bike. He leans down on his handlebars, flips his sunglasses down, and grins.

We stand at the top of a cracked, gray road. It goes straight down, at what you would think would be an impossible angle for a neighborhood street, for probably a hundred yards. Oak trees stand guard on both sides of the street, dousing the old houses in shade. But the street is completely exposed, and sunlight cooks our pale skin.

I had hoped I would never see this place. But I guess I always assumed that if I did, Asher would be here to suffer through it with me. Or die trying.

So, before I perish, let it be recorded in the annals of friendship that when called, Phillip Flowers, he of the still crackly ankle, answered.

And Asher, Mr. Perfect Attendance, shrugged and chumped out.

I mean, I hope he's okay? But he didn't look sick at lunch, and he didn't say anything about missing practice. He just didn't come.

On the muggy Monday afternoon that Ferret chose to exact his revenge.

"I'm sure you boys are wondering what you're doing here," he says. He grabs a red bandanna from his back pocket and dabs his forehead. "Well, congratulations. You made varsity!" He smiles and throws his hands up in the air.

We stare at him. The shithead.

He laughs. "You boys need a sense of humor. Especially if you're gonna be spending time with a funnyman like myself." He stuffs his bandanna back in his pocket. "Y'all are a disruptive presence. You horse around instead of doing your work, and it shows. Coach Heller and I spoke about this, and we don't want your lackadaisical attitudes to affect everyone else. So, to get you in the right mindset, you now have a personal trainer: Mr. Randall T. Farragut."

Mark and I glance at each other. He's gritting his teeth just like me.

Ferret smiles. "I can tell you boys are excited. Think of it as an opportunity, alright?"

We look past him, right down the potholed throat of Blood Hill.

People like us aren't supposed to train here. This place is for varsity runners. And even they talk about it with loathing and awe.

"It sucks going up," they say. "But it *really* sucks going down."

Supposedly people have broken limbs on this road, tripping on the ancient asphalt as they tried to make time.

This seems like a bad training method.

Where the *hell* is Asher?

"Alright?" Ferret says.

"Yeah," we say.

"Alright, then." He pulls out his chunky red stopwatch. "I'll give you fellas two and a half minutes to run down there and back up here."

Jesus. I pick my feet up and flex. My ankle is mostly better.

For now.

"And don't worry about your absentee friend," Ferret says. "He won't miss out on any of the fun."

Good.

Ferret presses some buttons on the stopwatch. It beeps and beeps.

"Go."

And we throw ourselves into the gullet of Blood Hill.

That night I pounce on Asher when he gets online.

so, I type, *wtf?*

hey. srry.

k. wtf?

i was at tryouts for academic team. i made jv.

Academic team? What? He's never mentioned that before, has he?

it was a last minute thing, he adds.

I want to say, "Then why were you all shruggy and silent and abandon-your-friends-ish?"

But he did endure youth group with me. So maybe they sort of even out. Barely.

So I just say:

congratz dood.

thx.

But he needs to know what he skipped out on.

ferret made us do blood hill.

shit.

yeah. my whole body is tired. but i somehow avoided ripping my ankle again. or breaking any bones.

haha. good.

We have the chat equivalent of an awkward silence. A chawkward silence.

Eventually, I say, *so does this mean ur not on the team anymore?*

yeah. sorry.

whatever. it's fine.

It's not, really. But I'm not going to say that. Now *he* owes *me*, though.

so ur going with me again on weds, right? to church?

Keyboard silence.

Finally he responds.

about that . . .

ELEVEN

I carry a crutch in one hand and a Bible in the other, like a sword and shield. Eyes linger on me as people pass by. I squint against the fading yellow light, scanning the crowd for Rebekah, hoping I don't see her so I have an excuse to go home.

Because how am I supposed to do this by myself? I've fooled her into thinking I might not be superawkward only because we've barely spoken to each other. If I stay here, she'll learn the truth and that'll be the end.

It didn't have to be like this. Asher could have come with me again, instead of giving me some bullshit excuse about academic team homework. I think he thinks he's doing me favor.

Well, it doesn't feel like a favor. It feels like Blood Hill. It feels like—

Shit.

There she is. Standing in the shade, under the covered porch that wraps around the youth center, leaning against a brick column.

She scratches her leg with the front tip of her bright blue flip-flop as she talks to someone.

Wow.

It's been a week since I've seen her. Baxter High is big—like, four thousand students big—and you can go a whole semester without seeing certain people if your schedules don't line up. Plus—and this is probably Ferret's doing—girls' cross country hasn't been running the same routes as boys' anymore.

I've missed her.

That doesn't make sense. I don't even know her. But now I want to go talk to her. I want to show her I brought the crutch, make her laugh.

And then what? Failure. Silence. Because I don't know what to do.

She's right over there and I can't just keep standing here but I don't know what to do.

"Go!" Asher told me last time. And that worked out okay.

Shit.

This is going to hurt. I hold tight to the Bible and crutch. I walk through the crowd, down the cement path, and up the steps. The person Rebekah was talking to—a giggly middle school girl with teeth-colored braces—sees me approaching and goes into the youth center.

I walk up behind Rebekah, not too close. "What's up?" I say.

She turns around. She sees me. She doesn't smile.

"Oh," she says. She presses her hand against her chest, and her eyes are wide and distant. It's like we've never met.

This already hurts.

"Sorry," I say. I hold the Bible up like identification.

She finally smiles, but it's toothy and fast and her cheeks are bunched up. She removes her hand from her chest like it was glued there. "Hey. Sorry. Phillip."

"Yup," I say, leaning a little more against the crutch.

Failure. Silence.

She tugs at a strand of her hair, pulling it straight and letting it spring back. "I'm sorry. You just surprised me." A laugh escapes from her throat. "Thanks for bringing those."

The crutch isn't really helping with the feeling of being kicked in the testicles, but I lean into it more anyway.

Quiet guitar chords float out of the youth center.

"I just wanted to give them back," I say.

She closes her eyes, and when she opens them, it's like they're new. Greener. She smiles a real smile. "I'm sorry. I'm being stupid. Don't leave." Footsteps clomp on the stairs behind us. She looks toward the doors of the youth center. "But can you not come in right away?"

I look at the doors too, to see if there's anything there that will make me understand. All I see is the same big room.

"I can't really explain right now. It's not a bad thing." She bites her lip.

The chords are louder. The rest of the kids stream in behind me.

"It's not a bad thing?"

She nods and looks at the doors again. "I'll come back out and get you. In ten minutes. Okay?"

"Okay."

"Thanks," she says as she slips inside the room.

I walk down the stairs, getting some more looks as I walk in the opposite direction of everyone else. A couple of ninth-grade stragglers run in from the parking lot. A minute later the doors shut and I'm sitting alone on a bench, wondering.

If it's not a bad thing, is it a good thing?

Three minutes pass. Five. Eight. Finally ten.

I still don't have an answer.

Eleven minutes.

Twelve minutes.

I'm thinking the answer is, "No."

Thirt—

The doors open, and she waves me in and runs back inside.

What does that mean?

It means I should have gone home, I think as I walk up the steps and into the youth center. The room is darkened, and Tim has already started his spiel. I spot Rebekah and sit down next to her, expecting an apology, or an explanation. But she acts like I'm not even here.

Finally youth group ends, and the lights go on, and we stand.

"So?" Rebekah says. She points at the Bible.

Wait. She wants to know if I did my assigned reading?

Hold on.

"What about the waiting outside thing?"

Rebekah rolls her eyes like I'm the one being weird. "Okay, I'll tell you. But you have to tell me what you thought about Revelation first."

"That's not fair."

"I know. But tell me anyway."

And she smiles, which is cheating. I act like I'm considering saying no. Then I say, "Fine."

I had put off reading it as long as I could. Then last night, as I

46

was brooding over Asher and my economics homework, I pulled her Bible out from under my mattress. Her initials—RFJ—carved into the cover caught my eye. I remembered how sure she'd seemed that I'd like it.

So I put the econ away and finally opened the Bible. The pages inside were soft, and so thin you could see through to the words on the other side. They spilled open to somewhere in the middle—Isaiah. "Woe to the obstinate children," it said.

I turned to Revelation. Because it's at the end of the book, the pages wouldn't lie flat, so I had to hold the end down with my fingers.

I stared at it. Not the words. Just the bookness of it.

And then I read it in one gulp.

"I kind of liked it," I say.

"Kind of? Come on."

"Okay, I liked it." I pick up the crutch and bounce it back and forth between my hands, trying to remember my favorite part. A lot of it was really boring, but it's a strange book about the world ending in terrifying and catastrophic ways, so of course I liked it. Plus, there were some awesome monsters.

"The eye-creatures were cool."

"Eye-creatures?"

"You know, the animals with the eyes all over them."

She smiles. "I knew you'd like it."

I squeeze the crutch cushion with my fingers. Great. So she has me pegged as a guy who's really into the Apocalypse. I'm sure that's a really good thing.

I glance across the room and somehow make direct eye contact with Ferret. He grins at me and looks like he's about to scurry over and gnaw on my ankle.

Go.

I turn to Rebekah. "Could we?" I nod toward the doors.

"Sure."

We dodge around clusters of people, and I try not to hit anyone with the crutch. That Amanda girl from last week smiles really big at me, and I wave and duck past her.

Outside, a haze of sunlight settles against the horizon. Lightning bugs hover and flash against the black backdrop of the pine trees. Under the awning the small porch is empty, except for the riot of gnats crashing against the light fixtures. Rebekah leads me around the corner to the right and leans against a brick column, exactly the way she was leaning earlier. I sit on the ledge next to her. The green of her eyes looks crystalline.

And I am suddenly really aware of something: I am by myself, talking to a girl about the end of the world, and it's not horribly, terribly, vomitously awkward.

"Do you believe all those things are going to actually happen?" I say. "In Revelation?"

"I believe what the Bible says is true."

"Okay," I say. I rub my finger along the craggy edge of the brick. "But do you think it's going to happen soon?"

"Well," she says, picking at an old-looking stain on her jeans. "I don't know. *Nobody* knows. That's what the Book says."

"But it also says 'the end is near.'"

Showing off the effort.

"Well, actually, it says 'the *time* is near.'"

"Oh."

"It's okay. It's different in some translations. And, anyway, it's said that for a long time."

We sit there for a few seconds, not talking. On the lawn, crickets chirp, mocking me.

"But," Rebekah says, and I hold my breath at the word. She crosses her arms over her chest, hugging the Bible against her. "I do think—sometimes—that it could happen soon. I mean, with everything that's going on in the world right now." She shrugs. "But it's scary to think about."

"Not necessarily."

"Ooh," she says, waving her hands around. "Mr. I'm-Not-Scared-By-the-Apocalypse."

"I didn't mean it like that. I'm just saying, there are scary ways the world could end, and less scary ways."

There's another silence.

"Plus, I'm kind of a badass?" I say, flexing a forearm.

"Really?" she says, leaning in to examine it. "I can't tell."

We grin at each other. I realize I just cursed at church and it was somehow not awkward. Maybe I'm better at this than I thought.

Rebekah holds out her Bible. "You should take this again."

And I'm right back to not knowing what to do. Does she like me, and that's why she wants me to take it? Or is she just trying to convert me?

"You should read Genesis," she says. "You can bring it back next time."

She points the book at my stomach, like last time, and I know what I'll do—whatever she says.

I take the Bible by the corner. My heart starts to flutter.

Is this when I ask her out?

No. Wait.

I don't even know if she likes me. I don't even know if this is a good thing or a bad thing.

I hold the book tighter and say, "Why did you ask me to stay outside earlier?"

Rebekah almost-smiles.

She takes a deep breath. "Sometimes I—"

And just then Ferret's head pops around the corner. Rebekah lets go of the Bible and I take it and hold it by my side.

"Well, hello there, friends," Ferret says. His cowboy boots clack against the cement. He nods at Rebekah. "Ms. Joseph." He nods at me. "Flowers. Good to see you. Though I feel like I haven't done my job if you're still able to stand."

I want to smack him with the Word of God.

"I'm just playing, Flowers. You know that." He looks at Rebekah. "This boy's been working hard this week."

I feel ashamed about the pride that swells up when I hear that.

From behind his back he whips out a clipboard and holds it in front of Rebekah.

"Ms. Joseph, did you get a chance to sign up for the Summit?"

Rebekah blushes. "I want to, Mr. Farragut—"

"Randy. Please."

"But money is tight right now and—"

He puts his hand on her shoulder. She flinches. "Rebekah, don't let that influence your decision. The Lord will provide. You know that."

She stares at his hand for a second, and he takes it away and pulls a pen from his pocket. He holds it out to her.

"Amanda's going?" she asks.

"Yes, she is."

He's bothering her. I should tell him to leave us alone.

Seconds drag past.

"Okay." She takes the pen and prints her name and email.

"Thatta girl," Ferret says, a devil's grin on his face. He takes the pen back and looks at me. "What you got there, Flowers?" he says, pointing at the Bible. "You ready to sign up too?"

I swallow. "What is it?"

"What's the Summit?" He laughs. "Oh, of course you're not familiar, Flowers. It's a leadership conference for young people who excel in their devotion to Christ. Don't know if it'd be your cup of joe."

Why does he have to be such an asshole *all the time*?

"Mr. Farragut," Rebekah says.

His grin fades. "I'm just teasing the man, as usual," Ferret says, patting my shoulder. "Flowers has always been my favorite misfit. I'm just glad I get to see more of him, now that his Indian friend left for academic team with you." He nods at Rebekah.

Wait. What?

"You're on academic team?" I ask her.

She blinks. "Yeah."

"Oh."

Why am I so bothered by that?

"Asher just hadn't said anything about it," I say, trying to explain the stunned look on my face. "But congratulations."

"Thanks. I'm glad he got me to try out."

There it is.

I'm so bothered because it finally adds up: Asher likes Rebekah too. That's why he's been acting shady. That's why he told me to go without him.

He knew I'd blow my chance to ask her out.

Ferret chuckles. "Y'alright, Flowers? You look a little thunderstruck."

I could still do it. I could still tell Ferret to leave us alone. He only came out here to screw with me.

I swallow.

"I'm fine," I say.

I swallow again.

Failure. Silence.

The smirk on Ferret's face.

The crickets swarming, crawling up the walls and beating their wings to drive the hot, sticky air toward me.

Rebekah looks at me, concerned.

Go.

"Yeah, no. I'm fine. Just. My ride is here," I say. I slide off the brick ledge, hand her the crutch. We say goodbye. Ferret reminds me he'll see me tomorrow.

I walk to the parking lot, out of sight from the porch, and wait for Asher's dad to show up.

TWELVE

I am full of hate. I hate that I'm standing in the sun wiping sweat from my eyes. I hate that Asher is at academic team practice with Rebekah right now. I hate that I didn't say anything to him about it today.

And I hate that I'm so pathetic.

I really hate that.

Oh, and I still hate Ferret.

"I scouted this place, gentlemen," he says, peering through his sunglasses down the rolling neighborhood road in front of us. "So I get to name it. Know what I'm calling it?"

Mark and I say nothing. I'm glad I still have him to be pathetic with.

"The Snake." Ferret leans back on the seat of his bike and points down the road. "See the humps? I almost called it the Camel. Then I realized, there's nothin' scary about a camel. The snake, on the other hand, is the devil's creature."

You're the devil's creature, you son of a bitch.

"I wouldn't say this to Coach Heller's face," Ferret says, "but I think the Snake is better than Blood Hill, training-wise. Sure, it doesn't look as scary right off. But it hurts more. You got *three* hills here, gentlemen. And what makes Blood Hill so easy is all those trees around it, so you can rest. At the Snake, there ain't a shady oak in sight."

We stare down the road. The asphalt gleams.

"So," Ferret says, "are you ready to ride the Snake?"

We continue to stare.

"I'll take that as a yes," he says. "Alright. I want you boys to run this down and back three times. Should be about one and a half miles. I'll be checking up on you."

This is going to suck so bad. I look over at Mark, but he's glaring at the road and shaking his head. Psyching himself up, I guess.

"Alright, boys. Ready . . ." Ferret raises his stopwatch. "Go."

"Fuck this."

I'm three steps into my stride before I process what Mark just said. I skid to a stop.

"Excuse me?" Ferret says.

Mark stands there, looks right at him. "Fuck this."

"You better watch your language, friend, and get moving. Otherwise I'm gonna have to let Coach Heller know—"

"Fuck you. I'm done." Mark spits on the ground and walks away, back toward school.

Ferret grips his handlebars like he wants to tear them off. "You get back here, son!"

Mark flicks him off without turning around. He's not getting back here.

And he's not looking to see if I'm coming with him.

"You bet your butt I *will* report you!" Ferret says.

Then he turns to me. His face is clenched. "You quittin' too?"

I watch Mark walk away. I wipe my damp face with my damp sleeve.

"No," I say.

Ferret nods, looks at Mark again, and turns back to me. "Better start, then."

THIRTEEN

Dad points at the water jugs with his pen, counting them. He's making an inventory.

"Two hundred," I say. We're in the basement on Saturday morning again. Chris is upstairs, taking a break because he "started earlier." I check another can of vegetables—this one's creamed corn—to see if it's expired yet.

"You know you can't throw off my count," Dad says, tapping his pen against his temple. "Mind like a steel trap. For numbers, at least." He laughs to himself and starts counting again.

I stack the corn on a column of other unexpired food cans and breathe deep. But not too deep. I took an allergy pill and an ibuprofen, but I still feel like there's a jagged piece of metal lodged in my forehead.

Asher and I were over at Mark's last night. We were ripping on each other like usual, but there was more of an edge to it, and we were joking *around* everything that happened this week, not about it. Though I'd calmed down from feeling betrayed by both of them, I still smarted like hell. And I could tell we all felt, maybe for the first time, that our friendship was broken.

When Mark whipped out half a bottle of some "doppelkorn" he'd gotten from two dudes in his German class, I thought it might help. But it was disgusting, like drinking pure alcohol, and it felt like liquid gloom. We got quieter, played video games we'd mastered in eighth grade, and went to sleep early. Then my dad picked me up at eight in the freaking morning.

"I'm not trying to throw off your count," I tell Dad. "That's how many there are." I grab another can from the unchecked pile.

Dad stops his pen again. "Did you count these already?"

"No. I just remember. That's how many there are."

We went five times that summer for water. Each time it was forty jugs. Mom told Chris to do the math.

"You sure?"

"Yeah." Another unexpired can goes on the stack. I rub my eyes and stand still for a second until my vision unblurs.

Dad scribbles in his notepad. He'll probably wait until I'm gone and then double-check the water jugs. "You feel okay?"

I pick up another can—green beans. "I'm just tired."

And hungover. And worried. And miserable.

From the quick rhythms of his pen against the paper, I'd guess Dad is drawing cubes. I wonder how many cubes he's drawn in his whole life. Tens of thousands. Hundreds of thousands. "Sorry I had to come get you so early," he says.

I shrug. "It's fine. I—"

I put the unexpired green beans down and sneeze. It feels and looks like part of my brain just fell out.

"Here," Dad says, grabbing a couple of tissues from a box he brought down. I blow my nose. "So, how's the study group going?"

I hide my sigh with another nose-blow. Ever since Chris started going to soccer practice and I started going to "study group," there hasn't been much conversation in the house. Dad and I did the game night thing a couple of times, but then a weekend went by and we just stopped. Which is okay with me, but apparently he wants to catch up now, while I feel like shit.

"Good," I say, hoping he'll drop it. I toss the balled-up tissues on the floor and pick up another can. Probably a hundred or more to go.

"Great," Dad says. "You know, Mr. Venkataraman doesn't have to drive you all the time."

I can't resist. "You're buying me a car?"

He laughs. "Nice try."

"I'm sixteen in a few months."

"And you're not driving until you're eighteen. The rule hasn't changed."

The damn rule. "So, what are you talking about?"

"I can drive you."

That can't happen. "Mr. V already said he would."

Dad and I are quiet. I fit one can on top of another with a metallic *plunk*. The hard plastic of Dad's pen clacks against his teeth.

He looks up and points his pen at me. "Hey, you're creative. I was thinking of calling all this stuff"—he waves his pen around the basement—"a 'survival pack' when we sell it. What do you think?"

I blink a few times and rub my fingers into my forehead. I'd forgotten about his little scheme. "I don't know."

"I think we'll make a mint off some Rapture nut."

He's got that making-fun-of-religious-people tone in his voice, but I don't get the reference. Still, I understand "nut." Doesn't he realize *I* think shit's gonna go down too? Doesn't he understand what *I* believe?

"Why do we have to sell it?" I ask, picking up another can. Peas, bursting from the pod on the label.

"Well, it'd be nice to have this space down here. And a little extra cash wouldn't hurt." He taps his pen against his thigh. "And I just figured we could, you know, move this stuff out."

We hear the door open and Chris's steps coming slowly down the stairs.

"But what if we need it?" I say.

"We won't need it, Phillip. Okay?"

"How do you know?"

Dad bites his bottom lip.

Chris walks in. "Did you guys finish?" His voice breaks a little.

"No, no," Dad says. "Just taking a quick break. Why don't you help Phillip with the cans?"

Chris stands next to me, picks up a can, flips it to the date, and stacks it. He looks at me from the corner of his eye.

I look at Dad, but he's suddenly done catching up.

Reluctantly I grab a can from a new stack. When I see what it is, I show it to Chris.

Baby carrots—our least favorite snack.

He shrugs and grabs another can like he doesn't remember.

JANUARY, THREE YEARS AND SEVEN MONTHS AGO

Mom shopped for groceries on Sundays. While Dad usually spent half the day on the computer, Chris and I would sleep in and make our own breakfasts—usually cereal. We'd sit in the kitchen and watch stupid shows on the little TV.

Mom would always bring a snack for us to eat after we helped unload the bags. Lately she wouldn't get back to the house until well after noon, but she almost never let us have real, sugary snacks during the week, so it was worth the wait.

That morning, or maybe afternoon, Chris kept switching the channel back to the weather. There was an ice storm in Tennessee, where Aunt Mara and Uncle Bill lived, and Chris kept saying we might see them if we just watched. I pretended to watch the report for a few seconds, and then I shot my hand over, grabbed the remote, and switched the channel back to some computer-animated show that Chris hated.

"Give it back!" He jumped out of his seat and reached for the remote,

hitting my cereal bowl. We tried to grab the bowl, but it spun away and shattered on the ceramic tile floor.

Then we heard the hum and roar of Mom's car pulling into the garage.

We both ran for the paper towels. I grabbed a few and shoved them into Chris's hands. But in the time it took Mom to get some grocery bags and walk in the door, we didn't accomplish much.

"Guys," was all she said when she walked in, the cold air right behind her. She put the bags on the floor, took the paper towels from my hand, and tore off two for me and two for Chris.

"Just clean up the pieces, guys," she said. "And be careful. Don't cut yourselves."

She soaked up the milk with Mom speed and precision and then helped us pick up the tiny crystals of bowl that lay in the gray cracks between the tiles. Finally she stood up, put her hand to her forehead, and sighed.

Chris and I crouched, looking up at Mom. She had gotten a new haircut just the week before. It had been long and straight and dark brown for as long as I could remember. But now it came down to her shoulders, and it was shaped or something, and lighter in places. She still looked a little weird to me, especially as she stood over us—a giant, scowling Mom impostor.

Chris said, "Do we still get a snack?"

And Mom laughed. Her head fell forward and her shoulders rose and she snorted.

"Yeah," she said. "If you guys get the rest of the groceries and put them away. But I don't think you guys should be eating that sugary stuff anymore."

Chris and I got all the bags in one trip, and we put them on the counter and started sorting the groceries and looking for our snack while Mom stood and watched the weather with her forehead crinkled. Aunt Mara was her sister.

The bags Mom had come in with were still sitting on the floor, so I walked over to bring them to the counter. An orange-pink piece of paper was sandwiched between the two plastic bags, and I picked it up.

SUNDAY BULLETIN, it read across the top in black type. The headline read PASTOR BAYLOR SPEAKS AT LOCAL CONFERENCE.

"Oh," Mom said. I looked up and saw her walking over with her hand already out, reaching for it. "Just something they were handing out at the store. Forgot to throw it out."

I picked up the two bags sitting on the floor and tried not to be obvious about it as I watched Mom open the trash can and hide the newsletter under the bowl shards and the crumpled, soppy paper towels. Mom reached inside one of the grocery bags and pulled out a bottle of low-fat ranch dressing and a bag of baby carrots.

"Who wants a snack?" she said.

FOURTEEN

I'm right in the middle of reading about atomic mass when I realize I've doodled. There, in the bottom right-hand corner of my chemistry book, just half an inch to the left of the page number, is a tiny heart blooming from a tiny mushroom cloud. The two sevens next to it are buildings bending in the nuclear breeze.

I didn't mean to do that. Did I? It's the first time in forever that I've doodled anything, let alone *that*.

I start to put my pen down on the desk. Then I look at the doodle again.

It's *good*. Just as good as the ones I used to draw, anyway. Right?

I get up and open my closet. I grab the stack of old sketches from the shelf and sit back down. It's an unruly pile of various kinds of paper—ripped notebook pages, real sketchbook sheets, the back of a syllabus from eighth grade. Each covered in drawings of guns and dragons and swords and explosions. And letters. Those medieval letters.

God, I miss this.

And in an instant I have it.

I shut my chemistry book, rip a page from my notebook, grab a pencil, and use the book as a base. First I draw a thin frame. The ruled lines help. Next, to fill most of the frame, a single letter, uppercase. There's a dangerous swoop at the end, but I nail it.

My pencil is dull. I yank open a drawer and rifle through years of school supplies until I find a little green sharpener. The ripping sound of the blade and the resistance of the pencil tip give me chills.

Now the ornamentation. A garden of tiny hearts inside the loop. A mushroom cloud here and there. An eye-creature floating off the end of the swoop, attached by a thread. A cross, dangling off the side. And a few basic vines to fill the remaining space.

I find a box of pushpins in the drawer, pick one out, and stick the paper to the wall, right above my desk.

The letter *R*, gazing down at me.

FIFTEEN

I bust through the shrubbery, and a branch claws my ear.

I shout from the sudden pain, then cover my mouth. We're supposed to be whispering.

Asher laughs through his nose and turns away. He walks toward the tall wooden fence that separates Baxter High School property from Baxter Estates, the neighborhood right next to the school. I follow him, dipping between the trees, which are pale, skinny, and slouching just like the kids that gather after school in this shady no-man's-land. The ground is littered with dozens of half-buried cigarette butts.

Asher and I have never cut class before. He's too good of a student, and I'm too afraid of getting caught. But today is Mark's birthday, and his parents gave him what he already knew he was getting, with the awesome bonus of a parking spot in a family friend's driveway in Baxter Estates. So we're cutting the final fifteen minutes of the last period today so we can go see it—our BMW.

This will fix us. Maybe.

Because if Mark tells the story of how he quit one more time, I'm going to cut the dude with my lunch fork. I mean, it's funny, and I don't blame him anymore, but I'm the only one of us left on cross-country now. So I kind of still do blame him.

And I'm even more worried about Asher. Since last week he's barely said anything about academic team, and neither of us has mentioned Rebekah at all. Does that mean he knows I failed? Is he trying to be nice by not saying anything? Or is he not saying anything because he plans to ask her out? Or has already?

I don't know. He's different now. It's harder to tell what he's thinking.

And I'm scared to find out.

We follow the fence away from school. Through the trees and bushes to our left, cars *fwum* by on Orchard Road. We look over our shoulders.

"I think we're okay," I whisper. Officer Terry, Baxter High's six-and-a-half-foot-tall security guard, doesn't ride this far out in his patrol golf cart. Probably.

"We should just go out to the sidewalk," I say, twitching my head to our left. "We're far enough."

So we bust through the shrubbery once more and walk in full view of the passing cars. Giddy with our audacity, and wanting to forget my worry, I ask Asher how he escaped from last period.

His story is so Asher. Since he's the perfect student, every teacher loves him. So he didn't even have to provide any proof for Mr. Tanger when he said he had to leave early to pick up supplies for academic team.

As I tell him, I had to fake a headache and stomachache all

during Mrs. Pell's English class in what I thought were very subtle ways, until about twenty minutes in, when she interrupted her own lecture about *Julius Caesar* to ask, "Phillip, do you need to visit the restroom?"

My face shot up full red. If I'd said yes, everybody would have thought I had diarrhea.

But when you gotta go, you gotta go.

By the time I'm done telling this story to Asher and he's done laughing at me and calling me an idiot, we almost feel like friends again. Like friends who can just double-check real quick that one of them didn't try to sabotage the other one because they both want the same girl.

We walk past the Baxter Estates sign and into the neighborhood.

"How's academic team?" I say, so casually.

"Good."

"Yeah?"

"Yeah. Good."

"Awesome."

And I guess that's going to be that.

But it bugs the hell out of me. We're minutes away from what could be *our* BMW. Or just *a* BMW.

Screw this. Either we're friends or we're not.

"Why didn't you tell me Rebekah was on—"

"Academic team?"

"Yeah."

Asher knew what I was really asking. Of course he did.

He scratches his nose. "I'm sorry. I didn't want you to think I was trying to, you know, get with her or something."

"Were you?"

"*No.*" He looks at me in disbelief.

I put my hands up. "Okay, sorry. You just kind of abandoned me."

"Because if you want to get with Rebekah, then you have to do it yourself."

"I know that. And I totally failed."

"You did?"

"I didn't ask her out or even get her number, and then I basically ran away."

We make a turn onto the right street, and we're quiet for a little bit. Then Asher looks at me and says, "Well, from what I heard, you didn't *totally* fail."

Holy shit.

"Yeah?"

"Yeah."

I look away so he doesn't see that I'm trying not to smile.

We're getting close to the house. Once we top this hill, we should see it.

"I have other plans, anyway," Asher says.

It takes me a second, but I get it. "No way. Who?"

"I'll tell you after I've executed the plans and they succeed."

"What if they don't succeed?"

"Then I'll never tell you."

"A-hole."

I punch his arm. He punches my chest.

And, just like that, we're friends again.

When we reach the top of the hill, I spot Mark's puffball hair in the distance, and then I see *it*—the slick black BMW shining in the sun, nose-out in someone's driveway.

Mark said he'd cut his whole last period and meet us here. I asked him what he'd be doing while he waited. He said, "Just looking at it."

Now I understand. It's gorgeous.

Our BMW.

But then two more figures pop up from behind the car. One a broad-shouldered shifter. One a wispy slouch.

"Who is that?" Asher says.

I think I recognize them, but I don't know them, even though Mark seems to. He didn't say anything about other people being here.

When we get close, Mark smiles and shoots his hand up. "Hey, jackasses!"

"Hey," we say.

Mark shoves his hands in his pockets and smiles at his car like he has a crush on it. The other two lean on the back bumper, not looking at us.

"Brilliant, right?" Mark says.

The blinding sunlight gushes across the flawless black surface. The radio antenna nub pokes out like a dignified pinkie. The tires and license plate glisten with newness.

"Yeah, dude," I say.

"Let's check it out," Asher says.

We walk to the driver's side. The other guys glance back.

"What's up?" Asher says to them.

"Y'all know each other?" Mark asks.

"No," the broad guy says. His voice is deep and apathetic.

"Oh, right," Mark says. "This is Dan the Man"—he points to the broad guy—"and Brad"—the skeletal one. "This is Asher and

Phillip." Asher and I each hold a hand up in silent greeting. Dan the Man gives a slight nod. Brad turns back around like he didn't see us.

"These are the guys from German class," Mark tells us. "Good dudes."

Yeah. Obviously.

"Anyway, ain't she a beaut?" Mark says in a voice I guess you'd call old-timey. Then he does the keyless ignition trick. And cycles through the satellite radio stations. And pops the hood and shows us the V-whatever engine.

It's impressive. But the whole time I'm thinking how much better this would be if Dan the Man and Brad weren't perched on the back of the car, talking in hushed voices.

"You sure you guys have to go back?" Mark asks us.

"I have practice," I say. "Remember?"

"Dude," Mark says to me, "just *quit*. It's so easy."

As easy as leaving your friend to fend for himself against a psychopathic coach.

As easy as inviting some random dudes to what should be *our* moment.

"I can't."

"You *can*, though." He smiles and taps me on the chest, but he looks nervous about it. His smile drops, and he sucks his teeth. "I hate that you guys have to go back." Mark nods back toward Dan and Brad. "Me and them are gonna drive around."

We look at the car, pick at our fingernails.

"The three of us should drive somewhere, though," Mark says. "Like, tonight?"

Tonight doesn't work. Asher has too much homework.

But if I can't get an apology from Mark, maybe I can snatch a favor.

"You can drive me to church tomorrow," I say.

Mark laughs. "Alright. And we can drive around before my party, anyway."

I totally forgot. Mark's birthday party is on Friday. His parents always go all out, and we always have a good time.

That will be our moment.

"We getting out of here?" Dan says as Brad steps off the bumper and hops around.

"Yeah," Mark says. "Just a sec." He tosses his plastic keypad in the air and grabs it. "So I'll see you guys later," he says to us.

We say yeah and start to walk down the driveway.

"Hey," Dan says. I turn back, and he nods at my head. "You've got blood on your ear."

I touch the top of my ear, where I scraped it against the bush, and rusty red flakes come off and stain my finger.

Dan stares at me.

"Uh, thanks," I say. Then I wipe the rest of the blood on my shorts, and Asher and I head back the way we came.

SIXTEEN

That night I fall asleep on the couch as I'm doing my homework. I snore myself awake about twenty minutes later, gather my stuff, and head up to my room.

I stop when I reach the doorway.

Dad is standing next to my nightstand. He wears his crinkled, yellowed undershirt and his baggy blue pajama pants. He scratches his armpit and squints at the shiny front cover of Rebekah's Bible.

I forgot to put it back.

"Um," I say.

He jumps a little bit and turns to me, giving my face the same searching look he was just giving the Bible. "What is this?" he says. His forehead is wrinkled like his old shirt.

"It's not mine." I walk over, reaching for the book.

He doesn't quite take it out of my reach, but he doesn't keep it where it was either. As I walk up to him, I realize he's still taller than I am, with wider shoulders.

That makes me angrier. "What are you *doing*?" I put my hand out for the book.

For a second Dad still squints at me. Then he looks down, and his shoulders sag. "I didn't mean to invade your space. You left the lights on—and then I saw this on your table."

"And then you just walked in and took it?"

"I didn't take it. I was just looking at it for a moment."

I hold my hand out again.

Dad exhales slowly. He places the book in my hand and says, "Alright." He walks off, but stops at the door. "Can you just tell me why you have that?"

I stare at the cover, the light from the fixture melting across its ridges. My arms and stomach and my whole body are rigid with anger.

"No."

He looks over and sees the notebook pages tacked to my wall, spelling out "REBEK" in medieval script and strange ornamentation. Then he leaves and closes the door behind him.

FEBRUARY

"I changed my mind," Dad said.

Mom's foot pressed down harder on the brake pedal. "What do you mean, you changed your mind?"

Dad huffed. "I don't want you to take Phillip and Chris to a church."

"Ben, we're already in the car and dressed. It's too late. We can talk when I get back." Mom reached for the gear shift.

Dad slapped his hand against the hood of the car, and all of us, including him, jumped at the loud thunk. In the second of stillness after, I looked up from the passenger seat into the rearview mirror, which Chris and I had been playing with a moment before. Now he stared into some place in his head as he sat stiffly in the backseat. I tried to force his eyes up to mine.

"I'm sorry," Dad said. He lifted his hand slowly from the car as if he had just dropped a weapon. "I just don't think it's fair how you sprung this on me."

"Hold on. I didn't spring this on anyone. This isn't a trap, Ben."

"I didn't say it was a trap, but you haven't told any of us about this, and now you're sending our children to be indoctrinated—"

"Indoctrinated?"

I stopped hearing what Mom and Dad were saying. In the mirror I held my eyes on Chris's, still trying to get him to look at me. But he was stuck.

After a while Mom stepped into the brake pedal again and pulled the gear shift into park. "Fine," she said. "Boys, we can all go some other time. I'll go by myself this morning."

Chris finally looked up, and his eyes grazed mine.

"Can you bring us a snack?" I said.

"Yes," Mom said.

"A real one," Chris said.

"Yes," Mom said.

SEVENTEEN

Her dot is green.

For nine minutes she's been "available to chat." To any of her "friends." Of which there are just 178, including, since a day and a half ago, me.

It's not the prize I thought it was. She just doesn't use this thing.

Her dot is never green.

And I am about to chat her. I have been about to chat her for nine minutes.

I should just chat her.

I remind myself that Jennifer Baylor said yes. Jennifer Baylor, who is pretty and smart and wears those kick-ass square-frame glasses and has been a low-level crush of mine for about two years and would have been a high-level crush if I'd had even the slightest indication she'd say yes, said yes to Asher. Which I still just cannot even believe.

But I have my own high-level crush. Who, from what I hear, doesn't think I'm a total failure. And her dot is green right now.

If only I could just think of something funny to say about Genesis before—

Her dot fades to blue.

Shit.

Say something. Anything. Maybe she'll come back.

so i read genesis, I type.

I press enter and watch the words sit there, alone in the chat box. They are so lame. They are the blandest possible words. I wish I could delete them.

The dot turns green again. Ohmigod.

hi, she says. *so what did u think?*

That question again.

After Dad left my room, I sat down on my bed and read Genesis furiously, crashing through verses and toppling whole chapters. Oceans and skies separated and plants sprung to life and humans rose and fell and lived and died.

I thought it was awesome. But that's not enough.

Why can't she just *tell* me what I should think? That would be so much easier.

My fingers hover above the keys. My palms sweat.

it was awesome, I say, hoping it looks like enough once I type it out. But it doesn't.

do i get a cookie? I add.

So lame so lame so lame.

if u want. we happen 2 have 2 boxes of the best cookie ever.

which is?

oatmeal raisin obv!

oatmeal raisin is obv not the best cookie ever.

ur obv wrong about that.

obv you've never had chocolate chip becuz that is the best. obv.

ur mouth is dumb, obv.

My mouth is dumb. We're flirting, I think?

so did u nerd out on genesis or what? she says.

i did. That doesn't feel like enough, so I add, *it was epic.*

yeah kinda. anything else?

Ugh. This is like a quiz. I don't want to just throw out another adjective, but I am drawing a total blank. I didn't have time to *analyze* it.

let me think about it some more.

ok.

I don't know what to do now. We had a good chat moment, and now it's gone and I don't know what to do. Shit.

sorry i left when ferret came outside after youth group, I say, desperately switching topics, loathing myself for choosing the worst one.

She's silent. I stare at the chat box, waiting.

it's ok, she says. *he's kind of weird sometimes.*

He's weird. Not me.

he's kind of my nemesis sometimes, I say.

haha.

She laughed.

I just made her laugh with my words.

I didn't fail.

I should ask her out.

Ferret isn't here. Asher didn't sabotage me. Jennifer Baylor said yes.

It's just me and Rebekah.

It's just me and her.

Just us, right now.

The box remains empty. My fingers don't move. The seconds tick away.

I hear it in my head: "Y'alright, Flowers?"

He isn't here now, but he'll be there again on Wednesday. Sneaking up, meddling, mocking.

What if he finds out?

sorry gtg, Rebekah says. *c u l8r.*

yeah. c u.

Her dot disappears.

EIGHTEEN

I actually like running by myself.

When Mark quit, Ferret's evil powers were unleashed exclusively on me for an awful couple of days. But on the third day he came up to me right before practice and told me, with "great anguish," that our training sessions would have to end because Coach Heller needed him to work with the varsity squad. He told me that if I used the tools he'd given me, I could excel on the team.

Neither of us believed him.

And now I run alone. I run as fast or slow as I want, because Ferret's busy most days. I run the streets and paths that I like, and I try new ones. I think, or I don't think. There's not much else to do when you run by yourself.

Today is a not-thinking kind of day. The air is just a little bit cool. My legs feel strong. My lungs feel clear.

So of course there he is, rounding the corner on his red bike.

His angular sunglasses glint in the sunlight, and he wears a tight-lipped smile. As he passes the group of girls ahead of me he sits straight up on the seat and lifts a hand to wave slowly.

"Ladies," Ferret says.

But his front tire swerves, and he grabs for the handlebars, his face locked in panic. He wobbles past the girls, and they cover their mouths, stifling their laughter.

I bite my lip to keep from laughing too. Maybe he's like an emotional T. rex—as long as I don't show any fear or happiness or react at all to him, he won't see me.

I focus on my breathing. I look straight ahead.

And Ferret rides past me.

Yes.

But behind me I hear him braking. And turning around. And riding up slowly.

No.

He rides beside me, standing on the pedals, pumping them once every few seconds to slow to my pace. The girls seem to have picked up speed—they're already around the corner.

"Gave 'em a scare, I think," Ferret says.

Emotional T. rex. Emotional T. rex. Emotional T. rex.

"Said I think I gave 'em a scare. You in there, Flowers?"

He touches my scalp with his claw. I mean, finger.

I jerk away.

Dammit.

"Yeah," I say.

"Yeah, you're in there, or yeah, I gave 'em a scare?"

"Both, I guess."

"I think that's a good guess."

I'm silent. I run a little faster, to make him pedal more.

"Ready for the meet?" he says.

Our first meet of the season is Saturday morning. Meets are brutal. You have to wake up early, get dressed in a tank top and tiny shorts that expose your pale flesh to the burning gaze of the sun and everyone else, wait and wait and wait until your race comes up, and spend the next twenty-five minutes (in my case) running so hard that the inside of your chest feels as if it's been set on fire.

You can't really be ready for that.

"Yeah."

Ferret rides quietly for a moment. "You should be, after all that hell I put you through." After that he's quiet again. But he doesn't leave. We move down the street together, side by side.

Is this a new form of torture? What does he *want* from me?

"Aren't you supposed to be with varsity?" I say.

"Afternoon off. You coming to youth group tonight?"

That's what he wants from me? I'm not giving it to him. Who knows what he's planning.

"I don't know," I say.

Ferret chuckles. "You'll be there, Flowers. I know why, too. A certain young lady, am I right?"

Oh my God. No.

"Let me give you some advice, Flowers." He pauses for effect. "Don't bother."

This is it. This is all he ever wants from me: a reaction. Preferably anger and fear.

I try to keep quiet. But I can't. "Why?"

"Because she just isn't right for you, Flowers. And don't get me wrong. You aren't right for her, either. You know, just 'cause a girl invites you to church doesn't mean she's interested in anything about you but your soul."

No.

"You don't know anything about it."

He laughs. "I'm just trying to save you a heap of trouble."

"Whatever."

"Whatever and ever amen, Flowers. *Amen.*" He raises both arms over his head, like a preacher overwhelmed with passion. "Y'know—"

He swerves into me. I try to dodge him, but my foot hits the curb and I trip onto the lawn.

"Ow."

My ankle. The same goddamn one.

Ferret rights himself and brings his hand to his forehead. "Aw, hell. I mean, dangit. That was entirely my bad. I got carried away and—"

"Shut up."

I stand, trying not to groan as I feel the sting. Maybe it's not as bad as before. Maybe it is.

Ferret takes off his sunglasses. Without them his face looks weirdly shaped and sun-damaged. I can see in his eyes how weak he really is.

He's not some master villain. He doesn't have anything planned.

He's just a dipshit who wanted to scare me.

But he can't anymore. Because I can tell him to shut up.

And he'll listen.

"You alright?" he says.

I don't move or flex my foot. "Yes."

"You sure?"

"*Yes.*"

"Alright, then." He slides his sunglasses back on. "I do apologize."

Ferret pushes off and rides down the street, the breeze flapping against his T-shirt sleeves. I watch him until he turns the next corner behind some squat pine trees, and then I run through the pain.

It's not as bad.

NINETEEN

It's 7:05.

7:05 still counts as seven-ish.

Seven-ish is when Mark and I agreed he'd pick me up before church. Seven-ish is what I reminded him about at lunch today.

I guess we won't have as much time to drive around. But whatever. We'll have plenty of time on Friday.

I check my phone: 7:06.

I did remind him. Even if punctuality and remembering are not things he does very well, he supports what I'm trying to do here, even if he thinks the religious thing is kind of weird. So he'll show up.

I sit in front of my computer watching stupid videos. I tap out drum solos on my desk.

7:12.

I get up, go to the window to look at the street and the driveway. He's not out there. He's not driving up. My fingernails clack against the windowpane.

7:14.

I'm calling him.

It rings. And rings. And rings. And rings.

He picks up, and I get a blast of bass notes in my ear. I pull the phone away. "Mark?"

He says something, but I can't make it out.

"Where are you?"

Yelling in the background. "What?"

"WHERE ARE YOU?"

He finally turns down the music. "Oh, shit."

"Oh, shit what?"

"Dude, I . . . It just slipped my mind. I'm in the car with Dan and Brad over by Best Buy, but we'll come and—"

"No. No. Forget it."

I hang up and hurl my phone at my pillow.

Shit.

I can't call Mr. V. By the time he got here, I'd already be late. Rebekah takes this stuff seriously, so if I just wandered in ten minutes after . . .

Actually, she might not care at all. Based on what happened last time, she might prefer it.

Mark calls back, but I let my phone vibrate on the bed.

This is my fault. I relied on an unreliable person to be my ride. I had multiple chances to ask Rebekah out, but I waited and waited, and now I've probably let it go too long. Because deep down, I think Ferret's right.

Why would *she* ever like *me*?

I look in the mirror to see if I missed something.

Nope. Still average as hell.

I look at the letters tacked over my desk. Each letter of her name on a piece of notebook paper, all caps and adorned in obsessive details.

Yup. Still weird as hell.

I step closer. I look at the *R*, hastily drawn, with the old mushroom-cloud hearts exploding out of it. Then I look at the *H*. The lines are precise. All around the letter oatmeal raisin cookies do battle with chocolate chip cookies, impaling each other on their swords, aiming for vital bits of raisin and chocolate. A lone, nervous sugar cookie hides in the bottom right corner, oblivious to the chip-studded ninja dropping in from above. At the top a disembodied mouth says to another disembodied mouth: "Your mouth is dumb."

I grab my phone. 7:18.

There's still time.

I take my book bag and walk downstairs to go lie to my dad again.

"This is it."

I point at a light blue house off to the right. A hulking SUV sits in the driveway in front of a small gray car. Standing next to them is a speedboat perched on a trailer.

I picked this house because it had the most stuff in the driveway. This is where I'm going to "study group," so it should look like there are people here.

And some of them came in a boat, I guess.

"The blue one?" Dad says.

"Yeah, right here."

The car crawls along as Dad takes us over the bright yellow

speed hump that lies across the neighborhood street. I zip my book bag zipper back and forth. Zip-*zip*-zip-*zip*.

Come *on*, Dad.

The back end of the car slumps down as we finally pass over the hump. We slouch toward the house. It's so close. I could just open the door and jump out.

"Looks like somebody sailed over," Dad says. "Or motored over, I suppose."

God, I hate it when Dad and I make the same joke.

Finally he stops. I unclick the seat belt and grip my bag by the top strap and move for the door.

"Doesn't look like there are a lot of people here yet."

Does he suspect what's going on? I'd hoped my urgency ("I have to *leave*, Dad") had been enough to distract him from my lying. But I bet he's still wondering about that Bible.

"I don't know," I say. "We're early or something." I open the door, start to step out.

"I thought it started at seven thirty. It's 7:29 right now."

I give him a death glare. "I don't know, okay?"

"Alright, alright. Just checking. Nine o'clock, right?"

"Yeah."

I close the door and step onto the lawn. Behind the house is a small clump of woods. Behind the woods is Wesley Road Faith Church.

I wait for Dad to turn around and drive back over the hump. I walk up the driveway and glance sideways at our car until I finally slip behind the boat.

And then I run. I hold my book bag to my chest and scurry into the thin woods behind the house, my shoulders bobbing back and forth. My ankle stings a little, but that's all.

Ferret can't stop me. Mark can't stop me. Dad can't stop me.

Tree branches scour my arms and face. I jump over some sticker vines and burst open an old hollow log as I kick through it.

And then I run out of the tree line and onto the church's lawn. A few stragglers hold the youth center doors open for each other. A couple of them see me and squint their eyes for a second before going in.

Rebekah's not out here. I guess I figured she'd wait for me.

But youth group has started. Her friends are in there. And as far as she knows, I flaked. So why would she wait for me?

"Phillip," someone says, far away. I look over at the parking lot and see Rebekah standing by the passenger side of a newish white Jetta. She cups her hands around her mouth.

"Phillip!"

I wave.

"Come with us!"

She waited.

I start to jog across the lawn.

"Hurry!"

I start to run across the lawn.

"I don't think this counts," Amanda says as she pulls into the Kroger parking lot.

Rebekah groans. "Amanda, Tim said it does. So it does."

"He was just being nice. He doesn't really want me to count this."

This may be the cleanest car I've ever been in. The windows are smudgeless. There aren't any papers or wrappers shoved in the back of the seat. Even the floor mats are immaculate. I think I'm making it dirty just by breathing in it.

"Now you're calling Tim a liar," Rebekah says. "*Tim*. See how crazy you're being about this?"

"I am not—"

"What did Tim lie about?" I ask, leaning forward. I have to speak up a little over the Christian pop radio, which isn't as bad as I thought it would be, but isn't good either.

Amanda rolls her eyes just a little. "I didn't say he was a liar." She turns down a lane, hunting for a spot. Just like that, her eyes brighten back up and she smiles as she looks at me in the rearview. "He said I could count our refreshments run as a service hour for the Summit."

"Oh," I say, trying to sound like I understand all the parts of that sentence.

Rebekah, of course, hears it. "If you want to go to the Summit, that leadership conference thing, you have to complete fifty service hours." She raises her eyebrows at me. "You know, volunteering."

The atheist word for it.

"And this shouldn't count because it's not real service and it's not an hour," Amanda says. She pulls into a spot and turns off the car.

"We'll see about that," Rebekah says, snatching the key out of Amanda's hand and ducking out of the car.

"Hey!" Amanda says, laughing and then chasing her toward the store.

I get out and walk after them. I feel lucky to be here, lucky that I made it just in time for them to see me, lucky that Rebekah yelled my name. But I am still obviously on the outside of things.

When I get inside, Amanda is holding a shopping basket and Rebekah is holding a shopping basket.

"Hey!" Amanda says. "Sorry we left you out there. *Somebody* tried to steal my car keys." She glares at Rebekah, and Rebekah looks off, as innocent as a lamb. Amanda knocks her basket against Rebekah's and then takes out the list Tim gave her. There was an oversight, apparently, and the Wesley Road youth group is in dire need of Tostitos and Mountain Dew, or whatever.

Amanda rips the list in half and hands a piece to Rebekah. "We'll meet you by the checkout. Phillip, you come with me. I need your muscular system."

But I was going to make Ferret- and snack-related jokes to Rebekah. I was going to be skipping church with her, except not really. I was going to be more inside.

I cross my skinny arms, and then feel embarrassed and uncross them. "My muscular system isn't very muscular."

"Close enough," Amanda says without looking up from her list. Then she drops it in her basket and puts her hand out. "Okay, team. Break!" She power-walks toward the soda aisle, then shouts back, "Phillip, grab a cart!"

"I think I should listen to her," I say to Rebekah.

She puts her hand up for a high five. "Good luck out there."

"You too, soldier," I say, and then make contact with about half of her hand.

Soldier?

She smiles and walks away. I grab a cart and steer it to the sodas, my hand tingling. It was awkward, and it was only a high two-and-a-half, but our hands *did* touch.

When I arrive with the cart, Amanda dumps a case of Sprite into it. Then she looks at the list. "I totally missed how much soda was on here. We need two more of those, three Cokes, three

Diet Cokes, and a thing of bottled water." She looks up at me and nods toward the shelves. "So?"

"Right. Sorry." I grab a Sprite case and plop it into the basket while she takes the Cokes. We work in silence for a little while.

Then Amanda says, "Do *you* think I should count this?"

"For the volunteer hours thing?"

"Yeah, the service hours." She slides a twenty-four-pack of waters onto the bottom shelf of the cart.

Why is she asking me? I should just agree with what Rebekah said.

"Sure. You're helping, right?"

"Yes, but not in a meaningful way. Tim gave me his credit card, so it's not like I'm paying for it. I'm not *sacrificing* anything."

"Like a goat?"

She stops and glares at me.

"Bad joke," I say, even though it was actually 3 percent serious. *I* don't know what they consider "sacrificing."

Amanda cracks a smile and looks at her list. "Follow me."

I follow her. To the chips. She takes control of the refreshments-grabbing, rendering me a simple cart driver, which I am cool with.

"I'm just stressing because the Summit is important to me," she says. I'm liking Amanda more than I used to, but I still don't get her. It's a fraction of a requirement for a "youth leadership summit." Who cares?

"It's just one service hour, right?"

She hooks her blond hair behind her ear and looks at me in a way that tells me I don't understand. But I already knew that.

I watch her grab and stash bags of pretzels and popcorn. "Phillip," she says, "why did you start coming to our youth group?"

Didn't Amanda used to be the most aggressively nice person I'd ever met? Why do I keep getting this feeling like she's actually just *aggressive*?

"Rebekah invited me."

"I know that. But why did you come? And why did you come back?"

She's done grabbing snacks, and now she's just looking at me. My palms feel slick against the plastic cart handle.

"I thought it sounded interesting." I scratch my ear. "And then it was, so I wanted to come back."

Still just looking at me.

"I didn't really go to church as a kid, so there's that, too."

Still. Just. Looking.

I clear my throat. "And Rebekah. I wanted to hang out with Rebekah."

"You know she's special, right?" Amanda says.

I give her a look back.

"As in, amazing," she says.

"Well, yeah—"

"Absolutely amazing, right?"

"Yes."

"You're sure?"

"Yes."

I feel like she's scanning my brain with her eyes. Long, awkward seconds pass.

"Good," she says finally, folding up the list and putting it in her pocket. "We're done here."

Back at the church we carry the refreshments over to a side door. Amanda pulls out a small ring of keys, unlocks the door, and props it open with a case of Diet Coke.

"Okay," she says. "I can take it from here, y'all."

"Wait," Rebekah says, "we can help you."

"Yeah," I say.

Amanda stands in front of the open door, keeping us out. "No, no. I've got it."

"Amanda—"

She holds up her hand. "I can handle putting pretzels in a bowl, okay? You two have fun. And be careful." She grabs four bags of snacks and hauls them into the room, leaving the door propped.

Rebekah whispers, "She wants to feel like she's being a good—"

"I heard that!"

"No, you didn't!"

Pretty soon it sounds like a crinkly plastic massacre in there. We shrug at each other and start walking toward the front of the youth center. I hold the straps of my book bag tightly.

It's weird how much difference one person's presence or absence can make. Rebekah and I were both around each other most of the time, but Amanda being there made it completely different. Especially because Amanda was acting like she's Rebekah's mom. She must have asked me to get the sodas and stuff with her just so she could quiz me. The weird thing is, I think I passed? Because I agreed Rebekah's amazing? But anybody could do that.

Do I believe it? I *think* so. It felt like I believed it. And I guess it looked like I believed it.

But I still barely know her. We just met a few weeks ago. There is so much about her I don't know. There is so much about me that she doesn't know.

We could ignore that when Amanda was around.

Now we can't.

We reach the front of the building. The big, flat space of the lawn and the volleyball and basketball courts looks so empty. Everyone is inside. I hear the faint echo of Tim's amplified voice.

"Do you want to go in?" I say.

"Sure."

Going inside will be safe. I won't have to think of things to say. It's what we'd be doing anyway, if we hadn't gone on our refreshments mission.

It's like letting her dot fade to blue.

"Or we could not," I say.

She arches an eyebrow. "Oh, yeah?"

"Just theoretically."

Ferret might come looking for us. But I almost want him to.

The cuffs of her dark purple long-sleeved shirt hang over her hands, and she gathers and twists them. "I don't know."

The air goes out of me. "Yeah, you're right. We—"

"We need a good reason." She smiles. "Like Amanda has."

I am so on the spot here. On the spot is not where I like to be. I like to be well off the spot.

I look around. For anything.

"Basketball," I say, like a Frankenstein, and point, like a Frankenstein.

She turns around, sees the basketball lying in the grass, and dramatically throws her hands in the air. "Somebody just left it out!"

"Very irresponsible." I shake my head. "I guess we have to clean up after those kids."

We walk over to the ball. Rebekah picks it up and squeezes it. "You know, somebody should test the condition of this ball. To make sure those kids didn't ruin it."

"I think you're right, young lady. I don't see anyone else out here, so I guess it'll have to be us."

"A game of HORSE, then?" She grins. "If you're up for it, Grandpa."

I swipe the ball from her hands. "You're goin' down, whipper-snapper."

And Rebekah and I start playing HORSE instead of going to youth group. I'm pretty sure I'll need to go easy on her, since, despite being uncoordinated and terrible at pretty much every sport, including basketball, I am usually pretty good at standing in one spot and shooting a ball through a hoop.

But then she keeps *nailing* them.

"I used to play," she says, handing me the ball after an outside-the-key swish.

I have *HOR*. She has *H*. This is ridiculous.

"You totally sharked me," I say, dribbling in place to prep for the shot. "Is there anything you're *not* good at?"

She scrunches up her forehead. "Um . . . darts?"

"I don't believe you." I take the shot. It arcs nicely but clangs off the rim, falling pathetically to the ground.

"Aw. There must be something *you're* good at." She puts her hand over her mouth like she can't believe she just said that.

I laugh. "No, I'm bad at everything." I retrieve the ball and pass it to her.

She cocks her head. "Come on. That's not true."

"Okay, I'm average at some things."

She smiles, but she doesn't look as amused anymore. "But really."

"Really. I thought I was good at *this*, but obviously not."

She bounces the ball hard. Once. Twice. "Tell me."

It was a joke, but now it's not. The thing is, it's true. I do okay at school, but I'm not great at it. I'm not athletic. Being obsessed with the Apocalypse isn't something you can be good at.

And I'm obviously not good at talking to girls.

Rebekah just barely shakes her head, like she's disappointed. She bounces the ball a couple more times and aims to give me my final letter.

"I draw."

I spit it out just before she releases the ball, which wobbles a bit on the way, and circles the basket, and gently drops through.

Rebekah's eyes are wide open, looking at me. "You *draw*?"

"Sometimes. Just as like a hobby or whatever. I'm not 'good,' but—"

"You didn't tell me you draw," she says. She walks over and gets the ball.

You don't tell people you draw. That's lame. Plus, I don't *draw*. I *have drawn* a few things recently. And if there's one person I didn't want to tell, it's Rebekah, because—

"What do you draw?" she says, tossing me the ball.

Exactly. I am not telling her about the letters. I'm just not.

"Stuff," I say, hoping that will be enough, knowing it won't.

"What stuff?"

"Just." I dribble a few times, trying to think of something, trying to calm down. "Stuff."

"Okay. When you miss this shot and I win the game, you have to draw something."

"We didn't say we were playing for anything."

"Well, we are." She smiles. "So shoot."

Shit. Shit shit shit. I can still pull this off. I am good at this. I can go on a four-letter streak.

I shoot.

Air ball.

"That's *E*," Rebekah says. "I win."

I look at her with pleading eyes. "Where am I even supposed to draw something?"

"You don't have any paper in your bag?"

I honestly don't. I just have my chemistry textbook and her Bible. "No."

For a second she looks like she might relent. Then her eyes perk up, and she points at the volleyball court. "There."

"Where? In the sand?"

"Yeah."

She isn't going to give up on this. I never should have mentioned it.

But I did.

"Okay. I need some time to think about it." I have no idea what to do. I've never drawn anything in sand before.

"Let's sit over there," I say.

"In the sand?"

"Yes."

She smiles. "Okay. You're the artist."

"No, I'm not."

We walk over together and sit down across from each other. The only sound is the quiet whooshing of cars going by. Out beyond the road, the molten orange sun dips behind the pine trees. Leaning back, I dip my fingers into the sand.

I still don't know how I'm going to pull this off. I need more time.

"You owe me a cookie," I say.

She laughs. "You're right. I can go ask Amanda for one."

"No. You'd bring back an oatmeal raisin."

A moment passes. Just like last time, I'm surprised at how comfortable this feels. How this feels even more comfortable.

I'm glad I came.

I lean forward. I touch the sand with my finger and let it drift, forming a faint drifting line. "Amanda seemed really stressed out."

"Yeah. Sorry she was sort of ordering you around. She's a really sweet person, but she also likes to be in charge."

"I noticed. I don't get why she was so worried, though. She asked me whether she should count the hour or not, and I was like, 'Why is this such a big deal?'"

Rebekah looks stunned. "Did you really say that to her?"

"Well, no, not really. But she did look angry at me."

"Yeah, going to the Summit means a lot to her. And not just her. There's no way you would know this, but the Summit is a big deal to some people. Especially people like Amanda who are really dedicated to being youth leaders."

There's no way I would know. Why does it sting to hear her say that? It's not an insult. It's true. I don't understand the Summit at all, even though it's been explained to me.

"Why?"

Rebekah scrapes out a hole in the sand. "I don't completely

know. It's been around for a while. There are a lot of famous people who show up and give talks and concerts."

"Famous people?"

"Famous in the Christian world." Rebekah fills the hole back in and pats the sand down. "And people seem to get a lot out of it. At my old church the youth pastors would always talk about how great it is. How important it was for them."

"So Amanda doesn't want to cheat to get there."

Rebekah laughs. "Right. She'd better count that hour." She turns back toward the side entrance as if to scold Amanda, then she shakes her head. "Crazy."

"Are you going to count it?"

"What do you mean?"

"I thought you were going too."

She looks down. "Yeah. No. I don't know. She wants me to."

"And Ferret wants you to."

"He practically forced me to sign up, right? It's not that I don't want to go. I do. It's just expensive."

"You have to pay to go?"

She laughs. "Yeah. Six hundred dollars."

"*And* you have to do community service?"

"Service *hours.*"

"Still."

I look up. The sun peeks over the trees, sinking fast. The air between Rebekah and me seems hazy and gray. I look down and see I've drawn a small heart in the sand beside my leg. I wipe it out quickly. I can't draw that.

"And with my dad gone right now . . ." She trails off and looks away.

"Your dad's gone?"

"He's a missionary in Indonesia."

A missionary? I didn't know that was something people even did anymore.

"How long has he been there?"

"Two years. Actually, he's been doing missions work on and off for the past four years. That's why my mom and I moved up here over the summer to live with my aunt."

"Do you miss him?"

Even as I say it, I regret it. I know how dumb that question is. How it kind of makes you hate the person who asked it.

"Yeah," she says. Somehow she doesn't seem offended. "We write letters. And he might be coming home over Christmas. But since he's not around, money's a little tight, even living with my aunt." She pulls at the cuff of her sleeve. "He'd probably freak if I didn't go to the Summit, though."

"Is he strict?"

"Not strict. Just good. Really good all the time."

"Good?"

"A good person. He witnesses in everything he does. He expects me to witness in everything I do." She digs another small hole with her finger and fills it back up just as quickly. Then she laughs. "Anyway. Too much information."

We both lean back. The air is so calm, I imagine she can hear my heartbeat. In the sky only the sun's wake remains.

I want to say, "No, it's not." Or, "I'm glad you told me." But even though those are true, they would sound so weak.

I can say something else, though.

"My mom died a few years ago."

Her eyes are calm. "I'm sorry," she says.

"Thanks. I haven't told anyone that in . . . I don't know."

"That's so hard. I shouldn't complain."

I feel my stomach tense up. She thinks I'm trying to top her story. She thinks I just used my mom's death as a weapon.

I don't do that. I would never do that.

"No, no, that's not how I meant it."

"I know." She dismisses me with a wave of her hand.

"Really. I wasn't trying to—"

"I *know*."

She looks at me, and even in the dim light I can see the intensity of her eyes. I don't want to ruin this night. I don't want some stupid thing I said to make me awkward again.

I still haven't drawn anything. Now, in the darkness, it might be too late.

I couldn't have drawn the mushroom-cloud-heart anyway. That was the first thing that popped into my head, but it just didn't make sense. It's my thing, not hers, or ours.

The letters wouldn't work either. Too elaborate. Too creepy.

I need something simple.

Something true.

"Do you still want your drawing?" I say.

"Yes," she says.

Taking a breath, I smooth out a space in the sand between us. I place my finger on the sand and push upward. One quick, straight line.

And another. Connected to another. I keep going.

In the dark they look smudgy and gray. Half-hidden.

"What are you drawing?" she says.

I don't answer. I lean in closer and finish the letters, which are simple and true:

I LIKE YOU.

Then I take another look at them and feel sick.

I'm a coward. I couldn't even say it. I had to write it in the sand. In the dark.

Then suddenly there's a noise like *choonk*, and light surrounds us, and Rebekah says, "Oh, God!"

The overhead lamps have finally turned on. The glare is harsh and white, and it drops multicolored spots into my eyes.

Rebekah holds her hand over her chest and laughs. "I can't believe how scary that was!"

"I know."

My words aren't hidden anymore. They are fully illuminated and unavoidable. We can't not look at them.

They're too much. They're too strong.

"Um, sorry," I say.

I reach forward to wipe the words away.

"Phillip," Rebekah says. "Don't."

I don't. I lean back, my heart pounding.

She leans forward. In the sand she underlines I, then LIKE, then YOU. She adds TOO, and underlines that.

She sits back, wipes her hands on her pant legs, and shoots me a stare like, *Look at what you just made me do.*

TWENTY

Mark screams into the wind. "AM I FORGIVEN?"

We shoot past a big green truck. Air pours into the car from all four windows and the moonroof, and it flaps and flattens our shirts and pushes into our faces like fingers. Some emo-punk song crashes out of the speakers.

I scream, "NO!"

Asher screams, "NO!"

Mark screams, "FUCK YOU, ASHER. THIS HAS NOTHING TO DO WITH YOU!"

Emo-punk screams, "COME ON, COME ON, COME ON!"

I scream, "FUCK YOU. YES, IT DOES!"

Mark screams, "FINE!"

And we go even faster.

Mark has been apologizing for the past two days for not picking me up. The next day at lunch he bought me an ice cream sandwich and told me that he had been about to come get me when Dan the

Man and Brad had made him drive them to the Best Buy parking lot for some dumb-ass stunt they were filming with their friends.

So he forgot.

It was a terrible excuse. And the sandwich was full of ice crystals. And I was feeling pretty cocky after what had happened on Wednesday night, and prickly about him ditching me for his goons. So I kind of left him hanging.

Now this is supposed to be his forgiveness present to me. No Brad. No Dan. Just Mark, Asher, and me in our BMW, finally, speeding down Steven Pillory Memorial Highway, going way too fast, playing terrible music way too loud, and giving way too many innocent people the finger.

I am finally starting to feel merciful.

I thrust my middle finger out the moonroof. "FUCK YOU, STEVEN PILLORY!"

"YEAH!" yells Asher, leaning in from the backseat to stick his own finger out the top. "FUCK YOU, STEVEN!"

Mark squints, confused. "WHO'S STEVEN . . ." Then he gets it. "OH, YEAH! FUCK YOU, STEVEN! FUCK YOU AND YOUR FUCKING MEMORIAL HIGHWAY!"

And still we go faster.

The music drowns in the wind. We blow past two cars in the right lane. The red arrow on the speedometer climbs to eighty-five mph. A yellow Mustang is in the left lane, in front of us. We are rapidly approaching it. It's not moving over. We're closer. It's still not moving. I grip the door handle and hold my breath.

Mark lurches us into the right lane. My stomach lurches to the left.

"FUCK YOU, AMERICAN PIECE OF SHIT!" Mark yells, flipping the Mustang off.

This isn't fun anymore.

"THAT'S ENOUGH!" I yell.

"WHAT?" Mark yells.

"SLOW DOWN!" Asher yells.

Mark laughs. He doesn't slow down. We pull into the left lane again. He turns off the music. He lifts his head and howls. "AM I FORGIVEN?"

I squeeze the handle and glance at the speedometer again. We're going ninety. I had forgiven him. Now I don't want to.

But I do want to be alive for his party tonight.

"YES!"

"WHAAAAT?" He's shaking his head, pretending he doesn't hear. A hulking white minivan chugs along ahead of us.

"YES!" I yell. "SLOW THE FUCK DOWN!"

"SLOW DOWN!" Asher echoes.

"ARE YOU SURE?" Mark says.

The minivan is so slow. We are so fast. We're going to hit it if he doesn't slow down right now.

"YES, YOU'RE FORGIVEN! NOW FUCKING SLOW DOWN!" I point to the minivan with one hand and switch my other to the oh-shit handle above the door.

We're almost on it. We're almost on it.

"OKAY!"

Mark hits the brakes and jolts the whole car and scares the shit out of me, and probably Asher, too, but I can't look back at him right now. We slow down enough. And we don't hit the minivan. And we're okay.

We drive behind the guy for five or ten seconds in silence. Mark presses a button, and all the windows roll up and the moonroof closes. I glance at Asher. He's pressing his palms into the seat leather.

I take a breath and turn to Mark, who has a worried grin on his face.

"Happy birthday, you asshole," I say.

"Yeah," Asher says. "I hate you, birthday boy."

Mark runs his hand through his bushy hair and laughs. "Thanks, guys."

I turn the music back on, and it's really, really loud.

Later, Asher and I walk along the side of the neighborhood clubhouse. Inside, Mark's party has been going strong for a couple of hours. Shane Geiser told us he brought a small bottle of tequila and hid it behind the electric meter box thing on the side of the clubhouse. And that we could have a shot each—"But that's it."

At this point that sounds awesome. Brad and Dan, the ones who were supposed to bring the booze, got here empty-handed about an hour ago, disappointing pretty much everybody who hadn't brought their own. Which, of course, includes Asher and me.

Mark said Brad and Dan still had some leads that might come through, though, and that we could share theirs when they got it. That's so obviously not happening that I've basically given up. But I'm happy for Mark. He's pretty drunk by now—he just poured a bunch of sparkles from a girl's present into his hair—so people must have been giving him birthday sips and shots of their stashes.

Asher and I do not have the connections or the charm or the correct birth date. Thank God for Shane Geiser, though. He's just as dorky as us.

"There it is," Asher whispers, pointing at a large metal box.

"Dude, why are you whispering?" I say. The clubhouse is surrounded by big lawns and tennis courts and the swimming pool.

"It just seems appropriate." Asher stops in front of the box and leans over it. I stand next to him and look behind us toward the front of the building and the parking lot. No one. I look toward the back, where the courts are. No one there, either.

Bass thumps out from the building, and I tap my foot along with it.

"There it is," Asher says. He pushes himself off the box and brings back a hand-size bottle with a brown label. He holds the label in front of his glasses, trying to read it. "Looks like . . . uh . . ."

"Come on, blindy," I say, snatching the bottle from his hand.

He crosses his arms and looks at me for a second. "Blindy? Seriously?"

"Shut up," I say. I hold the bottle up so the light from the parking lot hits it. "'Señor Salamander,'" I read.

"Señor Salamander?"

I double-check. "Yeah, Señor Salamander Tequila. It looks at least twenty years old."

Asher shakes his head. "This is going to be disgusting."

I twist the cap off and bring the bottle up to my nose. I recoil and hand the bottle to Asher. "Oh. Dude."

He sniffs hesitantly and then brings his arm up to cover his nose. "I can't believe we're about to drink this."

I take the bottle. "Let's just do it and get it over with."

"Hold on. We have to drink to something."

"To drinking!"

"I hate you. Seriously." He takes the bottle back. "Okay, I've got it." He raises the bottle in the air. The light from the parking

lot shimmers in the pale brown liquor. "To finally getting girls."
He swoops the bottle down to his lips and drinks for a couple of
seconds before thrusting the bottle at my chest. I grab it just as he
swallows and makes a noise like, *"Blugck."*

His toast gets under my skin, makes me hesitate, even though
he meant it to be triumphant. I told him what happened on
Wednesday, but I haven't told him what happened since. Or, what
hasn't happened since.

I take a deep breath, close my eyes, and drink. The tequila is
like burning oil in my mouth, and I feel it singe my insides. I rip
the bottle away and hand it back to Asher. We groan and spit, and,
eventually, we laugh.

"I knew it was going to be disgusting," Asher says, "but I really
had no idea." He twists the top back on.

We talk about how we think we can feel the buzz already. A car
drives into the parking lot, lets some girls out, and then drives off.
"Woooo!" the girls say, and the music inside spills out as they go
in. Asher leans back against the electrical box, placing the bottle
on top. I kick the ground, dig up a small patch of grass.

"Something wrong?" he says.

I shove my hands in my pockets. "No."

"Obviously there is."

I should just tell him.

"I think I fucked up," I say. And then I tell him.

Wednesday night I was in a state of levitational bliss. After
Rebekah and I said goodbye, I levitated back through the woods,
I levitated in the car as Dad drove me home (he didn't seem to
notice), and I levitated up to my room and finally sank down onto
my bed, my powers spent. I lay there in that half-awake brain space

just before sleep, until a giddy thought jiggled me awake.

I sat up and grabbed my phone, but then I realized I didn't have Rebekah's number. So I got online and wrote this message that I can still see, word for excruciating word, in my head:

> Hi, Reb. Can I call you that? No? That's okay. It's not a very good nickname. We don't have to be one of those couples that have stupid, cutesy names for each other.
>
> Anyway, Reb, I just realized that you didn't give me a new homework assignment for this week. Which book should I read? Exodus? Judges sounds cool. Are there eye-creatures in any of the other ones?
>
> And can you give me your number?
> Honeybuckets

I know she's not online much, but two days have passed and she hasn't responded.

And I don't blame her. I fucked up. I scared her away. "Honeybuckets"? It was a joke, but *Honeybuckets*? And calling us a couple?! It's like I was drunk. What the hell was I—

"Dude, stop," Asher says, interrupting me.

"What? You asked me to tell you—"

He points at my feet. "You're murdering innocent grass."

I look down. He's right. I've kicked up a whole extended family of grass roots. I try to stomp some back into place. "Sorry."

110

"Did you just apologize to the grass?"

"Shut up, asshole."

"Whoa!" he says, laughing. "I'm listening to your problems. I don't think I deserve to be called an asshole."

"Well, this is serious, and you don't seem to really care, so—"

"You're scared of her."

I freeze. "What?"

He pushes the bridge of his glasses with his thumb. "You're scared of Rebekah."

Is he *trying* to piss me off? "I'm not scared of her. I'm . . . Okay, fine. I'm scared of her. So?"

"Don't be."

"'Don't be'? Okay, I won't be. Just like that." As if Asher is some authority on girls? He has as much experience as I do: none at all. Actually, I "went out" with Kira Dooley for a week in sixth grade, so I have more than he does. If you don't count him and Jennifer Baylor, which hasn't even been going on that long.

Asher lifts himself onto the box and lies flat. "It's not that easy. But it's not as hard as you think."

I come and stand over him. "What is going on with you lately? When did you become such a fucking guru?"

He laughs, and his perfect teeth glow in the light. "Do you remember when I went with you to church?"

"Yeah."

"Do you remember what that guy Tim was talking about?"

I stare at the grass, trying to remember. I remember being bored with it. And I remember not really hearing much of it because I was constantly thinking about Rebekah and how she smelled and what the hell I was going to say to her when Tim was done.

111

"Sort of."

"I didn't think so," he says. "'The life you choose'? Remember?"

"Oh. Yeah." It was that standard self-esteem bullshit with a God twist.

"Okay, this is embarrassing, but for some reason, it actually made me think."

"About what?"

"About how I have to make things happen in my life. And maybe that sounds really obvious, but it's *true*." Asher smacks the edge of the box. "I would always just be nice and do well in school and obey my parents and hang out with you guys. But I wasn't happy. I was *content*, but I wasn't happy. I realized that to be happy I had to do what *I* wanted to do. Even though that's not exactly what Tim was saying."

"So you joined *academic team* to be happy?" I say.

"I know you think it's boring, but I think it's fun."

"And then you asked out Jennifer Baylor."

"Right."

"And you got this whole new philosophy in one night? At church?"

"Not all of it. But most of it, yeah."

"What does that have to do with being scared, though? Weren't you scared when you talked to Jennifer?"

"Yes! Of course."

"But you said don't be scared!"

"It's more of a mind trick. You know you have to do what you want to do. But sometimes those things are scary. So you're scared, but you tell yourself you're not scared, so you make the choice to do the thing that scares you. Then afterward it's not scary anymore."

Sometimes I can't tell if Asher really is smarter than I am or if he just sounds like he is.

He pushes himself off the box. "We should go back in."

"Wait," I say. "Thanks for the wisdom and shit, but how does this help me? I already sent that stupid message. Not being scared isn't going to let me travel back in time and stop myself from sending it."

"You're right. You did what you did. Maybe you screwed things up, and maybe you didn't. You don't know. But maybe even *she* doesn't know if you screwed things up or not. So when you talk to her tomorrow, not being scared will make it seem like you didn't screw things up, even if you did."

There are a lot of confusing things about what he just said, but there's one thing that's especially confusing. "Tomorrow?"

"You have a meet tomorrow morning, right? And Rebekah will be there."

"Rebekah will be there?" My heartbeat accelerates.

"Yeah. To *run*? You know?" He moves his arms back and forth.

"I thought she was on academic team."

He looks at me for a second. "How did you not know this? She worked it out so she could do both."

"She's going to be at the meet tomorrow. To run."

"Yes. And you can unscrew things if they're screwed. But you'll probably be okay."

"So you don't think the message was that bad?"

"It was pretty bad. But I think you're freaking yourself out. As usual." He leans over the box to put the tequila away.

That sounds right. All of it sounds right.

I would never tell him this, but I'm happy he's my friend.

Don't be scared. Just don't be scared.

113

Maybe if I say it enough times by tomorrow morning, I won't be.

"Hey," Asher says. He looks behind the bush to the left of the box. "What's that?"

He walks around the box and ducks down under the heavy leaves of the bush. They swish and crash as he digs around. I hear a dull metallic clang, and then Asher turns around, smiling, and holds up a can of Miller High Life.

"Holy shit," I say, grabbing the can from him. It's warm, but it's beer. A full can of beer, stout and sturdy in my hand.

"There are two cases back here," Asher says.

"What?"

"Yeah, man."

"Whose are they?"

"I don't know." Still squatting, he looks back up at me with big eyes, like he's suddenly lost his guru confidence.

"Well . . ." I say, stalling. This is obviously someone else's stash. And a stash is a sacred thing. It wouldn't be cool to steal from it.

But there's so much of it. They—whoever they are—wouldn't even miss two. They'd probably be happy to share, if they knew.

Then, toward the front of the clubhouse, the bushes rattle, and someone yells, "Ow, asshole!"

I turn toward the sound, beer in my hand, right as another voice yells out, "Hey, what the . . . ?"

Three dark forms stride toward us. It's Mark. And Dan the Man and Brad. And we were obviously just raiding what is now obviously their stash.

Dan tromps up, the sweat on his face refracting the dim light. "What the hell?" Then he notices Asher. "Look at *this* faggot tryin' to hide."

"I'm not hiding," Asher says as he slowly stands up.

"Then what are you doing? Stealing?"

Brad stands beside Dan, curling his fists up at his side. He's stringy but fierce. Mark stands silently behind both of them.

"This isn't what it looks like," I say, immediately regretting it. That's what you say when it definitely *is* what it looks like.

"Then what is it?" says Brad, his mouth tight.

These guys live for this—an excuse to kick somebody's ass.

"We didn't realize it was yours, and we weren't taking it, anyway."

"Bull. *Shit.* What is *that*, then?" He points to the beer in my hand.

"It looks bad, but I was just about to put it back."

"Yeah, right," Dan says.

Asher clears his throat. "I thought it was supposed to be *ours*, too. Right, Mark?"

Why are you doing this, Asher? Just let it go.

Mark shrugs. "We didn't know if we would have enough."

"Oh, please," Asher says. "You have two cases back there."

"Whatever," Dan says. "You didn't pay us anything. It's ours. Why would we give you any?"

"Here's your beer." I hand it to him.

He snatches it up. "Damn straight." He looks at Asher. "You probably already drank one. Right, faggot?"

Asher laughs. "I don't even know you, Dan, so I'm not sure why you think you can determine my sexuality. But since you apparently love to spit that word at other people, I'd say there's a pretty good chance that *you're* gay and—"

"The *fuck*?" Dan steps toward Asher chest-first, his arms cocked at his sides.

Mark throws his arm in front of Dan's chest. "Come on, man."

"No, dude," Dan says, huffing and sticking his chest out. "Get these kids out of here." He points at both of us.

"Dan, man, they weren't—"

"The hell they weren't!"

Asher steps back and crosses his arms. "It's fine. We're just going to leave."

I look at him and step back too. "Yeah."

"Good. Get out," Dan says, stepping down a little. Mark stares at Asher like he's trying to recognize him.

Asher and I walk around them on either side. As we pass, Dan turns his head and whispers to Asher, "Faggot." Just in case we didn't get it.

Asher laughs quietly. As we walk toward the parking lot, he yells, "I love your new friends, Mark!"

MARCH

They were really good at hiding it. I didn't even realize how bad things were until Mom told me she was going on vacation.

"Right now?" I said, clenching the top of my sheets in my hand. It was after ten thirty, and I had just started to fall asleep. It was a Tuesday night. I had school the next day, and so did Mom—at the high school library, where she worked.

Mom looked at the digital clock on my nightstand and made a face that I didn't understand. I thought maybe I had convinced her not to go.

"Yeah," she said. "I have to go right now, Phil." She laid her hands flat on her lap and stared at her nails. Only she called me Phil.

"No, you didn't."

"Phil."

But then she stopped and stared at her nails again. And then she sandwiched her hands between her knees and actually looked at me.

"Phil," she said, and now it actually sounded real. "I can't tell your brother this. But you're right. You're old enough."

I hadn't said that, but I knew what she meant, I guess. I pulled the sheets up a little higher, to my chest.

"Your dad and I have been together for a long time," she said.

Suddenly I knew everything.

I watched TV. I knew what happened to parents when they said stupid things like that. They divorced. My parents were getting divorced like idiots, like people on TV. Like parents whose kids had ADD and got sent to detention. I was going to detention. I was going to get ADD. This was stupid.

"Why?" I said.

She crinkled her forehead. "Why?"

"Why are you getting divorced?" I said.

Mom leaned toward me. "Oh no, Phil. We're not getting divorced. I'm just taking a little time for myself. When you've been with someone for as long as your dad and I have been, you need to be by yourself sometimes. And you don't always know when you need to do that."

I looked away from her at the wall next to my bed. I still had a Tony Hawk poster up there from when I thought I was going to be a skater.

"Okay, you're right again," she said. "I'm not telling you the whole story."

She paused, waiting for me to turn back, but I kept looking at the poster.

"You know when we were about to go to church and Dad stopped you?" Mom said. "Well, he wanted me to stop too, but I've been going to Crossroads Church for about three months now. It's important to me."

She looked at me like she expected me to respond to that, but I didn't do or say anything. She gathered her hair like a handful of grass. "But that's not the point. It's a big part of it, but there are a lot of other big parts. And small parts. And all those big parts and small parts can build

118

up over years and years. And that's why your dad and I had our argument tonight."

"I didn't hear you," I said.

"We went into the basement." Mom looked at the clock again, and then took my fingers in her hand. "I have to leave, Phil. Just for a little while. You guys are going to do great, and I'll call every day. And don't think that this is your fault. Or Chris's. Okay?"

I hadn't thought that. Why would it be our fault? Why would it be anybody's fault but theirs?

Mom kissed me, and she squeezed my hand, and she told me she'd be back soon. She closed the door behind her. I stood at the window, watching her car leave and then waiting for it to come back.

TWENTY-ONE

There are a lot of reasons why I just vomited in the woods.

For one, I do this pretty often before a race. At least, I did last year. Actually, I did it so many times that the seniors would hang around me, just waiting for it to happen. For a few minutes I would actually feel kind of cool. Then I would barf.

For two, whatever was in that tequila bottle was truly foul. My stomach was twisting in on itself all last night. I hope Shane Geiser is okay.

For three, the stress from what happened with Dan the Man and Brad has been swirling around in my intestines with the evil bacteria from that bottle. Some of it came up, but some of it's still down there.

And for four, Asher was right: Rebekah's here. And I'm scared.

I wipe my mouth and clutch my knees. Then I'm staring right at my puke, so I clutch my knees elsewhere. Our team's tent stands just outside the trees, and I can hear people warming themselves up, clapping sporadically to keep their energy going. The paths we're running don't have much tree cover, and the sun is bright and hot.

I could just not run. I could get Mr. V to take me home. He's such a ridiculously nice guy that, even though Asher isn't on the team anymore, he drove me here because Dad had to take Chris to his soccer game. Asher claims his dad is only looking for excuses to get out of the house, since he works from home, but I bet Mr. V would drive me back now if I asked him to.

"Hoo, boy!" calls a familiar voice. I cringe. "Something smells rank back here, Flowers. You up to your old tricks?"

I open my eyes and see Ferret's skinny shadow stretch out in front of me.

I push myself up and stand straight, blocking it.

I breathe.

"Nope," I say, and I turn and walk past him toward the tent.

There actually is a runner's high. It's just that it comes after twenty-one minutes and forty-three seconds of feeling like you're inhaling a can of pepper spray and your legs are being beaten with rolling pins. Still, that's a personal record for me. Thirty-two fewer seconds of that to get the same effect:

Lightness. Easiness.

Less-scaredness.

"You were very fast," says Mr. V as I rub my face with my towel. "Did you see me cheering?"

I'm sure a few people in the tent area are wondering if I'm adopted.

I nod. It's easier to lie if you don't say anything. I didn't look at the crowd at all because I was afraid I would see Rebekah.

"Good," Mr. V says. "Do you stay to watch the other girls?"

The "other girls" are the JV girls. They're last in the racing order today. Racing orders change, and we don't always run on the same days as the girls, but today it was varsity guys, varsity girls, JV guys (that's me), and then JV girls.

Rebekah is a varsity girl. I was wondering if Rebekah might just leave after her race, and what I would do—or not do—if she did. But I look over at the edge of the course, and she's there, about fifty yards out from the starting line, standing with the other varsity girls. They've switched into identical T-shirts instead of the sheer racing tops, but she's still wearing those tiny shorts.

Good Lord.

"Do you stay?" Mr. V asks me again.

I should stay. But as soon as I think about Rebekah, my lightness is heavier.

That stupid email. That stupid, stupid email.

Don't be scared.

Don't be scared.

Don't be scared.

I don't know if this is working. But I have to try.

"Let me go talk to someone real quick."

I walk across the grass, dry and crisp in the sun. Rebekah stands between a couple of other, older varsity girls who are also hot. Their T-shirts all say TEAM CARLY.

I walk up beside Rebekah.

Don't be scared.

"Who's Carly?" I say. My voice sounds loud and fake.

"Oh," she says, double-taking. The girls behind her glance at me and then turn back to the course. "You scared me."

"Sorry."

Classic move, creeping up on her like that. Always very charming.

"It's okay," Rebekah says, but she looks away when she says it. "Anyway, she's this girl on JV who's made a lot of progress lately. We're all supporting her."

A few of the girls yell, "Team Carly!" A short red-haired girl at the starting line waves at them and smiles nervously.

"The varsity guys would never do something like this," I say.

"Would you want them to?" she says, kind of sharply.

I'm silent, trying to figure out the right answer.

Don't be scared.

"I wouldn't admit it if I did," I say.

Her mouth is tight like she's trying not to laugh. Or she's angry.

So I did screw things up.

But I maybe almost made her laugh.

And she likes me. She wrote it in the sand.

Don't be scared.

"So, how was your race, Reb?" I say.

Her slow smile is a backhanded compliment. "Pretty good . . . Honeybunches?"

"Honey*buckets*," I say quietly.

"Right."

I pull at the fringe of my shorts. "Sorry about that message. Was it, like, too much or—"

"No, no, no," she says, but she looks away again. "It was fine. I've just been busy with everything."

"Yeah." We watch the JV girls crush up against each other

behind the starting line. Rebekah and the other girls start cheering for the whole Baxter team.

I'm not scared. I'm so not scared, I'm about to barf. Again.

"Do you want to meet somewhere after this?"

She looks at me like she thinks I'm playing a prank on her.

"I'm serious."

"Where?"

Oh, shit. "Um. We could . . ."

"You're hopeless."

"Pretty much."

She smiles again. Thank God.

"I know where we can go," she says. "But I have to watch this race first."

"Yeah, okay. Yeah. I'll just. Wait." I point behind me, maybe toward our tent or maybe not. "I'll be here."

The starting gun fires, and Team Carly roars.

"You are such a dork," I say.

"Shut up, Honeybunches."

"Honey*buckets*."

The glass doors slide open, and we walk side by side into the cold lobby of the East Baxter Public Library, just a short walk from the park where we were racing. The roar of the air conditioner is like the *shush* of a librarian giantess.

"I have to drop some books off," Rebekah whispers, and she walks toward the circulation desk, taking a few things from her bag and giving me a chance to breathe.

I asked out Rebekah.

I did it. Finally. Finally finally finally.

124

I had to tell somebody. Right then. And the only person right there right then was Mr. V, who I had to tell anyway since he's my ride. He slapped me on the back and said, "That's my Phillip." Then he offered to pick me up at the library later because "coincidentally" he had a few errands to run in the area.

I should have said no. Whatever his reasons, he's my ride, not my dad.

But I didn't want to call my actual dad. I don't want him involved. So Mr. V is picking me up from my "date."

He called it that, not me.

But I think he's right.

"Hey," Rebekah says, "come on." I follow her as she walks to the history shelves. Squinting just a little, she scans the rows of books, searching for something about the fall of the Roman Empire for a presentation. I think that's what she told me on the way here. I was a little too screaming-and-jumping-up-and-down-inside-my-head to comprehend everything she said.

She grabs a book. She flips the cover toward her, reads it, and replaces it. Then she moves on to the next one.

"I can't believe you've never been here," Rebekah says, searing me with her eyes. "You should be ashamed." She's joking, but she's also not joking.

"I read books."

"So you claim."

"Yeah, I claim that I get them *at the bookstore*. Or online. Like a normal person."

"Oh, so I'm weird for checking books out of the library. How *weird*."

"Yeah."

"*You're* weird."

"So are you."

"Fine. We're both weird."

This is what Asher was talking about. This is Rebekah and me, wearing dirty track pants, our hair matted with sweat, not caring that we're in a library on a Saturday afternoon. This is what happens when you tell yourself you're not scared so you do the thing that scares you and then you aren't scared.

This is what I wanted to do, and I did it.

Though even if I'm not technically *scared*, I am *nervous* as all hell. I didn't know there was a difference until now.

"Now you," Rebekah says. She's collected a short stack of sources. "What?"

"It's your turn to get something."

"I don't have a library card."

"They're free. Or you can just use mine."

"I don't really need anything right now."

She sighs. "You're not very good at this."

I open my mouth, about to ask what she means. Then I realize: You're on a date, idiot. You're supposed to *do stuff together* on a date.

An idea pops into my head, but it's a bad one. I immediately try to think of something else.

But now it's all I can think of.

What the hell. She already knows I'm weird.

"Is there, like, an Apocalypse section?" I say.

"Oh, yeah, definitely. Every library has an Apocalypse section."

"You know what I'm saying."

"Actually, I don't."

"Let's just look it up."

"Wow, you know how to do that?"

I think of my mom. I think about the times she would take me to her job at the Central High Library. How she showed me to use the catalog computers. How cool it was to grab any book I wanted and hang out in the staff room and read and be fawned over by the other librarians. I was pretty young then.

"Yeah," I say. Turning quickly to hide my blushing, I walk to the computers. Rebekah stands behind me as I search for the book, secretly hoping they don't have it. But they do.

As we walk through the aisle, between the towering shelves, the dry, dusty scent of old paper grows strong. Midway down the aisle, on a high shelf, I see the book. I slide it out from the shelf and flip it so the familiar block letters and tiny mushroom cloud heart face up toward her.

"'*It'll All Be Over Soon*,'" Rebekah reads.

"Yup," I say, the word catching in my throat.

"What is it about?"

"Well," I say. I don't know how to answer that. Where to start.

"It's funny," I finally say. "It's actually really funny, even though it's about, you know, the world ending or whatever. It's this guy"—I point to the cover; my finger shakes—"writing about all the different ways the world could end and how people predicted the world would end throughout history. But it's also about him and how he's kind of obsessed with all that stuff. It's sort of like a memoir but also a nonfiction book. I know that sounds like the least funny thing ever, but it's not."

"So," she says, cautiously, "is this your favorite book?"

It was basically my obsession for a year of my life.

"Maybe," I say. "One of them, probably. Part of it is, I like the art." I take the book and open it, flipping through for a chapter opening. A big *I*, adorned with curlicues and vines and spikes, blares out of the page. Then I close the book and point to the mushroom cloud heart.

"I used to draw this all the time." Technically I drew it just last week, but that still counts as "used to."

"Why?"

I open my mouth, feeling as if I know the answer, but then I realize I've never thought about it before. "I don't know. It's this thing that can kill millions of people. But then it's also . . . love? I think it makes more sense if you've read the book."

She takes it from me. "You're really into this Apocalypse section stuff."

"Is that weird?"

"Yes. But we're both weird, remember?"

We're both weird.

But we're both here.

I get an idea.

I put my hand out. "Team Weird."

She laughs and places her hand on mine. "Team Weird."

We hold them there. Then she says quietly, "Break," and we pull our hands back.

We're standing face-to-face. Her hair is pulled back, revealing the full shape of her face. Her freckles pop. Her eyes are dark, marbled green. I could lean down and kiss her right now.

"I think you'll like the book," I say. I lean against the shelf so I'm not looking right at her anymore. She searches through her books like she's double-checking that she has all the right titles. Something between us dissipates.

"I want to read it." She grabs the book, and for just a half second our fingertips touch underneath the back cover.

I follow her as she goes to the circulation desk, and stand behind her as the woman smiles and greets Rebekah by name. She checks Rebekah's books out and says, "See you soon."

We walk out into the humid air. Blinding smears of sunlight reflect off car hoods in the parking lot. Rebekah and I squint at each other.

I guess the date's over already.

But wouldn't Mr. V be disappointed if I called him this soon? Wouldn't I?

"I don't have to go yet," I say. "Do you?"

"No," she says. "I can stay."

"Good."

I don't have a plan, though. There's nothing around here except the park, and we spent most of the day there.

She sees me struggling.

"Come on."

Rebekah leads me along a concrete pathway to the side of the library. We turn the corner, and I see what's hidden here—a narrow lawn stretching alongside the library, enclosed by a wall of tall shrubberies and trees. Benches lean against the trees and along the wall of the library. No one else is back here.

We sit down on one of the benches, in the shadow of an enormous dark green and red-tinted bush. I feel apart from the world.

"This is cool," I say.

"Thank Alex," she says, pointing to a small plaque on the bench that reads ALEX NEIGHBORS, EAGLE SCOUT PROJECT 2008.

"Do you know him?"

"Just his gardening."

"Then how do you know he really exists?"

She smiles. "He does."

"Sorry, I can't believe in Alex without more proof."

She grimaces. Maybe it wasn't as witty as I thought.

For a while we just sit together, watching the squirrels scamper along the grass, and the way the light changes when a breeze rattles the tree branches above us.

Alex may have made this, but I did too.

Eventually Rebekah reaches into her bag and pulls out a pen, a piece of scrap paper, and a book. Then she plops them in my lap.

"You still owe me a drawing."

"But I already—"

"That was nice, but it wasn't a drawing."

"That's not fair."

"Yes, it is. I won, fair and square." She picks up the pen and stands it upright in my hand. "You owe me a drawing."

I poise the pen above the paper.

I look over. She's watching me.

I look back at the blank page.

This is not cool. How can she expect me to just *draw* something? Right now. With her staring at me.

I move the paper a little and realize that I'm drawing on the copy of *It'll All Be Over Soon*. I see the mushroom cloud heart in the corner. I could draw that. Put her initials inside the heart.

But no. I just told her it means love. Death and destruction and love. I don't want her to think I love her. I definitely don't want her to think I want to destroy her.

I place the tip of the pen against the page, hoping the drawing will just flow out of me, like that one night. Instead my hand shakes. The pen makes wispy lines until I pull away again.

Why is this so hard? Just draw something. *Anything.*

But I don't draw anything other than mushroom cloud hearts and medieval letters.

I glance over, and she's still looking at me.

I can't do this. I can't do something real.

I know what I'll do. This will be cute.

I draw a house the way a child would draw it, with a door right in the middle, a window on each side, and a chimney with a curlicue of smoke twisting out the top. I write the words "Youth Center" on the roof, then beside the building I draw a stick figure in a dress, with a big smile. I write her name and an arrow pointing to the girl.

I hand her the drawing. I think it's pretty funny.

Again she proves me wrong.

"Phillip," she says. Her face is still, but her eyes can't hide her disappointment.

"I never said I was *good*." I wait for her to laugh, but she doesn't. "Sorry. It's just a lot of pressure. I didn't have time to think about it. Let me draw you something good. Later. At home. I promise."

Slowly she folds the paper and puts it in her bag. Then she takes the pen and points it toward my throat like a dagger. "You better," she says, but there's no energy in her voice.

How was that my fault, though? Drawing's not a *trick*.

When she takes the book back, she examines the cover before putting it in her bag. She pulls a leaf from the bush and folds it in half. And then again.

"I wanted to ask you something, Phillip."

"Sure," I say, my voice wobbling.

"When you read the Bible, do you think it's fiction, or do you think some of it might be true?"

She lets the quartered leaf flutter to the ground.

I feel like I just walked into a trip wire. That I helped set.

I figured she might ask me something like this eventually. I knew I should come up with an answer. But I didn't. I basically just hoped she wouldn't ask.

And now the only answer I have sounds like the wrong one.

"I think some of it might be real," I say. "Probably. Why?"

"You called Genesis 'epic.'"

"Well, it *is*. It's a compliment."

"It's not when you're talking about something that a billion people believe is true. Not just a story. It's like you're reviewing it online or something. 'Four and a half stars for Revelation. Epic!'"

She can't even look at me.

"Is this about what I said about Alex?"

"No, it's—"

"Or the message I sent? I'm sorry. I was in a weird mood and I was just joking—"

"I know, Phillip." She looks at me like her gaze might push me over if she tried hard enough. "You're funny. That's one of the reasons I like you. But this stuff isn't a joke to me, and I'm not sure you get that."

"I get that. I've read the books you asked me to read. I come to church even though my dad doesn't want me to."

She leans back a little. "I didn't know that."

I shrug.

"But is that just because you want to hang out with me?" she says.

132

"Is that a bad thing?"

"No, but it's not the only thing."

"So I have to believe what you believe?"

"I didn't say that. I just want to know that you believe in *something*. Or that you think about those things. You seem kind of wishy-washy sometimes—like you can't make a decision for yourself."

What? We're only here because of a decision *I* made.

"Yes, I can. And I believe in things."

"Then, what do you believe in?" she says gently.

What's in my books. Asher, mostly. My dad, sometimes. This secret place behind the library. Her. These are all things that I believe in, but I don't know what to call that. I don't know how you could ever come up with one word to explain it.

"Reality?" I say. But I know that's not it at all.

Rebekah hangs her head just a little. Then she gathers her hair, fans her neck, and exhales, long and slow. "I'm sorry. We barely know each other, and I'm asking you to—I'm not even sure what I'm asking."

Barely?

"Is this why you made me stay outside last week?"

She doesn't say anything for a while. I look over. She's let her hair go. Tears shine in her eyes.

"No," she says. "That was . . . I was singing."

"But I've heard you sing."

"Not in front of everyone. Alone onstage. It made me nervous that you would see me. It's very personal."

"So is drawing," I say, too loud.

I wish I could take it back.

I don't want to be angry at her.

133

I really don't want her to be angry at me.

What can I do? *Think.*

Genesis.

"You were in Genesis," I say.

I remember. There's a character named Rebekah in there. She only comes up a couple of times, but in one of the stories, Rebekah deceives her old, blind husband, Isaac, into giving her favorite son, Jacob, his blessing, which her other son should have received. I didn't really understand it.

"You were named after a . . . after someone in Genesis."

She nods.

"Why?"

"Phillip, I don't want to go into that right now."

"I'm just trying to ask a question about what you believe."

"And it *shows*," she says, looking right at me.

I sit back, grind my teeth. She thinks I'm wishy-washy. Amoral. Or maybe just ignorant.

"I think about things," I say. "I read."

"I know you do." She sighs. "I guess I'm also worried what my dad would think."

"Why?"

"Because you're not Christian, and he would freak out if he knew."

"But he doesn't know. He doesn't even know I exist."

"That doesn't matter."

So this is what it really comes down to: Rebekah's dad. After all that. After the crutch and the Bible and the basketball and the sand, she says no because her dad wouldn't approve. This was never going to work—unless I converted.

"You could have told me earlier," I say.

Her mouth drops open. "Why? So you didn't have to waste your time?"

"I didn't say that."

She rolls her eyes. "You pretty much did."

"Well, you're suddenly remembering you can't go out with me because of your dad."

"That's not what I said."

"It is, basically."

I wait for her to deny it. I wait for her to tell me all my effort was worth it. I wait for her to tell me that what we think about God is irrelevant.

I wait for her to tell me it's not over.

But she doesn't.

Well, how's this for a decision?

I get up. "I should go," I say.

And she doesn't tell me to stop.

So I don't.

I walk out front and reach for my phone to call Mr. V, but I see he's already here. I open the passenger side door and slide in.

"Can you take me home?" I ask.

"Yes, of course," he says. "I'm sorry, Phillip."

He looks as stunned as I feel. How does he know what happened? Is it that obvious?

"It's okay. She just—"

"Your father is very angry with you, and it's my fault. I'm sorry." He turns the key in the ignition, and the van rumbles to life. "I'll explain as I drive you home," he says.

TWENTY-TWO

I walk into the kitchen, and Dad leaps out of his chair.

"What've you been doing?" he says, holding his arms out in front of him, almost like he wants me to jump into them.

"You know what I've been doing. You interrogated Mr. V already." I open the fridge and grab the orange juice.

"I had no idea where you were. Will you *look* at me when I'm talking to you?"

I put down the glass I got from the cupboard and turn around. Dad's face is red, and the strings of his neck muscles bulge.

"What is with your attitude recently?" he says. "When Chris and I got home from his soccer game and I saw that you weren't home yet, I let it go. And then I waited. And I waited some more and you still weren't home, so I was *worried*, alright? That's why I 'interrogated' Mr. Venkataraman and found out you've been lying to me for the past month."

I shake my head and pour some juice. I *knew* he would do this.

Dad throws his hands up. "You're shaking your head because you have nothing to say. You've been lying to me, and not only have you been lying, you've been lying about something pretty goddamn important."

"Important? Like what I'm doing on a Wednesday night?"

"Yeah, like going to a fundamentalist church."

"*Fundamentalist?* You don't even know what you're talking about."

"I drive by that church all the time, Phillip. It's nondenominational, and that means fundamentalist, and that means crazy people."

"'Crazy'? Listen to yourself, Dad."

"I know perfectly well what I'm saying." He steps toward me. "And it's shocking that not only would you lie to me, but that you don't have a problem with it and you don't have a problem with going to a place like that. After what this family has been through."

"Oh, please. Come *on*, Dad." I walk toward the stairs. Take my stupid orange juice I don't even want.

"Phillip, stop."

I stop. I don't look at him.

"Is this about a girl?" he says.

Not anymore.

"No."

"Well, good. Then, maybe you'll listen to me. I've never had to ground you before, but I will, because you don't seem to understand that you've done something wrong. You can't go to that place

137

anymore, and you can't go out on weekends for at least two weeks."

I almost laugh. I can't go to "that place" anymore. As if he's the one stopping me.

"Whatever." I walk out of the room.

"We're not finished talking about this."

Dad can do what he wants.

But I'm finished.

TWENTY-THREE

"My dad feels really bad about it," Asher says. He rips the plastic wrap off his PB&J and splits it down the precut middle. "He's been sitting alone in his office for the past two days."

"Seriously?" My eyes flick over to Mark's chair to get his response. But he's not here.

"Seriously. He slept in his chair."

"Well, make him stop doing that. It's not that big of a deal."

Asher pushes the bridge of his glasses up his nose. "It's not?"

He and I haven't talked about what happened yet. Asher chatted me yesterday to tell me about his date with Jennifer Baylor. They went to dinner at La Bruschetta, the "fancy" Italian restaurant in town (which means it's not the Olive Garden). Then they walked over to Nelson Park. They kissed. It was Asher's first kiss.

The whole thing was just really super and great.

And then he asked about Rebekah and me.

I didn't want to talk about Rebekah and me.

But I'm over it now.

"It's not," I say. "All that happened was my dad got really angry and he said I couldn't go to church anymore."

Asher stops midbite, and his eyes open wide.

"But it doesn't matter, anyway," I say.

"It doesn't?"

I tell him what Rebekah said and what I said.

"Oh, man," he says. "Sorry."

I tear open my sandwich. Ripping the plastic wrap is very satisfying. "It's not a big deal at all. I actually feel kind of stupid for drawing it out this long. She was never going to be okay with—"

I notice that Asher's eyes have locked on someone behind me.

"Hey," says Mark. I look up at the tall bastard. He stands beside his empty seat, holding the strap of his book bag with one hand and his pink plastic tray with the other.

Asher waits a couple of seconds and says, "Hey."

Mark tugs on his book bag strap. "Sorry I didn't text you guys."

"Okay," Asher says.

Mark looks at me, but I say nothing.

"That was messed up on Friday night," Mark says.

"Yeah," Asher says.

Mark looks at me again, but I say nothing. He runs his hand through his hair.

"Alright, so—" Mark says, stepping away.

"That's it?" Asher says, dropping his sandwich on his tray. "You're not even apologizing?"

"*I* didn't do anything," Mark says.

"Yeah, I *know* you didn't. You let Brad and Dan just—"

"What was I supposed to do?"

"*Something.*"

"You were stealing their beer!"

"You really think that?"

"Even if you weren't, you were pissing them off on purpose."

"They've been total assholes to me *and* Phillip."

Mark breathes out heavily, and he looks around the cafeteria like he's trying to find the right thing to say.

"Alright," Mark says. "Sorry."

"Okay," Asher says.

Mark looks at me *again*, but I say nothing. He stands uneasily.

"Are you going to sit down?" Asher says.

"Actually, I was gonna do this thing where I sit with them one day and then you guys the other day."

"*What?*" I say.

He looks at me like he's never heard me say anything before. "I was just gonna, like, switch off."

"No," Asher says. "That's ridiculous. If you want to sit with them, then sit with them. You can't switch."

"Why are you being such a dick?"

"Why am *I* being such a dick? Why are your new best friends the most dickish dicks who ever dicked?"

"Shut up, Asher. You think you're better than everyone else. It's really boring. *You're* really boring. At least Dan and Brad know how to have fun. You guys just leave the party."

After that, none of us says anything for a while. Finally Mark walks off to sit with Dan and Brad. A couple of the other people at our table look stunned, but we don't comment. We just eat.

When the lunch bell rings and everyone jumps up, I remember

what I was going to do earlier. I unzip my book bag.

"Hey," I say to Asher, "give this to Rebekah." I hand her Bible across the table.

Asher grabs it but doesn't take it. "You sure?"

"Yeah, dude," I say.

As he takes the book I feel the grooves of her initials slide under my thumb.

TWENTY-FOUR

On Saturday night I read the Book of Matthew because I knew it had Jesus in it. I thought maybe He could do it. Maybe I just needed to finally read about Him and that would be enough. The Holy Spirit would fill me and I'd get down on my knees beside my bed, clasp my hands together, and ask God to wash my sins away.

I could be a Christian. Just like that.

So I closed and locked my door and I opened a Bible site. I recognized the big stories of Jesus's life. Mary, Joseph, the star, the three kings, Bethlehem. And then when he was older, all the miracles.

I wasn't feeling anything.

The Crucifixion was coming up, though. Maybe that could be it for me, I thought. I mean, I'm an outsider. Basically. People don't really make fun of me or hit me or torture me to death, but they don't really like me either.

I perked up when, right before the Crucifixion, somebody asks

Jesus about "the end of the age." When will it be? How will we know? What are the signs?

He gives some vague descriptions at first, but then he finally gets to the point: "Therefore keep watch, because you do not know on what day your Lord will come."

So, nobody knows. Except Him. It could be tomorrow. It could be a couple thousand years from now.

Which is what Revelation said. And it didn't piss me off then, but hearing it from Jesus did. I *liked* him! But what he said sums up exactly what I hate about religion: It's fear.

He's coming, so you better act right.

He's coming, so you better believe that some boring stories written thousands of years ago are the Truth.

If you don't, *you're* the crazy one.

And you're not one of us.

I closed the site and pushed myself away from my desk and lay flat on my bed with my arms crossed over my chest. I stared up at the rippled white ceiling.

Rebekah liked me.

But she didn't even give me a chance because she was scared. Of her dad. Of God. Of us.

I won't believe in that.

Hell, no.

TWENTY-FIVE

My lungs feel cavernous. The cement beneath me feels springy. I am a much better runner now that I run alone.

And I'm proud of it. I want all these people driving on Silver Street to see me and be reminded that they are too lazy or too fat or too old to do what I can do.

By myself, I am stronger than any of them.

And then I hear it. The whirring sound of rubber on cement. Coming up behind me.

I don't even have to remind myself that I'm not scared.

"The Lone Ranger," Ferret says as he rides up beside me. "Guess that makes me Tonto."

I drift a couple of feet away so he doesn't knock me over again. "You're not supposed to ride your bike on the sidewalk," I say.

"You a cop, Flowers?"

"Nope. But there might be one around the corner."

"I got a lot of buddies on the force. They won't bother me."

After a couple of seconds, though, he turns his front tire just a little and rides on the grass. We keep going, side by side, in silence. I bet he heard about me and Rebekah somehow. Now he's waiting for the right time to say he told me so.

"Anyway," Ferret says, "I'm not here so you can perform a citizen's arrest on me, Flowers. I just wanted to congratulate you."

"For what?" I say.

"On your personal record this weekend. I didn't know you had it in you."

"Thanks," I say, trying to make it sound like "Get away from me."

"I think you've shown some real gusto lately, Flowers. You coming to YouthLife on Wednesday?" he says.

"No."

"Rebekah didn't tell you about this? Monthly thing at Risen Church? Bunch of youth groups getting together?"

"No."

He rides in silence. Finally he says, "Something happen?"

There it is.

"The hell do you care?"

"Wait a tick, Flowers. I care."

I stop just as the sidewalk starts to curve. He brakes, skidding on the grass.

"No," I say. "You don't. You just wanted to tell me how right you were."

He bows his head and lets his sunglasses fall into his hand. He folds them up. "That's not why I came out here. I'm sorry if things didn't work out, but—"

"Bullshit."

"Whoa, now. Maybe I made it seem like I didn't want it to

146

happen. And maybe I didn't. But Rebekah, God love her, is a little strange. And you're *really* strange, Flowers. Sometimes strange people go together." He coughs. "But sometimes they don't, I guess."

I think of Rebekah's hand on mine. Then she says, "Break."

"You made fun of me right in front of her," I say. I start walking.

"Flowers, maybe—"

I run. Away.

TWENTY-SIX

On Wednesday practice is canceled due to heavy rain, so I ride the bus home. I watch TV for a few hours, then I go to my room. Online there's a message waiting for me:

> Phillip, I thought a lot about what I said at the library. I know it probably seemed like I was coming out of nowhere with that stuff, but it's been on my mind. I felt like there was this whole side of me that you wanted to pretend didn't exist or didn't matter. I meant what I said, but I didn't mean to hurt you.
>
> Sorry it took me so long to say any of this.
>
> I'm singing at this event tonight at Risen Church, and *It'll All Be Over Soon* is helping

with my nerves. You were right. It's funny. But smart, too.

"Sorry it took me so long," she says.

Not, "Sorry I won't go out with you because you're an atheist." Not, "Sorry I do whatever my dad tells me, even though he's on the other side of the planet."

Not, "Sorry. I want to see you again."

I look down at my trash can and the letter drawings I buried inside it a couple of days ago. I was starting to think that might have been a mistake. But now I stick my foot in and push them down even farther. The crackle of crushed paper sounds so good.

I realize the wall space above my desk looks empty, as if there had always been something there. So I rip a sheet of paper out of a notebook and start to sketch a mushroom-cloud heart, but then I leave out the heart. I tack the explosion to my wall.

She didn't mean to hurt me, she says. But she did.

I hope her voice squeaks tonight.

I hope she loses that copy of the book and has to pay a big overdue fine.

I hope she realizes—

There's a knock on the door. I check the clock.

"I have five minutes, Dad."

He's getting me to do more work in the basement so I can fulfill my groundage. We've been doing this every night. So often that I'm not even allergic anymore.

The door, not entirely closed, starts to open.

"Dad."

"It's not Dad," Chris says as he walks in, spinning some wiry bracelet on his wrist. I guess it's a middle school thing.

This is strange. I basically never see Chris anymore. Partially because of soccer—it's Wednesday, so he would usually be at practice, though that must've been canceled too.

But it's also just awkward. Ever since school started. We're different now.

It's harder to talk to each other.

"What're you doing?" I ask.

He leans against the wall. "Bored," he says, shrugging. "You still have to work in the basement?"

"In a few minutes."

"It's something to do." He brushes his hair out of his eyes.

"I guess."

He looks at the sketch on the wall. I think he's going to try to make fun of me, but he doesn't say anything. We watch the rain.

Then he snorts with laughter. "You lied to go to church?"

I smile. "Kind of."

"Weird."

"Yeah."

Just a minute or two until Dad comes in.

Chris glances into the hall and turns back. "I heard what Dad said. When he was yelling at you. It was pretty stupid." He spins his bracelet. "You should be able to go to church if you want to."

I shrug. "Yeah. Doesn't matter, though."

"I'm just saying. He shouldn't bring Mom into it."

My mouth opens to say something, but I don't know what it is. So I close it.

There's another knock.

"Hey, guys," Dad says, smiling to see the two of us in the same room. "It's really coming down out there."

We don't respond.

Dad pokes Chris. "You're more than welcome to help us out if you're bored."

Chris fixes his hair and actually seems to think about it. "I'm not that bored."

Dad laughs. "Alright. Fair enough. Phillip, you want to start?"

"Fine."

"Oh!" Dad says, poking Chris again. "I was thinking about a fun project for the three of us. After we're finished with the basement, we could go down to the Land for a few weekends. Fix it up a bit. What do you think?"

Chris and I lock eyes. We think the exact same thing.

But he's the one who says it.

"No." Then he goes back to his room.

"Look," Dad says, tapping the top of a stack of canned goods, "I know there's a place you'd rather be, but we both know you need to stay here tonight. So stop worrying about it and let's get this done. If we do it right, we can finish it quickly, and then I'll order some pizza. Okay?"

The lightbulb hanging from the ceiling casts weak shadows, stretching the box corners into dark, sharpened points on the basement walls.

"Okay?" he asks.

"Fine," I say.

He thinks he knows what's going on with me. He thinks he knows where I want to be right now. As usual, he has no idea.

"Hey," he says. "You think we should pack the generator up? It's pretty sturdy, I think, and—"

"Yes," I say.

"Okay, then," Dad says, smiling. "I like to hear that definitive tone."

His cheer is infuriating. He's forcing me to help him sell this stuff. He's imprisoning me for going to church. And he doesn't care what I think.

He's always been like this. The Land is this piece of property somewhere south of Macon that Dad inherited from his dad. When Mom still hadn't come back after a few weeks of staying with her friends, Dad got this great idea that it would be fun to "get out of the house" and go camping on the Land, even though there was a cold snap that weekend.

By the time we got there, the air was frosty, and the only light was from our headlight beams, shining across the meadow and fading into the woods. We eventually got a fire going, but the flames never reached higher than half a foot, so we got in the sleeping bags to try to warm up. My pillow felt like a pile of snow. I remember thinking we might actually freeze to death.

Dad finally relented when Chris started to cry, and we spent the rest of the night in the car. In the morning Dad apologized—for not renting a camper. Like that was the problem.

"Come on back," he says, beckoning me farther into the basement.

And now what Chris said about Mom is making me think. About how she had to live with someone who stopped her from doing what she wanted. A man who thought she was crazy. And two kids who weren't sure.

How much that must have hurt. To be with someone who thinks that what you believe, what you're trying to do with your life, is stupid.

How every time Dad makes fun of "Rapture nuts" and Christians in general, he's making fun of Mom.

Shit.

Rebekah was right. I didn't think about Revelation or Genesis or even Matthew as anything other than fiction. I was only looking for what was cool about them—or what was stupid about them. I was only reading them because she told me to, or because I forced myself to. I never thought of them as something that could be real.

And she never said she wouldn't go out with me because of her dad. I decided that's what she said and then I asked her to deny it. I basically demanded she choose me over her beliefs right that second. And when she didn't, I left, scared.

But even after all that, she still read *my* book.

And said it was funny.

But smart.

Oh my God. I completely missed it.

She still likes me.

She's giving me a second chance.

She wants to see me tonight.

I know exactly where it is too. It's just a mile from here, maybe a little more.

But I'm trapped down here with him.

"Phillip, you alright?"

It's pouring outside. Anyone who went out there would be drenched in seconds.

What if I'm wrong, though? Why couldn't she just tell me what she meant?

Dammit. I have to make a decision.

"I'm fine," I say. I turn around to walk upstairs. "Going to the bathroom."

Lying again.

"Alright, but be quick," he says. "We can get this done in a jiff."

I rush up to my room and put on my running shoes. Chris stands by the door and says, "Where are you going?"

I knot my laces and stand up. "Church."

TWENTY-SEVEN

"Where's the bathroom?" I say, dripping on the lobby carpet of Risen Church.

The kid has short bleach-blond hair, baggy black jeans, and a wallet chain. He slouches in a chair and plays a game on his cell phone. He keeps pressing buttons as he looks at me with an open mouth.

"On the right," he says, and nods back with his head.

"Thanks." I squish past him, leaving a damp, spotty trail. I hear the muffled sound of a man's voice coming from beyond the closed doors in front of me. That must be YouthLife. I haven't missed it. Maybe.

I walk to the bathroom. My fingers are wrinkled, my hair is limp, and my T-shirt sticks to me like a wetsuit. I look like a fugitive.

I flip the nozzle of the air drier up and blast it on my face. The air rushes into my nostrils, into my ears, into my hair, but it's not going to be enough—my whole body is wet. I unwrap a fresh roll of toilet paper and work with it and the air dryer for about five minutes.

Now I look less like a fugitive and more like a normal damp person.

Or, potentially, a crazy damp person.

I walk out of the bathroom toward the hall. The man's voice is gone. Now a quiet guitar echoes inside. I don't know why, but I suddenly feel like this is it. This is her thing.

A voice from behind me yips, "Flowers?"

Ferret.

I turn. I freeze.

"What the—?" he says.

I run to the doors and open them and slip inside.

The worship hall is enormous. The walls stretch up and up and up and finally meet at a point far above everyone's head. The room is dimly lit, except for the stage, which gleams under the power of the lights hanging from the ceiling. Four columns of folding chairs, many rows deep and full of kids, file toward the stage. Above the stage, hanging from scarily thin black wire, is a ten-foot cross.

And beneath the cross Rebekah stands, holding a microphone in both hands like it's a porcelain doll. She wears a knee-length dark green dress, and her hair is loose and tucked neatly behind her shoulders. She looks tiny up there.

The acoustic guitar player nods at her. She smiles back at him and then looks out to the crowd, right toward the back of the middle aisle, where I'm standing.

But the lights are too strong. She can't see me.

Then for a moment she is completely still. Slowly she raises her hand above her eyes. She squints. And now I'm sure of it: She sees me.

I got it wrong. She doesn't want me here. I'm just making her more nervous.

But her shoulders drop. She relaxes her grip on the microphone. And she closes her eyes and sings.

I know instantly why she didn't want me to see this before. This isn't *for* me.

But she's letting me see it. She's letting us see it.

No one moves.

Her voice rises to the ceiling.

> *"In Your love I find release,*
> *A haven from my unbelief.*
> *Take my life, and let me be*
> *A living prayer, my God, to Thee."*

I don't know how I know, but I know she is seeing God. Alone, on a stage, in front of all these people, and she is somewhere else.

The back of my neck tingles.

Is this what Mom saw in this? Why she had to go to church?

It's not the destruction of the world or the creation of the world or fear or miracles.

It's you and God.

It's your voice.

Rebekah breathes deeply and lifts her face so she's looking at the topmost point on the ceiling. She opens her eyes and releases her entire voice.

"Take my life, and let me be
A living prayer, my God, to Thee."

The guitar fades. Rebekah steps back. An older man, maybe in his forties, steps in from the side of the stage. He wears a white-and-blue-striped button-up shirt and jeans. He speaks softly into the mic.

"Thank you, Rebekah." They smile at each other.

The man onstage paces as the guitar plays softly. "Everybody here tonight," he says, "I hope that you can take something from this. I hope that you know that God loves you. That He wants to talk to you, to be in your life. And that even when no one else will listen, He will. You can live in God's love. It's true."

He stops and scans the crowd. "Anyone, anyone here tonight. If you want to live in God's love, please come forward and pray with us. Even if you already believe, but you've strayed and want to come back into His arms, join us."

I stare at Rebekah, who now stands at the side of the stage. I want her to smile at me, or shake her head at me, or even point toward the doors and mouth, "Go!" But she doesn't look at me.

"Christ makes all things new," the man says.

My face feels hot and prickly.

A couple of kids near the front walk toward the stage, their heads low.

"Join us in Christ," the man says.

More go to the stage.

I look at Rebekah, and she's still not looking at me or anyone else. But I feel like she's especially not looking at me.

There's a lightness in my chest.

"Christ makes all things new," the man repeats.

I walk. My feet pick themselves up and move my body toward the stage. Rebekah is not looking at me. I walk forward. The lightness is in my head. I look back at Rebekah, but she's not onstage. She's walking off. Where is she going?

I keep walking. I crush in behind the others who came forward. I look at them for clues. I don't know what to do. They close their eyes, and some raise their hands in the air. Some whisper.

I stand and shove my hands in my pockets. I feel sick.

"Join us in His love."

A hand touches my shoulder. I turn, and it's Rebekah.

"Are you sure about this?" she says.

I wipe a tear from the corner of my eye. "I think so."

"I need to know if you're sure."

I pull a lock of damp hair off my forehead. "I'm sure."

She smiles.

"What do I do now?"

She grabs my hand and squeezes it. "Pray."

APRIL

Mom came back. So we went to Stone Mountain.

"I see it," I said as Dad drove us farther into the park. Tall pine trees lined both sides of the road. I knew that what I'd seen—a flash of granite between a couple of trees—didn't actually count as seeing it. And so did Chris.

"Shut up," he said. "No, you didn't."

"Yeah, I did."

"No, you didn't."

"Double or nothin'!" Dad called out from the front.

"Yeah!" Chris said, not knowing what he was agreeing to.

There wasn't anything at stake anyway. We had taken a day trip to the park at least once every summer as far back as I could remember. Stone Mountain is this mile-high scoop of granite sticking out of the middle of a forest in middle Georgia—like God meant to use it in the Appalachians but dropped it on the way there. The area around it is a state park, and there are attractions and rides, not to mention the enormous likenesses of Confederate heroes carved into the front of the mountain itself.

It was almost an hour away from the house, so it counted as a fake vacation.

And this one felt like the fakest yet.

"How about it, Phil?" Mom said, looking at me in the sun visor mirror through her black sunglasses.

"What?" I said.

"Play again." She smiled.

These were the kind of games we played on family vacations, ones where you had to be the first to spot something. At Stone Mountain it was the mountain itself, then the village, then the steamboat, then, at the laser show projected onto the face of the mountain at night, it was who could spot the first laser.

When I was a kid, I thought those games were so much fun. I thought I really could see the first laser. That I could catch something that fast if I just looked hard enough.

But I was getting too old for all that.

"I already won," I said.

"Come on, Phil. Next winner gets an ice cream."

"Ooh, can I play?" Dad said.

"No," Mom said, poking his shoulder. "Watch the road."

I kept quiet. I knew what Mom was doing, and it made me angry. She was trying to act like everything was okay again. Like she could just leave for a month and we could go back to playing games with each other.

I watched the tree trunks as they filed past. When I looked back, Mom pushed her sunglasses up onto her head. She looked at me in the mirror again. She needed my help.

"Okay, fine," I said.

"It's on!" Dad said. Mom clapped. Chris hunkered down and squinted at the top of the tree line.

"There!" he said, and he pointed toward Dad's side.

We turned our heads and saw the rounded top of the mountain looming between a gap in the trees. It was always surprising how big it was when you got close enough.

"Yup," Dad said.

"Ha-ha!" Chris said, taunting me.

"Ice cream for everybody!" Mom said.

"Mom!" Chris protested.

She looked at me in the mirror again. Then she flipped her sunglasses back down.

"Ice cream for everybody," she said.

TWENTY-EIGHT

"Just wait until you're ready," Dad says.

Two cars whoosh by, leaving an open space behind them. I ease the car's nose down toward the main road.

I start to turn.

Dad's hand clutches my shoulder. "Ah-ah-ah. Look." He points down the road at an approaching car. A *distant* approaching car.

Behind me, two sharp blasts of a horn. I look in the rear-view mirror and see a mom in a light blue minivan glaring at me. Behind her is a growing line of cars, driven by parents impatient to get home after a Thursday of work followed by a humid JV cross-country meet, possibly the least exciting spectator sport in the world.

We are in their way.

"They can wait," Dad says. "Let's be safe."

This is embarrassing.

It's a right turn. A simple right turn.

I look down the lane. There is still room for us, and time. The ticking of the turn signal is maddening.

"Dad, I think we can go." I raise my foot.

Dad's hand clamps down on my shoulder, and I stomp on the brake. Our heads jerk back. "Don't go until you're *ready*," he says.

"*They* think we're ready."

"It doesn't matter what *they* think."

"Fine." I wait for the approaching car to pass. Finally it does. The mom blasts me again.

"I'm *going*."

"Phillip!"

I hit the brakes, stopping with my nose in the road. On the other side a car had started to turn into this lane. Now it's blocking that side of the road, and a car is coming toward it.

I don't know what to do.

Horns blare from all sides.

"Put it in reverse, Phillip," Dad says.

I reach for the shift to put it in reverse. Dad's hand grips mine. I look in the rearview, and the mom has already taken our spot.

"But, Dad—"

"Put it in reverse or go, go, go!"

I hit the accelerator, and we wobble from the parking lot into the lane. Dad grips the armrest and the emergency handle. There is an open road ahead of me.

I go go go.

My whole body is one clenched muscle. I don't look back.

"Is it okay?" I ask after a while.

"I don't know. I didn't hear anything." He glances back. "It's fine."

He looks like a sneeze quit on him halfway through.

"Dad," I say.

"What?"

"Look. I'm driving."

For the first time ever on an actual road, five miles below the speed limit and with my hands at ten and two, after just a few weeks' lessons, I am driving.

He starts to laugh. And then I start to laugh.

"You're driving," he says, as if he just read an interesting factoid about space.

"I'm driving," I say, as if I already knew that factoid.

We're okay.

After I called Dad from the church that day and told him where I was and what I was doing, he didn't do anything I expected him to do. He didn't yell. He didn't threaten more groundage. He didn't have me arrested.

He just came and picked me up. And then he asked me to explain.

I did, as well as I could. And I said I was sorry, but running to that church right then was something I had to do. Not just for a girl. For me.

He started crying.

"*I* should apologize," he said. He'd been "bullheaded." He'd made me hide myself. He'd tried to separate me from someone I cared about.

"I already did that once before," he said. "I won't do it again."

Then he really started crying.

I could remember only a couple of other times in my whole life when I'd seen him so upset. I stood up and sat beside him and hugged him. He hugged me back, harder, and we sat there awhile. Eventually he wiped away his last tears. He looked at me, his face streaked red, and said, "I won't stop you from going to church. Okay?"

"Okay," I said.

"And I'll support you in whatever you do. Okay?"

"Okay."

"And—" he said, shaking his head just slightly, his eyes searching for something. "I'll teach you how to drive, okay?" Those words came rushing out of his mouth, almost on top of each other, as if he were trying to sweeten a deal. One he thought I might actually turn down.

Until then I hadn't understood what I'd really done so I could see Rebekah that night: I'd run away from my father, when all he has is me and Chris.

And he felt like he had to bargain with me to get me back.

I started crying too. I felt awful. I didn't deserve a reward. I'd done something *wrong*.

But he wanted me to say okay. If I did, he'd be happy. And *I'd* be really happy.

This would bring us closer.

"Why don't we pull in here?" he says, pointing to a strip mall parking lot.

I don't mind. I drove—that's what I wanted to do. And between breaking my personal record by more than thirty seconds this afternoon and barely escaping destruction just now, my mind and body feel hollowed out. I just want to lean my head against the window and close my eyes.

I pull into a spot and put the car in park. I start to unhook my seat belt, but Dad puts his hand on my shoulder, gently.

"You have to be careful, okay?" he says.

I let the belt zip across me. "Yeah."

166

TWENTY-NINE

"I'm sorry," Rebekah whispers, "but this movie is terrible."

"Yeah, I know."

"I thought you were into it."

"No. I've been bored out of my mind for the past hour."

"So have I. I thought you wanted to see this?"

"I thought *you* wanted to see this."

We stare at each other in the dark for a moment. Then we laugh. The woman in front of us glares as we grab our stuff and leave. We walk out of the theater, debating who is responsible for wasting an hour of our lives on a romantic comedy about lobster fishing called *Newfoundland Love*.

I swear it's her. But it's probably me.

In the lobby, arcade games and grab-a-prize machines vie for attention. The smell of sugar and butter is smothering. Everything is lit up.

I am with my girlfriend at a movie theater on a Friday night.

In the past few weeks I have discovered something: Going on dates with a girl you like who likes you is awesome.

We went to the park and yelled gibberish at geese (and then we fed them). We got ice cream and ended up flicking chocolate chips at each other. We played putt-putt, and I hit her in the shin when I swung my club back too far. She still has the bruise and, according to her, a license to hit me whenever she wants to. We did pretty much all the going-out things that people do.

Except two:

1. We don't hang on each other in the hallway and text each other every minute. In fact, we still rarely see each other at school, even though we are aware of each other's locker locations now. I like that we're sort of above it all.
2. This one, I'm about to do.

"Let's go outside," I say.

I push open one of the lobby doors and hold it for Rebekah as I scan the parking lot and the sidewalk. I don't see the Venkatara-van anywhere. I feel bad that Mr. V has basically become my driver, but he insists on atoning for getting me grounded. And it's a lot better than having my dad sit in the passenger seat and make bad jokes and correct my driving.

The front of the theater is packed. I lead us down the sidewalk. We stop at the corner just before Washburne 18 Stadium Theaters ends and the strip mall begins, away from the lights and the crowd.

I need a little space to do this.

"What are we doing?" Rebekah says.

I take her hand. "You know how I still owe you a drawing?"

She smiles. "Yes."

"Well, now I don't anymore." I reach into my pocket and take out a folded piece of notebook paper. I give it to her. My hand shakes, just a little.

"Had some free time in chemistry?"

I blush. "And geography."

I feel like an idiot. Of course I drew this at home, not at school, and I practiced at least twenty times to get it right. But then I decided to put it on notebook paper and fold it so all my effort wouldn't be obvious. Now it just seems shoddy.

When she unfolds it, and I see it again, I want to take it back. The drawing is supposed to be Rebekah's hands, clasping each other and holding a microphone. Beneath it is a quote: "'I will sing to the Lord, for he has been good to me.' Psalms 13:6."

It's corny. And sloppy. I forgot how hard it is to draw hands, and I didn't quite get them right. Her right pinkie finger looks like a claw.

It makes me ill.

"This is so good," Rebekah says.

"What? No, it's not."

"Yes, it is."

"I kind of screwed it up."

She sighs. "Here. Take it back, then."

"No, no. Keep it."

She looks at the drawing again, then carefully folds it and puts it in her pocket. "Thank you. That's a good quote."

I shrug, but inside I'm high-fiving myself.

After the running to church thing, she gave me her Bible back.

I asked her what I should read next, and she said that I should explore on my own but Psalms was a good place to start.

When I started reading it, I felt overwhelmed. There's a lot of heavy praising and talk about destroying enemies and being forsaken. I don't think I'm ready for that. But that one quote was so simple and so true. Like it was written with Rebekah in mind.

"I thought you might like it," I say.

"I do."

I take her hand again, holding it tighter this time. I have imagined doing this for so long now. I have held back because it didn't seem right. I have stopped myself because I was still too scared.

I'm doing it now.

I lean toward her and close my eyes and push my lips out and pray.

Rebekah pushes her hand against my chest. I stop, and I open my eyes. I'm so close.

"Not yet," she whispers.

I step back and drop her hand, but then she takes mine.

"Is that okay?" she says.

"Yeah. Yes. Definitely."

"Good."

After a few minutes Mr. V picks us up. We make fun of the movie, and Mr. V laughs. He drops her off, then me.

Not yet. Not *yet*.

It bangs around in my skull for the rest of the night.

THIRTY

Saturday night Asher and I are in his room.

"We could call . . . Ben Hasting?" he says.

I scoot back on Asher's bed and shove a pillow under my neck. "Why would Ben Hasting have alcohol?"

"I don't know. But we might as well ask him."

I stare up at Asher's ceiling fan as it chops the air. "Yeah, but if we ask him, then he'll want to hang out."

Asher snaps his cell phone shut and sighs. "Ben Hasting's not that bad. You don't even know him."

"I *guess*."

"Fine. I'll see if anybody's online."

I pick my head up. "What about Mark?" I say. He'd be a sure thing. In fact, the only reason we don't have a stash is because we stopped hanging out with him. Or he stopped hanging out with us. Or both.

Asher tries to wither me with his eyes. "Seriously?"

"I don't know. Sort of. It's been a while."

"I don't care. I'm done with him." He turns back to the screen.

I flop my head back down. "Done?"

"Yes, *done*. I'll try Wen." He punches a bunch of keys, chatting with Wen, but I wish he'd give Mark a shot. We've been friends for years. We don't have to be *done*.

The new Asher doesn't really compromise, though.

"Jennifer?" I say.

He winces. "Maybe not tonight."

"Why not?"

"We're kind of in a fight."

"About what?"

He lets a moment or two pass and then clicks over to the music software he's all excited about lately. "I don't really want to talk about it."

That's strange. He usually tells me everything that's going on with them, even if I'm tired of hearing about it.

"What about Rebekah?" Asher asks. "Some Communion wine?"

"Some what?"

"Communion wine. It was just a joke."

I consider telling him what happened last night, asking his opinion of why she wouldn't kiss me. But if he's keeping secrets, then why should I tell him anything?

"Do you even know what Communion is?" he says after I'd thought we'd moved past that.

Sort of. "Yes."

He turns all the way around in his chair. "Own up. This conversion thing is a scam."

"Yeah, it's part of my master plan."

"Is it?"

I sit up and stare at him. "Are you serious?"

"What? You can tell me."

He *is* serious. I throw the pillow at him, but he swats it away. "It's not a scam, a-hole."

"I'm not blaming you. It makes sense. You wanted to be with Rebekah, so—"

"You don't think I could be a Christian?"

Asher tries to push up the bridge of his nonexistent glasses. He switched to contacts a few weeks ago, but he still has his glasses-related tics. "I'm just saying, it seems convenient." He's smiling.

I'm not. "Fuck off."

"I'm sorry. But did you really change your whole philosophy in one night?"

I look him right in the eye. "*You* did."

He's looking for something to say, but he doesn't have anything because he knows he's wrong. He *does* think he's smarter than everybody else. Sometimes.

"That's right," I say. "Go back to your remix, DJ A-Hole." I flop back down.

He laughs. "Okay, that was good. Really, I'm sorry. I believe you."

"I don't believe *you*."

"I'm sorry. I know you wouldn't do that."

I peek up at him. He's looking at me with that sincere Asher face.

"Fine," I say. He turns back around and types and clicks and types and clicks. Ten seconds later a robot voice groans from his speakers, "DJ A-Hoooooooole."

I can't help but laugh.

And just like that, we're friends again. As always.

THIRTY-ONE

The lobby is packed. Dozens of conversations echo off the low ceiling. Men in jackets and ties and comb-overs stand at the doors that lead into the sanctuary, handing out programs.

So this is church on Sunday morning.

Asher and I never found any sources last night, and even though Ben Hasting did come over after all, he's pretty quiet, and we all crashed early. I actually woke up at nine this morning. The sun peeked over a broken blind in Asher's room and stared me right in the eye, so I couldn't get back to sleep.

Then I remembered Rebekah's open invitation to go to Sunday services. I hadn't taken her up on it because I'd figured it would be like going to youth group for the first time—frightening and confusing and probably involving a lot of singing.

But the sun ray felt like a sign. Or a reason, anyway.

So here I am, in this salmon-colored trash bag of a dress shirt

I borrowed from my dad, with my Bible—Rebekah's Bible—under my arm, feeling frightened and confused. But also like a Christian. And I probably don't have to sing if I don't want to.

Now, where is she?

I poke my head up above the crowd, searching. My thumb rubs nervously over the familiar initials carved in the Bible's cover: RFJ. I realize I still don't know what the *F* stands for.

There. Near the right-hand doors. Rebekah and a woman who must be her mom. Rebekah is wearing a milk-chocolate-colored dress that is somehow appropriate for church but still blazing hot.

Her mom has a kind smile. I push through the crowd, and when I'm halfway there Rebekah walks through the open doors into the sanctuary. I pause, wondering if I should wait, but then I press on. I can introduce myself like a gentleman, like an upright young man who deserves to hold the hand of her daughter and maybe eventually, with permission, kiss her daughter.

I walk up to Rebekah's mom, extend my hand, and smile big. "Hi. I'm Phillip."

She takes my hand slowly. "Hello." Behind her eyes she's searching for the name Phillip and coming up blank.

"Phillip Flowers."

She smiles. "Nice to meet you."

We're still shaking hands, and now we're nodding in unison.

She has no idea who I am.

"I'm Rebekah's . . . friend."

"Oh," she says, in a way that's supposed to sound like she finally understands, but she obviously doesn't. We're *still* shaking hands.

"Mom, let's—" says Rebekah, coming out of the sanctuary.

Mrs. Joseph and I let go of each other's hands quickly, as if we've been caught doing something wrong.

"Rebekah!" Mrs. Joseph says. "This is your friend?"

In a second's time Rebekah's expression quietly asks me what the heck I'm doing here, realizes what I'm doing here, and then replays the likely events of the past thirty seconds. Even in panic, she looks graceful. "Yes," she says. "The one who's been coming to youth group?"

Mrs. Joseph's hand goes to her chest as she finally places me. "*Oh.* The *friend.* I thought you were a girl!" She taps me on the arm.

"*Mom,*" Rebekah says.

"What? You never told me her name. *His* name."

"I'm sure I did, Mom."

So that ends, and now it's a new kind of awkward. The watching-someone-else-bicker-with-her-parent awkward blended with a growing awareness that your girlfriend's mom doesn't even know her daughter *is* a girlfriend of anyone.

I fan my collar and smile politely and shift the Bible, which is getting slick with nervous hand sweat.

Mrs. Joseph looks down at the Bible, a curious look on her face. "Is that? I'm sorry, can I see?" I show her the cover, realizing that me having her daughter's Bible potentially adds another bit of awkward into the mix, but there's no stopping it.

Mrs. Joseph squints, turns to Rebekah. "Is that your father's?"

"I let Phillip borrow it because he didn't have his own."

"Of course." Mrs. Joseph manages a smile. A hard silence follows.

Her *father's* Bible?

"Five minutes!" calls one of the men at the door.

"Better get moving," says Mrs. Joseph. "So nice to meet you, Phillip."

"You too."

She squeezes Rebekah's arm. "Meet me inside."

"Just a second."

Mrs. Joseph leaves us. Rebekah puts her hand to her forehead and shakes her head. "I'm so sorry."

"That's okay," I say, even though I'm not clear on what exactly just happened.

"I just wasn't expecting you. You didn't tell me you were coming." She smacks my arm, kind of hard.

"*Ow.* I thought it would be a nice surprise."

"It is. But—" She looks at the doors. "Come on."

She walks toward the sanctuary, waving me on. She takes two handouts from the man at the door and gives one to me. Printed on it is a roman-numeral list titled "Today's Sermon." The topic: "Standing in the Fire."

I follow her inside. The roof soars above our heads while the aisle slopes down, making me feel woozy. The pews fill quickly. Rebekah stops next to one. Her mother sits in the middle, a space saved next to her. "We'll talk after, okay?" She points farther down the aisle. "You can sit with the youth."

"Okay." I wave and walk away.

I feel hurt. But why? Because I had assumed we would sit together?

I guess I had assumed a lot of things this morning.

I squeeze into one of the youth pews, three rows from the front. I hold my Bible, Rebekah's Bible, Rebekah's dad's Bible, on my lap, with the handout on top. Light organ music picks up and smothers the noise of the worship hall. Church starts.

"Let's go over here," Rebekah says. She leads me through the post-church crowd outside and down one of the walkways. On the grass away from the path sits a hump of rock shaped like a big gray tortoise shell. A sign next to it reads SITTIN' STONE.

We sit on the stone. It's perfectly sized for two people, and the smooth granite is surprisingly comfortable, for a rock. I wrap my arms around my knees and pull them toward my chest. My mind is numb with worry.

Rebekah looks like she's trying to figure out what to say.

I'll start. "I'm sorry."

"*You're* sorry? Wait, no, *I'm* sorry. What are you sorry about?"

I still don't completely know. I just felt like I should be. "Why don't you go?"

She sighs and runs a hand through her hair. "I'm sorry my mom was so cold."

"She wasn't *cold*. It was kind of awkward, though."

"I *have* told her your name. I know I have. I haven't told her that we're . . . what we are."

"Team Weird?"

"Team Weird."

We put our hands in the middle and break.

"My parents are weird about that stuff," she says. "Weird in a bad way. Especially my dad."

"My dad's weird too."

"In a bad way?"

"In every way."

179

We both laugh, and things feel a little more normal—or weird, I guess. I stretch my legs out and lean back. The Bible starts to slide off the side of the Sittin' Stone. I grab it just before it falls to the grass.

"Good catch," she says.

I hold it in front of me, staring at the cover, at the initials. "So—"

"Oh, yeah. That, too. It was my dad's Bible, originally. That's why it looks kind of beat-up and old. It's mine now, but my mom still thinks of it as my dad's."

"Even though it has your initials on it."

"They're both our initials. My dad and I are both RFJ. I'm an only child."

She says that like all only children have the same initials as their fathers. "Then what's the *F*?"

"Frances, okay? My middle name is Frances."

I grin. "Frances?"

"Yes, she was my great-aunt. Shut your mouth, *Flowers*."

"Very original. Nobody's ever made fun of my last name before."

She smacks my arm, but she's smiling. "You made fun of my name first. Now you have to tell me your middle name, so I can make fun of it."

"Fine. It's Desmond."

"Desmond?"

"Yeah."

"That's a good middle name. How do you have a good middle name?"

"It was my grandpa's name. He was pretty cool. I have stupid initials, though."

She looks up as if she's finding something in her brain. "PDF. Ha-ha, you're a file format."

"Shhh, don't tell anybody." We watch the crowd for a little while, then I take the Bible and plop it in my lap. I'm not upset anymore, but I feel like there is still so much that's tangled between us. "Your mom seemed surprised that I had this."

Rebekah scratches her nose. "Don't worry about that."

"I do, though. Worry about it."

"Yeah, you're good at that."

"I know."

"Well, it was my dad's Bible for a long time, but then he gave it to me. And now he's been away for a while, and my mom is always telling me to 'remember' him. Like I could forget. Like I could 'forget' my dad by giving you that."

"Right," I say. Still, I feel like this Bible is something I've taken from him, *won* from him—the guy who almost stopped me and Rebekah from being me and Rebekah. There's a sick pride in it. And maybe too much of someone else's tricky family history.

"I should probably give this back," I say. I scoop up the Bible and lay it on her lap. "I can just buy my own."

"No," she says. "You should keep it for now."

"Are you sure?"

She hands it back to me.

"Okay," I say. "Thanks." I look at the initials on the cover of the Bible. His Bible. Her Bible. My Bible.

I run a finger across the shallow dips in the stone beneath us. The feel of it—the smooth, cool rock—reminds me of something.

"This is like a tiny Stone Mountain," I say, patting the sliver of rock between us.

"Yeah," she says. "Amanda told me the youth group bought laser pointers last summer and had a tiny laser show here one night."

I want to tell her something, even though my stomach tenses and my heartbeat picks up just at the idea of speaking.

"I used to go the laser show with . . . with my family. In the summer."

I can tell that she heard me stumble. Maybe even heard why I stumbled.

"Yeah?" she says, in a small voice.

"Yeah. My mom would always take us. And my dad. We did all that family stuff—climbing the mountain, playing games in the car, buying those glow-in-the-dark rope things."

I barely said anything, but I feel like I said too much.

"I love the laser show," she says. "We always went to the Christmas one, though."

"Wait. There's a Christmas laser show?"

"Uh, *yeah* there is."

"How did I not know about that?"

"Well, you're a heathen."

With incredible speed I poke her in the stomach. She *eep*s like a startled bird and claps her hand over her mouth. "Not fair. You don't have a license to poke me." She hits me with her Bible. I halfheartedly block her.

After, we're quiet. Behind us brittle leaves rattle in the wind. A calm settles around us. I should be happy with this, but there's still one big knot that just won't come undone. Rebekah was joking when she called me a "heathen," but I still feel like one sometimes.

"That was Communion, right?" I say. "At the end?"

After the sermon the men who had been standing by the doors walked down the aisles with silver trays.

"Yeah." Her eyes open wide. "Was that your first Communion?"

"I guess so."

"You never went to church with your family? Even when you were a kid?"

The true answer is a little complicated, but the easy, close-to-true answer is much simpler. "No."

"But that shirt is too ugly to wear anywhere but church."

"Thanks. It's my dad's."

"He *is* weird."

I smile. "So, I should have taken it, right?"

"The shirt?"

"Communion."

"You didn't?"

"No, but I should have."

"Phillip, that's your choice."

The assistant pastor stood at the microphone and said that if we hadn't "acknowledged" Christ, then we should let the trays pass us by. I didn't know what that meant. So when the tray came to me and I paused, looking at all the tiny rectangular crackers, and the guy next to me gave me a look like *If you have to think about it, you probably shouldn't do it,* I let the tray pass me by. And the next one, filled with small plastic cups of wine.

When the assistant pastor said, "Do this in remembrance of me," everyone but me tilted their heads back and ate. And as everyone in the church drank the wine, I didn't.

"But if you're a Christian, you should do it, right?" I say.

"It's a personal choice. That's all I can say."

I need her to know I'm not scamming. I need her to know I'm trying to do this the right way. And I need her help.

"I'll do it next time," I say.

She doesn't say anything. She just taps my knee.

THIRTY-TWO

On Monday morning Dad drops me off at school. Walking up the steps, I see Asher and the dangly straps of his book bag flapping on either side of him. Asher thinks he's pretty awesome these days, with his DJ software and cute girlfriend, but he's still got dangly straps flapping.

I duck down, grab a pebble, and chuck it at him. It only grazes his arm, and he glances at it and keeps moving. I pick up another one and throw it, this time nailing him on the back of his neck. He swats at it and looks back, pissed.

"What the hell?"

I catch up to him. "Sorry. I didn't mean to throw it that hard."

"Why were you even throwing it in the first place?"

"Just messing around."

We walk into the E Hall lobby. On both sides the freshman and sophomore skaters slump against the wall.

"My bad," I say, trying to catch Asher's eye, which looks blood-shot to hell.

Asher grabs the skin above his nose and lets go. "It's okay. I'm just tired."

We trudge into E Hall, slipping past the Roadblock—the immovable hot sophomore girls who stand in the middle of the hall and *squee* at each other until the bell rings. Asher's locker is just past them. He stops and tries to open it but overshoots his combination numbers. He hangs his head and curses, then finally gets it open.

He's obviously more than tired. But I don't want to bug him about it.

Maybe he'll perk up if I appeal to the guru.

"I went to church yesterday," I say.

Asher unloads books from his bag, not saying anything.

"I introduced myself to Rebekah's mom, and she didn't have any idea who I was."

That cocks his eyebrow.

"Is that weird?" I say.

"I don't know."

So the guru's still asleep.

Well, I didn't want to tell him this. But I might need to prod him.

"Okay, is *this* weird?" I look in both directions for eavesdrop-pers. If there were any, they'd be my first. Still, I whisper. "She hasn't kissed me yet."

"You're supposed to kiss *her*."

"I tried."

He stops, his hand deep in his bag. "She denied you?"

"She didn't *deny* me. She said 'Not yet.'"

"Well, that's something."

That's what I thought. "Yet" means "soon." Right?

"So I'm just freaking out again," I say.

"Probably. Maybe."

"Maybe?"

He rubs his eyes. "How long have you guys been together? A month?"

"Less than a month."

"About a month. Most people would have kissed by now."

"You're the expert on this."

"You're asking me what I think."

"So what should I do?"

"Just wait. After a while, if she still hasn't kissed you, then maybe something's wrong. Or maybe you have to up your game."

"The hell does that mean?"

"It means you have to prove that you're not scamming."

"I'm *not*."

"I'm saying *she* has to know."

"She *does*."

"Then don't ask me for help." He says it straight to my face, and a few people passing by look at us and then at their friends like, *Nerd fight*.

I look at the floor, feeling stupid for getting angry.

"Maybe I don't know what I'm talking about, anyway," Asher says. "Jennifer and I broke up."

I stand there with my mouth open.

I have no idea what to say.

"Dude—"

He shuts his locker, and it's not a slam but it almost is. "Not that you care."

He puts on his book bag and merges with the flow.

THIRTY-THREE

"Love your brothers and sisters in Christ," Pastor Tim says, ending youth group the way he always does. The lights go on, and Rebekah and I stand up. My spine pops as it uncurls.

Rebekah knocks my arm. "Why don't you ever sing?"

"Why don't you ever stop hitting me?" I say.

"Because I still have that bruise from putt-putt." She rolls the right leg of her jeans up a little and points to a small, grayish spot.

"That's a birthmark."

"That's an *injury*. A serious injury."

"You're right. I think you might need a cast."

She makes a fist. "*You* might need a cast."

It's crazy, but I want to kiss her right now, with the entire youth group surrounding us.

"Really," she says. "You never sing. You hum, but you don't sing."

"I'm a good hummer. I'm not a good singer."

She rolls her eyes. "It doesn't matter how good your voice is."

"It does, though. Your voice is really good. I would just mess it up, singing right next to it."

"Doesn't work like that."

Why is she bugging me about this?

"You haven't really sung either," I say. "Not since—not lately." YouthLife was the last time, that I know of, that she sang in front of people.

"You're changing the subject."

"I know. But still. It's true."

Rebekah chews on her lip. "I will. But you owe me another drawing."

"Why?"

"We're even now. You have to go first this time."

A drawing for a song. A tooth for a tooth.

"Sure," I say.

"It better be good." She pushes me.

"Oh, it will be." I push her back.

"Hey now, hey now. Stop the violence, y'all."

Somehow Ferret is standing right beside us. Pastor Tim is next to him.

I step away from Rebekah, feeling busted. I don't even know Tim personally, but I don't want to disappoint him. He's got this relaxed smile and intent gaze. He's too confident, too upright, too cool.

And Ferret—what the hell is he doing here?

"I don't think we've met," Tim says, offering his hand. "I'm Tim."

I swallow. "Phillip."

"Very nice to meet you, Phillip. How are you liking it here?"

"It's good. I like it."

"Fantastic. We're thrilled that you're here. And if you ever need anything, let me know." He claps me on the shoulder and turns to Rebekah. "As for you, Ms. Joseph, we have a little surprise. Do you have a second?"

"Sure."

"Let's talk over by the stage." They start to walk away.

"I'll just hang here with Phillip," Ferret says. Tim looks confused, but he just nods and keeps going.

Leaving me alone with Randall T. Farragut.

Who just called me Phillip. And said we were going to "hang."

Between cross-country and youth group, I see Ferret practically every day, but we never speak or even look at each other anymore. I had hoped that wouldn't change.

"I need a wingman for the refreshments station," Ferret says. "You game?"

Two collapsible tables against the wall are the "refreshments station," and they seem well stocked with sodas and snacks, as usual. What about that requires a wingman? Or even a main man?

I thought I made it clear that I hate him. Why won't he just *leave me alone*?

"By the way," he says, clearing his throat, "I'd like to apologize for being an all-around pissant."

A what?

"A dipwad. A turd burglar. Et cetera, et cetera."

This is painful. I could go to the other side of the room and pretend I have friends here. I don't want this.

Ferret hooks his thumbs through his belt loops. "I'm sorry. That's what I'm saying."

I shouldn't care. Ferret is annoying, careless, and mean. His apology is for being him, but *he's still him*.

He looks like a damn shelter dog, though.

And I guess I'm supposed to forgive people now, whether they deserve it or not.

"Thanks," I say.

The grin on his face tells me he knows how hard that was for me. "Wingman?" he asks.

I don't have anything else to do. "Fine."

"Hot *dog*. Come on, then."

I wait a few seconds before following him. At the tables he grabs two bottles of water by the neck and offers one to me. "Have a cold one, Flowers." He clears his throat again. "Phillip, I meant. An athlete like you doesn't need to be drinking sugar and caffeine." He takes a deep swig.

"I don't really think I'm an 'athlete.'" I open my bottle and take a sip.

Ferret shakes his head. "Don't talk like that." He takes another drink and gasps with satisfaction. "Okay, wingman, help me uncooler these drinks in here." He drags a cooler from beneath one of the tables and opens it. Inside, bottles of water and various teas and low-calorie drinks rest on bags of ice. Ferret grabs a few and slides them in front of the columns of soda cans already lined up on the table. I do the same.

"I'm trying to push these right now," Ferret says. "No more of this soda crap. I know that's practically sacrilegious in the state of Coca-Cola, but I doubt you'd see Jesus drinking this garbage."

I know Ferret didn't bring me over here to tell me about Jesus

Christ's beverage preferences. Or, I hope not. What is this really about?

We finish uncoolering, and Ferret stands next to the drinks, me by his side. He looks like he's waiting for someone, and soon enough, two seventh-grade girls walk up, chatting happily. Before they reach for sodas, Ferret grabs a bottle of water and holds it out. "Try an ice-cold water, Beth Anne."

Beth Anne looks at the bottle like it's a girl wearing too much lip gloss. "Uh, no thanks." She grabs a soda.

Her friend pipes up. "I'll take it." And she does.

"Valencia!" Ferret says. "Right on." The girls walk away, and Ferret turns to me. "If you offer people something better, sometimes they'll take it."

Okay, you freak.

Ferret chuckles. "Now I have to apologize again. I am a numbskull sometimes, you know that. And a fan of the grand gesture, when I should just tell it straight up."

I tap my foot on the carpet, waiting for him to finally insult me so I can go.

"I'm proud of you," he says.

Proud of me? Like he's my grandpa or something? I stay, despite myself, just to hear what he's talking about.

"And I think you've got a lot of potential."

Barf.

"And quite honestly, it's been inspiring watching you grow in Christ, Phillip."

I don't want to feel the satisfaction I feel when he says that. It's weak. And it's uncomfortable. He's been *watching* me?

"You've had the biggest drops in race times of anybody on the JV team this year. Me and Coach Heller have noticed. Did you know that? And you've made some huge gains here, too. Do you think that's a coincidence?"

"I don't know."

"It ain't."

I didn't know about my race times. And I never even thought about *that* and *this* together. If it's true, good. But so what?

"Why did you bring me over here?" I say.

"Rebekah's getting a scholarship to go to the Southeastern Youth Leadership Summit. The church is paying her fees." Ferret nods toward the stage. "That's what that's all about."

She must be excited. The money was the only thing in her way. Now she and Amanda can go together. "Good, but—"

"But what does that have to do with you? Well." He smacks his lips. "If you wanted one too, we could probably make that happen."

The bottle falls from my fingers and smacks against the carpet. Water glugs out, darkening the blue and gray fibers. I pick up the bottle and look for paper towels on the refreshments table.

Ferret pats my shoulder. "It'll dry on its own. Didn't mean to shock you. Do you know about the Summit?"

From what Rebekah and Amanda have told me about the Summit, it's for kids who are gifted at God. It takes place once every three years over just one weekend, the first one in November—not even a convenient holiday weekend. You have to be willing to give up three days, and fly in if you live out of state, and spend all that time and money learning how to be even better at God. Plus there are some concerts.

"Yeah, I know."

I know I don't belong there.

"Good," he says. "So you know you're not ready for it right now."

"Yes."

"But you could be. If you got more involved. If you worked for it."

"No."

"Yes."

"No."

"Why would you say that? When I've seen the strides you've taken."

"Because it's crazy."

"I wouldn't have brought this up if I didn't think you could do it. I know it seems like a lot, but I can help you." He strikes an action hero pose. "Randall T. Farragut, Spiritual Trainer. How about it? Water or soda?"

Okay, that's it. I screw the cap back onto my bottle and step back.

"Sorry," I say. "I can't."

"Fear is the mind-killer, Phillip."

I go searching for Rebekah.

MAY

Forty jugs of water. At first that's all it was.

"Can you boys help me with this?" Mom called from the garage. Her voice was strained. Chris and I jumped up from the living room couches and ran through the kitchen. Mom was back from her "Sunday time," and at her feet sat four plump water jugs.

"I need some strong boys to help me," she said, a little out of breath.

"Phillip is a weak boy," Chris said, laughing. I punched him, not too hard. We both took one jug in each hand, then we waddled into the kitchen and plopped the jugs on the counter.

"You can just leave the others on the floor for now, guys," Mom said. "We're putting them down in the basement."

"Why?" Chris said.

"Let's get all of them in here first, and then I'll give you the scoop."

When we'd finished and Mom had closed the minivan's back hatch, Dad popped his head into the garage. "Need some help?"

As a family we brought all forty jugs down to the basement and arranged them in a tight six-by-six square with a four-jug expansion on the side. When we finally finished, Dad didn't even ask the obvious question.

"So," he said, "how was . . . ?" He circled his hand in the air like he couldn't remember the word "church."

"Very nice," Mom said.

We all stood there, looking at our neat little creation.

"Mom," Chris said finally.

"I know," Mom said, rubbing Chris's shoulder. "I just want us to be prepared for any kind of minor emergency where we need to have water on hand. We're very vulnerable when it comes to droughts, not to mention power outages. So I thought we could keep this down here. Just in case."

Dad nodded vigorously. "Sounds good. Smart thinking." He poked a finger at her head. Mom smiled and batted his hand away.

I couldn't imagine us ever being in a situation where we'd need to drink from jugs we kept in our basement. And if we were that desperate for water, would forty jugs be enough?

Mom was planning for a catastrophe, but I felt relief. It meant she planned on staying with us.

THIRTY-FOUR

This isn't driving. This is parking. Ahead of me, as far as I can see, Highway 124 is just one long traffic jam. I groan and rest my forehead on the steering wheel.

"This suuuuuuucks." I bomp my head against the wheel a few times.

"Sad to say, but this is as much a part of driving as driving is."

"Taking you to get printer ink is part of driving?"

Dad laughs. "It is until you can afford your own car."

The truck in front of us creeps forward a few feet. I lift my foot from the brake and let us glide for half a second to close the distance. Glad we're making progress.

He drums on the window. "You know, since we're stuck here, there was something I wanted to mention. I've been reading a lot about climate change recently."

He starts talking about all the articles and books he's been reading lately, making sure to mention what he's found particularly interesting "from an engineering perspective," and I block out most of it. I want things to be cool between us, but I've had this mental fuzz in my head ever since Wednesday night, and Dad delivering a monologue while we crawl to Best Buy on a Saturday afternoon is amplifying the problem.

The light up ahead turns green, and we actually move a little bit.

"So," Dad says, "I think you're right. We should keep it."

"Keep what?"

"What I was just talking about. All the items in the basement."

When did he get to *that*?

"Okay," I say.

He snorts. "I thought you'd be a little more pleased than that. This is what you want, right?"

That is what I want*ed*, I guess. But how is he so late on this? I know he's been in my room to get my laundry. Hasn't he noticed the drawings on my wall? They're not about surging methane levels in the atmosphere. They're not about canned goods.

They're about God.

The world still might end soon. But it doesn't feel like that anymore.

We roll to a stop, just a few cars short of the light. A mile away, twenty minutes or more from here, the Best Buy sign rises above the highway.

"I just haven't thought about it lately," I say. "I've been thinking about going to this conference."

"What kind of conference?"

"A Christian conference."

I'm not really thinking about going. Ferret's offer was bonkers. It was like saying that not only was I ready for the varsity squad on cross-country, but also I could finish in the top ten if I trained with him. Ridiculous.

I just want to see what Dad says.

"This is through . . . your church?"

"Yeah. It's for people from youth group. You stay in a hotel in Atlanta over a weekend and learn leadership tactics and stuff. I have to do fifty service hours to go. And there's a fee."

"How much?"

"Six hundred."

Dad coughs. "Six hundred dollars?"

"The church might pay for it, though."

"Okay. Well." He's drumming on the window again. "This all sounds like a lot, Phillip. And very sudden. You just started with this church thing."

Church thing. *Church thing.*

Dad allows me to go to church, and I'm happy about that, but he doesn't *want* me to go. He thinks it's a fad. Interchangeable, like a favorite band or movie or book.

Ferret, as crazy as he is, actually treated me like a Christian. He didn't doubt my sincerity or my commitment. He thought I could go to the Summit, even though I didn't. And maybe still don't.

Isn't this something he knows about? Not like running, where he rides around on his bike barking at people. This is his real job. Being a professional Christian.

The fuzz is starting to clear up, and I think I understand why.

My brain was trying to cope with the terrifying idea of taking Ferret up on his offer. And now I'm thinking I might actually do it.

Dad sighs and points at the road. "This happens *every* Saturday. It's unbelievable."

Then why did we come out here?

The traffic light gives the turn lane next to us a green arrow. That road leads out to the start of Steven Pillory Memorial Highway, a *real* highway, not this strip mall service road.

"Then let's go around," I say. We can take Steven Pillory to Moon Place and then the road after that, whatever it's called. Skip the whole mess ahead of us.

Dad sees what I mean. "No, Phillip. That will take longer."

"No, it won't." I check the side mirror, start to turn the wheel.

"You're not prepared for that kind of highway driving."

I lift my foot off the brake.

"Phillip, no!"

I press it back down.

Dad stares at me, pissed, but obviously trying not to be. "Please don't do that. Let's take this slowly."

The arrow turns yellow. Then disappears.

I didn't take it. But I could have.

THIRTY-FIVE

I call Rebekah on Sunday night. She picks up.

"So, sorceresses were real?" I say.

"What?"

"Sorceresses. They actually existed."

I hear only the faint background roar of the phone.

"Sorry," I say. "I've just been reading Exodus. 'Do not allow a sorceress to live.'"

"Okay."

I can practically see the blank expression on her face.

"It just sort of surprised me," I say. "That sorceresses were in the Bible. I was kind of nerding out about it. I wasn't making fun of it."

Rebekah sighs into the phone. "I know. Sorry. You caught me in a bad mood."

I think that means it's not my fault. But maybe I did something

wrong at church this morning? Again? She didn't mention anything. . . .

"Between school and cross-country and academic team," she
says, "when am I supposed to fit in fifty service hours and a whole
weekend away?"

Wait, this is about the Summit?

"I thought you were happy about the scholarship."

"I *was*. Then I thought about what it meant."

Um. I thought she was definitely going. She really did seem
excited about it before. Just, like, a couple of days ago.

"Is there anything I can do?" I say.

She laughs. "That's sweet, but I don't think you can do my service hours for me."

"Well, I was thinking about going too."

"Hmm?"

"Ferret offered to help me go to the Summit. He said there were
some funds available. If I did the work."

"Phillip, that's . . . Why didn't you say anything?"

"I didn't know what to say. I didn't know what I wanted yet."

"You want to go to the *Summit*?"

"Yeah."

"You know it's a lot of work. And it's only a month away."

"I know."

"It's intense. For dedicated Christian leaders. I'm not even sure
I should go."

"But you *are* going, right?"

"Yes, but—"

"We can go together, then."

Silence. The phone speaker sounds like a seashell against my ear.

"Okay," she says.

A thrill passes through me.

"Team Weird, right?"

"Right."

THIRTY-SIX

The basketball court is empty. The volleyball court is empty. The stairs and benches and lawn are empty. Strangest of all, there are barely any cars in the parking lot. I step quietly and cautiously, like I might interrupt the church's slumber if I make too much noise.

Ferret is probably playing an elaborate joke on me. By the time I told him I was interested in going to the Summit, he'd had plenty of time to come up with this CORE thing, which he called "the student government of youth group." Supposedly they meet on Wednesdays before everyone else gets here.

But even though I want to try harder to be a leader, it's hard to see why people would show up early to do chores. And even though Rebekah is allegedly a CORE member, she's never mentioned it to me, even when she told me she wasn't coming tonight because she has to study for academic team. Plus, Ferret told me CORE stands for "Christians Offering Real Energy," which made it sound like he came up with "CORE" first and then shoved words into the acronym to make it work.

It would have been way too much work. But I bet he'd do it just so I'd walk into that big empty room where he's crouching, waiting to throw a rubber spider at my face.

"He made it!" Ferret yells from the youth center porch. Shamefully, I jump, just a little. He comes down the stairs to meet me.

If that was the prank, it sucked.

Ferret grins and shakes my hand like I didn't see him just three hours ago at cross-country practice. "You showed up."

"I showed up."

"Fantastic. We're about to start, so let's get in there. I'll introduce you around." He gently pushes me inside.

Pastor Tim sits on the edge of the stage, and about fifteen youth group kids sit in a scattered semicircle facing him. As we approach, some of the kids turn around, and I feel warm with self-consciousness. I recognize all of them, but I only know Amanda.

"Hey," Ferret yelps, interrupting people's conversations, "for those of y'all who don't know, this is Phillip Flowers. But you can just call him Flowers."

"Or Phillip," I say.

"Right," he says. "I was just kidding."

Everyone waves and says hey, though they look a little confused by our exchange.

"Take a seat," Tim says. "Glad to have you here, Phillip."

"Thanks," I say. I want to get as far away from Ferret as I can, though I worry that I'm now and forever his friend "Flowers." Thankfully, Amanda offers me the empty floor space next to her. I sit down, and Ferret plops down next to Tim.

Tim claps his hands once and then rubs them together. "Okay. We're going to have a shorter session today 'cause I have to meet up with our guest speaker and go over some things. So let's review some stuff real quick, and then I have a brainstorm for you."

First they talk about paintball this past Saturday. Pretty much everybody agrees that it was awesome. They talk about how quickly some people got shot, and who got angry, and how Ferret was "like an assassin out there," which is not surprising at all.

I don't have anything to contribute.

Then they talk about alternative spring break, which they're already planning for. They are going to Key West to build houses. There are lots of cats there, or so some guy says. It is going to be awesome.

I have nothing to contribute.

I shouldn't be here. These people know each other—some of them seem to have grown up in the church together. They have lots of plans with each other. Maybe I should just focus on getting service hours by volunteering outside the church. My schedule is busy, but not as busy as Rebekah's. I could fit in fifty hours soon enough.

I'm tired of feeling like the new kid.

Tim claps his hands again. "Okay, guys, let's brainstorm. I know we're already a little ways into fall, but our activities calendar for the next few months is a little bare. Right now we've got a few service projects and the lock-in after homecoming, and that's not enough. So I want you guys to come up with some ideas for fall events. Just shoot out whatever comes to mind."

"Hell house," says a chirpy girl.

Tim nods and scrunches his face at the same time. "Not a bad idea, but we haven't really done those in the past, so—"

A few more people speak. Some ideas are okay (Thanksgiving canned food drive); some are not okay ("We really should do a hell house"). Tim jots a few things down but doesn't seem impressed yet.

I'm not even trying.

Amanda taps my elbow and whispers, "Any ideas?"

"No," I say, feeling a rush of warmth for her. She's trying to include me.

But I'm still trying to exclude me.

"Just whatever comes to mind," Tim says.

How does something *come* to mind? Unless somebody puts it there, isn't it inside already?

You just have to find it.

I look up. Ferret senses that I thought of something. He nods at me and motions with his hand like, *Out with it.*

"Um," I say, and I feel everyone's eyes lock on me. The words "Never mind" try to push out of me, but I swallow them. "I don't know if you guys already do this or if it would be boring or whatever, but what about the Christmas laser show? At Stone Mountain?"

My stomach feels like a loaded spring.

Then Amanda says, "Ooh!" and claps her hands three times.

Tim nods. "That's a good one, Phillip. It's been a while since I've been to the laser show, but it's always a great time."

I hear a few quiet "yeahs."

"Al*right*, Phillip," Ferret says.

I feel my face flush.

Tim scribbles something on his piece of paper. He looks up. "Okay. Any others?"

♥ ♥ ♥

After youth group ends, I wait by the parking lot for my dad to pick me up. Still feeling triumphant, I text Rebekah.

i sang 2nite.

liar, she says. *i wdv hrd abt ppls ears meltng.*

melted their fones 2. hows study?

A minute or two goes by.

ok. waffles make it harder.

waffles?

Another couple of minutes.

yeah @ waffle house w asher.

My thumbs hover above the keyboard.

sounds fun, I say.

I see Dad driving into the parking lot.

I wait to see if she texts back.

I'm not going to invite myself.

Dad pulls up in front of me.

want to join? she says.

"I still don't understand why you never get hash browns," Asher says. He sits on the other side of the booth, a brown plastic cup of ice water in his hand.

"I just don't like them. That's all there is to understand."

"But how?" says Rebekah, sitting next to me. "They're potatoes. Fried potatoes."

"Fried potatoes are good," Asher insists.

"I just don't like the stringiness. I don't like the format."

Rebekah laughs. "The format?"

"The format."

"You're weird, man," Asher says.

This Waffle House is the busiest in town. Even on a weeknight there can be a wait. Dishes clank and waffle makers steam as truckers curse, hipsters argue, and waitresses shout out orders. The whole place smells like meat and syrup.

I can't believe I convinced Dad, even as much of a pushover as he can be, to drop me off here on a school night.

"So," I say, "how'd the studying go?"

Asher and Rebekah look at each other for a second and then bust out laughing. They're still laughing when our waitress, Brittany, brings me my orange juice.

"What?" I say.

Rebekah leans back into the corner of the booth and hangs her head in mock shame. "We didn't get any studying done. Neither of us."

"I was just sitting at my desk in my room, staring at my notes," Asher says.

"Me too," Rebekah says. "So then Asher called me, and we thought we might force each other to study if we met up."

"But it turns out Waffle House is not a good place to study in."

I snort. "What a surprise."

"My dad would flay me if he knew I didn't study tonight," Asher says.

"What?" I say. "He's not like that."

"Just because he's your freaking chauffeur . . ." Asher says, looking only at me. He shakes his head and trails off.

I grab a piece of pulp dangling from the rim of the cup and squish it. I had no idea his dad driving us bothered him.

"Anyway," he says, turning to Rebekah, "I'm not worried about us. I am worried about Colin."

"Colin, Colin, Colin," Rebekah says, shaking her head.

They move on and talk about this guy named Colin and some girl named Raina and their coach and the teams they're worried about and lots of other team-related stuff. This is like CORE all over again.

I drop out of the conversation, waiting for them to remember I'm here. When it seems like they're done, I turn to Rebekah. "I went to CORE tonight."

She spears a clump of cold hash browns (scattered with onions) and dangles it in front of her mouth. "You didn't tell me. Again." She eats.

"I didn't know for sure if I was going to do it. Again."

"Did you like it?" She sounds skeptical.

"Not at first."

"What's CORE?" Asher says.

"It's a church thing," I say. I turn back to Rebekah. "But we were supposed to come up with ideas for youth group activities, and I remembered when we were talking about the laser show. Anyway, I said it, and Tim thought it was a good idea."

"Awesome." She picks up her coffee mug and swirls the dregs. "So are you going back?"

"Yeah."

"You're really diving right in."

I glance over at Asher. He picks his fingernails and pretends to read the menu.

"Yeah. Well, you know, Team Weird." I put my hand out. She bats it down and looks embarrassed.

The waitress saves the moment by bringing my waffle and eggs. I salt the eggs, syrup the waffle, and tuck in. Asher taps my side of the table and motions behind me. I turn back and see Brad hulking near the entrance with a bunch of other dudes. None of them is Dan the Man.

"Where's his BFF?" Asher says.

"Yeah," I say, shoving a drippy bite of waffle in my mouth. "Or Mark."

"Maybe they broke up." Asher makes a fake pouty face. "So sad."

Rebekah nips a bit of egg off my plate. "*Why* aren't you guys friends with Mark anymore?" she says.

I've told her a little of what happened, but Asher and I tell the full story. He kind of exaggerates what Mark did at his birthday party and at the lunch table, but I don't correct him.

"I get it," Rebekah says. She nips another bite.

I grumble at her. "Yeah, but I think we should let it go now."

"You're still on this?" Asher says.

"Well, so are you."

He shakes his head at me again.

"Why not?" I say. "He's our friend. He did something stupid, and, yeah, he might still be friends with those jackasses, but he's still Mark."

"Maybe that's the problem. And, look, just because you 'have the faith' now doesn't mean you have to forgive people who treat you like shit."

That again? In front of Rebekah?

"That doesn't have anything to do with it," I say. I glance at Rebekah and think twice about what I just said. "Or not everything. I just want to let it go. I don't get why it's such a thing for you."

"It's *not*. It's a thing for *you*."

"Come on, boys," Rebekah says. "Settle down."

"Yeah, Phillip," Asher says. "Settle down."

And that's when I start to think we weren't really fighting about Mark.

THIRTY-SEVEN

Yeah, I definitely have chemical burns. The clots of sticky black liquid clinging to my legs are now cooking my skin in the late morning sun. I wipe a sheet of sweat from my face, tilt my head back, and groan.

"Look at that," Ferret says. "Beautiful."

He's looking at a partially resurfaced church parking lot.

He's *not* looking at the casualties behind him—me and the other two youth group kids who made the mistake of showing up on a Saturday for some service hours. Reagan, a freshman, sits in the grass, trying to pluck tar spots from her jeans. Jared, probably a junior, is so red-faced from the freak fall heat that I'm worried he might pass out.

Somewhere in Tennessee, Rebekah's running a varsity 5K in this weather.

Lucky.

"Okay, y'all. That's it for today," Ferret says cheerily. Then he turns around and seems to actually see us for the first time, after standing by and directing us most of the morning. His face drops. "Sorry, gang. I didn't realize that stuff was so . . . sticky. Why don't you come back to my office real quick to cool down? I've got waters. Just leave the rollers and stuff."

I really want to go home, but I want water more. Jared and Reagan look like they're thinking the same thing. Silent with exhaustion, we follow Ferret as he leads us to a side door beneath the main church building.

This is not what I thought service hours would be like.

This is not what service hours *should* be like.

This is Ferret's fault. Again. Why did I think I could trust him?

He holds the door for us, and we walk into an air-conditioned hallway. It feels incredible. "I may have some stuff for that stuff," he says, pointing to my legs, then he hustles to another door inside and unlocks it. A sign on the wall reads RANDALL T. FARRAGUT, ASSISTANT YOUTH PASTOR.

Ferret flicks on the lights and starts scavenging. The room is small, but it seems even smaller because it's so messy. His desk and shelves overflow with papers, books, and random items—a foam Atlanta Braves tomahawk, rolled-up posters, a green plastic light-saber, a kite that looks like a dragon, a Taco Bell bag, and a stack of blue T-shirts, among other things. Next to his keyboard is a dog-eared copy of one of my favorite books, *Dune*.

When he told me "Fear is the mind-killer," he was stealing it from that book.

I wonder where he steals the rest of his little sayings from.

"I got that stuff in here. I know it." Ferret opens and closes a few drawers, but no luck. "Oh, hold on. I got waters for you." He opens a mini-fridge underneath his desk, takes out bottles of water, and tosses them at us, not accurately, so that we each barely catch them. He goes back to searching for his magic medicine.

"My dad's probably here," Reagan says. "I don't want to keep him waiting."

"Yeah," Jared says.

Ferret stops. And deflates before our eyes. "Of course. I understand."

Jared and Reagan step out. I want to follow them, but I don't know them. Ferret yells out, "Thanks again, guys. Y'all were awesome out there."

A couple of weak goodbyes float back. Then the faint sound of the door opening and closing.

Ferret sits down and rubs his forehead. "I really messed this thing up, didn't I?"

I open my water and swallow it all in one long gulp.

"Yes," I say with a gasp. He did mess this thing up, just like he messes up pretty much everything with his aggressive awkwardness. I used to think that maybe he wasn't liked only on the cross-country team, but I don't think he's liked here either. Even Tim, who's respectful to everybody, usually treats him like a troubled child.

And he's supposed to be my spiritual trainer? No way. I'll see if I can get my service hours through Tim.

"I'm sorry," Ferret says. "I really am."

My skin is still burning. He's too late.

He sighs. "Alright. Let's take care of the paperwork." He pushes aside some magazines and picks up a clipboard. "This is your service hours tally sheet. Right now you've got zero." He flips it around and shows me. My name is at the top, followed by a table with columns for entering activities and number of hours earned.

He finds a pen, clicks it a few times, and enters my information. "Now," he says, "you've got two."

"Two?" I say. It just bursts out of me. How could that have been only two hours?

"We got things started a little before nine. It's 10:46 right now."

He's right. But all that work and sweat? All these chemical clumps in my leg hair? All the scraping and tearing it'll take to get them out?

That's only two hours? Out of fifty? With less than a month until the Summit?

"You know what?" Ferret says, reading my thoughts, which must be written in seventy-two-point font all over my face. "For your troubles, we can add another hour."

"What about CORE?"

He looks up at me slowly. "Now you're pushing it."

I'm pushing it?

"I showed up early," I say, ticking off the points on my fingers. "I came up with a good idea. I helped set up, afterward. None of that counts?"

"Service is more than just brainstorming and refreshments, buddy."

Okay, I'm done.

I put my empty bottle on his desk. "My dad's waiting too." I turn to leave.

"I didn't think you were afraid of a little hard work," Ferret says.

I almost keep going. But I stop at the door. "I'm *not*."

"Where you running to, then?"

"Home. So I can get the tar off my legs."

Ferret is still. Then he clicks his pen. "Fair enough. Just this one time, I'll mark you for CORE. That's four hours, okay? That's pretty good."

Four hours is . . . eight percent of the hours I need.

"It's alright."

Ferret looks away and tosses the clipboard and pen onto the desk.

"What about Reagan and Jared?" I say.

"What about them?"

"You aren't giving them three hours?"

"They aren't going to the Summit."

"What?"

Ferret makes fake sign language as he talks. "They. Aren't. Going. To. The. Summit."

I wait for him to explain.

He raises his eyebrows. "Not everybody's trying to *get* something from giving."

I want to feel outraged at what he just said. I want to flip him a double bird and storm out.

But I don't.

Ferret laces his fingers together and looks at his hands. "I did say in the email to bring sweatpants, just in case."

"You didn't say why. I thought you meant in case it was cold."

He nods. "I was unclear."

And then he completely forgot about it once he was playing Commander Parking Lot out there.

"Look," he says, "I know I'm a jerk sometimes. But I really can help you if you give me a shot. I'm not a total screwup."

"Really?"

He gives me an angry look for a second, then points to a framed document above his desk. "My seminary diploma. I graduated from college magna cum laude, Phillip. How could I be a total screwup and graduate from college magna cum laude?"

"I don't know what that means."

"I have two jobs. An apartment. A cat, for crying out loud."

I can't help it—I laugh.

"I know I sound like a fool right now," he says. "But you can't do this alone, Phillip. Trust me, it's not that easy."

"I didn't think it was."

There's a pause.

Did I? I guess when I pictured what I'd be doing for service hours, it was raking some old lady's leaves or . . . setting up refreshments.

"Maybe I did," I say.

As soon as I say it, I regret it. Ferret's going to jump all over a confession like that.

But he leans back and says, "For the casual believer, it is that easy. But if you want a real relationship with God, you can't be afraid to accept guidance. And you can't be afraid to get your hands dirty."

I glare at him. "What about my legs?"

He has a nervous little grin. "I set myself up for that one."

I want a real relationship with God.

But the guy begging to introduce me is practically buried in his own trash.

"One more shot," Ferret says. "If I screw up again, you can kick me to the curb."

Maybe I do need help that badly.

Plus, he *did* tell us to bring sweatpants.

I look at Ferret's tattered copy of *Dune*. He sees, and his eyes light up.

"I'm not afraid," I say.

Outside, the air smells like a marker.

THIRTY-EIGHT

Dad sits down across from me and slides my ice cream over. "Vanilla with jimmies. Cup." He holds his up, catching a drip with his tongue. "And blueberry cobbler. Cone."

I scoop out a small bite, eat it, and plant my spoon like a flag.

"Not hungry?" Dad asks, already well into his.

I shrug.

After we took care of my resurfacing wounds, Dad and I did some parking practice at the school lot. Then we hit the local roads for some slow driving. I thought that would be it, but Dad directed me to 124 and then the left turn that leads to Steven Pillory Memorial Highway.

I was freaking out. Finally I would get to really drive. Finally Dad understood that I could do this.

But then he told me to take the next right into the Jimmies Ice Cream—as a "reward for a job well done."

I'd rather just go home. I mean, I like ice cream, but it's kind of babyish as a "reward." And it's just weird, in a bad way, to eat ice cream in public on a Saturday afternoon with your dad.

He clicks his tongue. "Jeez, that looks painful."

And it's flat-out embarrassing to have your dad comment on your legs in public. I pull them back under my chair. "They're fine."

Scrubbing the clots off my legs revealed a bunch of angry red splotches. We put some aloe on them. Now they're dull red, and they really do just barely sting.

"Do I need to be worried about unsafe working conditions there?"

I look up at him. "Dad. No. It was partially my fault anyway."

"Maybe so." He dabs some drips that fell on his wrist. "I just don't want you to get hurt trying to get to this conference."

Does that mean he's okayed it? This is the first time he's mentioned the Summit all week.

"So, I can go," I say, trying to make it not sound like a question.

He twists his cone around, looking for the next chunk to bite off. "I don't know yet," he says.

I stir my ice cream with my spoon, trying to think of a good argument. I don't want to spend all this time on service hours only to have Dad say I can't go. I don't want it to come to that. Again.

Maybe if I get Tim to call him. Not Ferret, that wouldn't—

Sppppp.

Um. Dad just basically spat a glob of ice cream onto his chin. Now he's wiping it off and laughing. I look around, just to make sure no one from school is here.

"Dad, what—"

"I'm sorry. I'm sorry. I just." He dabs at the corner of his eye. "Do you remember that pink coat your mom always used to wear?"

Yes, I do. But where the hell did that come from?

"A little."

"She got that coat here. Right at that table over in the corner. This was shortly before you were born. Anyway, somebody had left it, but it looked like new, and your mom tried it on and loved it. So she just *took* it." He starts to smile. "We got in the car, and we'd pulled out into the parking lot, when we see this woman get out of a truck near us. She looks right at Mom, who's holding this pink coat in her lap, and her eyes get really big." Dad makes his eyes go cartoonishly large.

"We all knew right then that your mom had more or less stolen this woman's coat. I was ready to get out of the car and tell her how it was a misunderstanding.

"And then your mom says, 'Floor it!' And I did!"

Dad and I both laugh pretty hard.

Sometimes I remember: I like Dad. He tells funny stories. He has a goofy laugh that makes those stories funnier. He's sort of okay with stealing somebody's coat. He's capable of bringing up Mom and not being awkward about it.

"Do you ever think about your mom?" he says.

And he's capable of ruining everything with one dumb question.

"Dad."

"What?"

"No."

"No, you don't think about her?"

"Just *no*. Stop."

"I don't mean to bring up painful memories, Phillip. But we don't talk about Mom very often, and I wanted to hear what you have to say."

Other times I remember: I don't like Dad. He traps me. He tries to understand me but doesn't trust me. He gives me something but wants too much in return. He's not capable of bringing up Mom and not being awkward about it.

I don't want to run away from him. But I have to push him back. He's making me.

I push my spoon deep into my half-eaten ice cream and slide the cup away.

"No," I say.

THIRTY-NINE

On Monday after school I find Mark at his locker. He's alone.

He glances at me and slides a notebook into his bag.

I cross my arms and lean against the locker next to his. He can't stand long silences. I can wait him out. I know I'll win.

Then one of the Roadblock girls stands in front of me, looking at me like she wants something.

"Excuse me," she says, pointing at the locker.

"Oh, sorry."

I hear Mark snort and try to hide it. The girl opens her locker, and I have to stand behind Mark now. I lost.

"I'm not apologizing," Mark says over his shoulder.

"I'm not apologizing either."

"So what do you want?"

"I want things to not be like this."

"Not my fault."

"I didn't say it was your fault. Even though it kind of was."

He slams the locker shut and turns around.

"You were a dick," I say.

"You guys were dicks too."

Roadblock girl gives us a sideways glance, closes her locker, and hurries away. Mark puts on the oversize army jacket he pulled from his locker. I see him wearing that thing all the time now. "Mostly Asher," he says. "But you, too."

"You called me 'boring.'"

"I did?"

"Pretty much."

He works a few kinks out of his hair. "Sorry."

I shrug.

"So," he says.

"So." I'm going to have to say it. "Let's not be enemies."

We bump fists and walk down C Hall.

"How's church girl?" he says. "You guys still together?"

"Yeah."

"That's awesome, dude. That's huge."

"Whatever."

"Does she ever do bad things?"

"What does that mean?"

"I'm just joking, dude. Sort of." He stops me in the middle of the hall and lowers his voice. "My parents are gone this week, so I'm having a party at my place on Friday. You guys should come."

Rebekah wouldn't do that. Would she?

"I'll ask."

We walk some more and I contemplate how sad it is that Mark

is having a house party and I only *just* got the invite. At the end of C Hall, we say see ya, do a dude hug, and then turn away.

Mark taps me on the shoulder. "I shouldn't invite Asher, should I?"

My mouth hangs open long enough to catch a fly.

"No," I say.

FORTY

A couple of days later Rebekah and I walk side by side toward the youth center for CORE. The setting sun lights a massive sheet of gray clouds from underneath.

"So I finally get to meet the mysterious Mark," Rebekah says.

"There's nothing mysterious about Mark."

"Maybe not to you."

I was kind of hoping she'd say no. Mark and Rebekah are different and distant spheres in my life, and now they're getting all Venn diagram-y. It makes me uncomfortable.

"It's cool if you don't want to go," I say. "I don't want you to feel pressured."

"I want to go."

"Even if there's alcohol?"

She looks at me out of the corner of her eye. "I can handle it."

"Even if there's smoking?"

"Uh-huh."

"Even if there's 'grinding' and 'rap music'?"

She hits me, which is basically what I was going for.

"I know I must be blowing your mind right now," she says. "But I like going to parties. This will be my first one since I moved here."

Honestly, sometimes I forget that she hasn't been here all along. We walk up the stairs.

"Is Asher coming?" she says.

Hmm.

"I don't think so."

"They're still not friends?"

"You saw how Asher got."

"Yeah," she says, reaching for the door handle.

I grab it first and hold it. "Actually, probably don't mention it to him, okay?"

She furrows her brow but says, "Yeah, okay."

We go inside. At the front of the hall, the CORE kids sit in clusters of two and three. A few of them watch us discreetly as we walk in together.

Once we cross the big empty floor, Amanda jumps to her feet and hugs Rebekah. "Hey, girl!" Then she just about squeezes my rib cage open. "Hey, boy!"

We sit down next to her. Amanda and Rebekah chat.

Ferret, leaning against the stage, gives me a wink.

Near us Jared sits with another guy whose name I don't know. Jared nods and says, "What's up."

Tim walks in from a side door and greets everybody. He notices me and then points and smiles.

I belong here. That quickly.

Tim gives a one-clap, and everybody quiets down. "Okay, gang. Let's get down to business. First of all, we're starting to move on some of the ideas you all came up with last week. Thanks to everybody for your help on that."

Ferret gives me another wink. I give him the stink eye.

"Now, moving right along, Baxter High School homecoming is coming up really soon. Pretty much everything's taken care of for the lock-in afterward, except we need a few folks to be what we call youth chaperones. And, no, that doesn't mean 'narcs.'"

A few laughs.

"Some of you probably remember this. We've done it for a few years now, and it's just a way for you guys, the ones with heads that are *mostly* screwed on right, to help, uh—"

"The less fortunate," Ferret says.

"Sure," Tim says. "Let me stress: You probably won't have to do anything at all. We have good kids here, and to my knowledge we've never had an incident. But it's an exciting night, and sometimes when people get excited, they want to do dumb things. So you can try to help them make the right choice. That's all.

"So, any takers? If you're going to the Summit, these would count toward your service hours."

Amanda raises her hand.

Tim smiles. "What a surprise." He takes a pen and paper from his pocket and writes her name down. "Anybody else?"

Jared raises his hand. Tim writes his name down.

"Just need a few more."

How have Rebekah and I not made homecoming plans already? I guess neither of us really cares about that stuff, but still, it would be fun.

I tap her leg and whisper, "You want to?"

She looks surprised. "I don't know. Do you?"

"Yeah. You need hours, right? Let's do it."

Amanda pushes her from the other side and whispers, "Do iiiiit."

Rebekah shrugs. "Okay."

I raise my hand.

Throughout the rest of CORE and youth group, Rebekah's pretty quiet. After the last praise song of the night, Rebekah takes her phone out of her pocket. "I've got a lot of homework, so I can't really stick around." She stands up and calls her mom.

"I'm going to go wait outside for her," she says when she's done.

"Okay," I say. "I'll come out there."

She walks outside without a word. I follow, wondering what happened.

Outside, she lifts herself up onto the ledge enclosing the porch. The back of her jeans scrapes against the brick. "I know," she says. "I'm not being nice."

"Why not?"

"Because I'm mad."

"Why?"

"Because you made plans for homecoming without even asking me."

"I did, though."

"You ambushed me."

"I just assumed you would want to go."

"Exactly."

Rebekah's voice has an edge to it that I haven't heard before. I know she's right, but I don't think I deserve this.

And why doesn't she want to go?

"I have a match that day," she says. "Did you know that?"

"No."

"And you have a meet."

"I do?"

"Yes. I know because I'm skipping ours, and they're the same day."

"Well, it'll be in the morning. You'll have time to get ready and—"

"So we can get some service hours?"

"No. I mean, yeah, but not just that."

She looks over her shoulder at the parking lot.

"We don't have to go," I say.

She folds her hands in her lap and sighs. "I don't know if my dad would want me to go to homecoming, anyway. You know, boys and cars and drinking and being bad and getting pregnant. They all go together with homecoming to him."

"That sucks," I say.

A breeze flows through, and goose bumps rise all over my arms. In the parking lot a white compact SUV pulls up to the curb.

"I think your mom's here," I say.

Rebekah turns, finds the car in the dark, and waves. She slides off the ledge and lands softly on her feet.

I take a folded piece of paper from my pocket and hand it to her.

"Here's what I owe you," I say.

She takes the drawing. "Thank you." She looks up at me and grabs my arm. Goose bumps flare all over again.

"Sorry I was so lame just now," she says.

I grind a pebble with the sole of my foot. "It's fine. I'm sorry too. For ambushing you."

She bites her lip. "Let me ask you something."

"Okay."

"You know you don't have to do all this stuff just because Ferret wants you to, right?"

"I know. That's not why I'm doing it."

"I saw him give you a thumbs-up after you raised your hand."

"You think that's why I did it? So Ferret would give me a thumbs-up?"

"Then why are you doing it?"

I have no idea where to even start with that.

She lets go.

"We'll talk later," she says. And she walks away.

FORTY-ONE

Ferret crushed me.

"Cold one," Ferret says, taking a couple of bottled waters from his mini-fridge. I grab one and hold it against my face to keep from melting in his office chair.

Ferret smiles and leans back. "Told ya."

I don't want to laugh, but I do. Because for once, he did tell me. He told me exactly how much better he is at running than I am. I feel the telling in my legs and lungs.

And I made him tell me too. He just wanted to go for a "friendly run" before a Saturday afternoon of service hours. I thought I would punish him for last time. For all the times. I wanted to prove he's not in control of me. I'm in control of him.

So I ran ahead. But then he ran ahead of me. And stayed there, no matter how hard I pushed. Then, for three-point-one miles, I punished myself.

I open the water and guzzle it. It feels amazing. I am drunk on pain and endorphins.

"Phillip, I've been running long distance for years. I used to compete in 10Ks and half marathons. Did you think just 'cause I don't run at practice that I don't run at all?"

I don't want to give him the satisfaction, but he's earned it.

"Yes."

He shakes his head. "Just 'cause you can't see it don't mean it ain't there."

"But why the bike?"

"So I can sniff out slackers like you."

I hold the bottle against my forehead and glare.

"Just joshing," he says. He grabs a bag from beneath his desk and stands up. "Okay. I'm gonna jump in the shower real quick and change. You stay here, rest up, and we'll get started on something slightly less painful."

"There's a shower here?"

"Yeah, there's a little workout room and a small bathroom. Exclusive membership, so stay out. No gayferds allowed."

He winks at me and leaves. Gross.

Also, "gayferds"?

I sit in silence and pick at the few scabby splotches still on my legs. At this point it's my fault they're still there. I need to focus on something else.

I look at the junk that's piled on every surface. Mounds of useless, forgotten crap. Precarious stacks of paper.

That copy of *Dune*, on the desk right next to his computer, like a reference manual. Beneath it, his Bible.

And standing next to them, tucked away on the other side of his monitor, something I didn't see last time—a framed photo of him, several years younger, posing with an older woman. Who must be his mother.

Ferret has a *mom*.

I realize that, even after his list of life accomplishments last week, I've never thought of Ferret as having a childhood or a family or a life. That's why these things in here are startling—they are proof of Randall T. Farragut's existence.

A few minutes later Ferret walks in, rubbing a towel on his head. He's changed into jeans and a gray T-shirt. "You didn't touch anything, did you?" He pretends to be concerned.

"I tried to, but I got lost."

"Hilarious. Actually, that's what I was hoping you could help me with. Sort through some of this stuff."

I'm relieved that what we're doing doesn't involve burning flesh. But, based on what he said last time, I'm a little wary.

"And this counts toward the Summit?" I say.

"Well, you're helping your assistant youth leader be a more organized individual so he can get more work done and bring more people to God's love." He looks around. "And it certainly ain't gonna be easy. I'd say that's service."

Good. That's why I came here today. It wasn't for the company.

But I am curious.

"Who is that?" I say, pointing to the photo.

He drops the towel on the floor and sits in his chair. "Most important person in my life. Aside from Jesus, of course."

"Your mom?"

"That's Momma. The one who bore and raised me all herself. The one who gave me this." He taps the spine of his Bible. "And this." He taps the spine of his *Dune*.

"Your mom gave you *Dune*?"

"I'm guessing you've read it."

"Yeah."

"Second-greatest book ever written. Perfectly fictionalized model of self-discipline."

"I just thought it was cool."

"It's that, too."

He was talking about his mom almost in past tense. I want to ask. It feels like picking a scab.

"So, is your mom . . . here?"

"In Baxter? No, she still lives where I'm from. North Georgia mountains."

He misunderstood me. But it's better that way. "You talk to her?"

"Every day. She gave me everything." Ferret spreads his arms wide, as if to encompass his life, his wisdom. But he's actually encompassing his office. "And I want to pass it on to others," he says.

"I don't want all this." I point to his shelves and file cabinets and desk.

He blushes. "That's not what I'm talking about. That stuff's not important." He puts his hand on the *Dune*-Bible stack. "What you keep closest is what's important. That's what I want to pass on to you."

"I already have a Bible. I already have *Dune*."

"But do you know what to do with them?"

Sort of. "Do you?"

He shrugs. "I have some ideas."

Maybe for the first time, I believe him.

It feels like a shot of Señor Salamander Tequila.

"Why me?" I say.

"Why you what?"

"Why did you choose me for this?"

"Because you can do it."

"You believe that I'm a Christian."

"Aren't you?"

I crack my knuckles. "I'm not sure Rebekah thinks so."

His mouth drops open. "No. Wrong."

"I think she thinks I'm doing this stuff to impress you."

He laughs. "We know that ain't true."

"Yeah."

"You know who I think you're doing it for?"

My heart stops. "Who?"

"God."

I feel a wave of relief. "Really?"

"Heck, yes. Look, I don't mean this in a creepy way or nothin', but I was watching you at that Risen Church event a while back. What I saw that night was a young man eager to know God. A young man who wants to better himself." For a moment he looks embarrassed. "You know, I see some of myself in you. Not the screwup part. Well, maybe a little. But mostly the kid who was searching for the Truth. That's you."

He shrugs and leans back in his chair.

Is that me? It *was* me. I felt like I'd been looking for something and found it.

But I haven't felt that way since that night. Now I kind of feel like I'm searching for something I lost. So he's right about the screwup part.

I already knew that, though.

"I guess it is me," I say.

"There you go," he says. "You watch. Things will work out just fine. This stuff with Rebekah—don't worry about it. Seek God. Smart girl like her, she'll come around."

"Yeah?"

"Oh, yeah. And think about that. What an incredible opportunity to let *your* love grow in *Christ's* love. Going to the Summit, becoming leaders here and at school together, going on to college, maybe even seminary. Who knows, maybe even getting married someday."

Um.

I swallow, but it goes down the wrong tube and I start a coughing fit.

When it dies down, Ferret says, "Sorry. I'm getting ahead of ourselves. Let's just make sure you get to the Summit, alright? You'll need to put in a fair amount of time over the next few weeks." He picks up his clipboard and looks at my sheet. "But you'll be fine. And Rebekah's on track—" He flips to her sheet and freezes.

"What?"

He puts the clipboard down, a smile on his face. "Just realized I need to pencil in some hours she earned this summer. She's a real go-getter, that one." He stands up, grabs a big trash bag from beneath his desk. "Anyway, where do we start?"

I look around. "How about anywhere?"

FORTY-TWO

I will not lose to Dan the Man.

I will not lose to Dan the Man.

I will not lose to Dan the Man.

The pool cue slides between my fingers, tapping the cue ball, which glides across the felt at just the right angle and speed. The three ball drops in.

"Nice," Mark says, cheering me with a plastic cup full of keg beer.

Now I'm just one ball behind Dan. And the six is perfectly in line.

"I don't know," Dan says. "This Ferret dude sounds gay."

I chalk my cue, refusing to take Dan's bait. I was trying to explain to Mark about how things are different with Ferret now, when Dan sauntered into the room and made me play pool against him. I kept trying to talk only to Mark, but Dan's been drinking since before the party started, so his natural dickitude is amplified.

"Dude, shut up," Mark says. "If you knew Ferret—he's just *not*."

I will not lose to Dan the Man.

I take the shot. The cue ball hits a little too hard, dropping the six but overshooting for the final setup. It's just the cue and the eight ball now.

"Seems a little queer," Dan says. "That's all."

"Shut up," Dan's girlfriend, or whatever, says, finally piping up in the corner. She's makeup-hot, though I feel bad for thinking that now. "You think everybody's gay."

"Everybody *is* gay."

"So *you're* gay. That explains things."

He steps to her, and they make out a little.

I swig from my water. I'm going to end this.

I will not lose to Dan the Man.

The shot is tricky. I have to hit the eight ball just right so the cue ball doesn't drop in too.

My phone vibrates. It's a text from Rebekah.

coming up driveway :)

My heart beats five times as fast.

"She here?" Mark says.

"Yeah," I say.

"Awesome. I want to meet her."

I ready the shot. Slide the cue back and forth.

"Phillip's got a woman?" Dan says.

I will not lose to Dan the Man.

"Wonder if she's jealous," he says.

I will not lose to Dan the Man.

"Or if she's got a dick," he says.

I slam the shot. The eight ball falls in. And the cue ball right after it.

I lose by default.

"Uh-oh!" Dan says.

"Dude, I'm cutting you off," Mark says.

"What?" Dan says. "Just trash talkin'. No hard feelings."

I ignore him and head for the stairs. Mark stops me.

"Forget him. Tonight's your night, dude. Crush it."

"Thanks," I say, wondering again how he can be friends with that jackass.

I head up through the house to the garage. Almost the entire first floor is packed with people. Dance music groans out of Mark's family's surround sound system. The kitchen counters are strewn with glass bottles and fallen towers of plastic cups.

These people shouldn't be here. This is *our* house—Mark's and mine and Asher's.

I know it doesn't make sense to think that anymore. But I do.

Thankfully, the garage is quiet and dark. A couple of smokers stand by the open garage door, their bodies outlined in the light from the driveway.

Rebekah and I could just stay out here. And talk about things, finally.

Since Wednesday night, we talked on the phone once, but not about what happened, and we weren't joking like usual. I wasn't even sure Rebekah really was coming tonight until she texted me an hour ago and told me she had a ride.

She hasn't mentioned the drawing at all.

But that's fine. This will be better. It can just be us out here, alone. Mark can meet her later.

I walk down the stairs into the garage and see two new figures outlined in the open door. Squinting into the dark, they can't see me yet, but I can see them.

Rebekah.

And Asher.

Together.

He was her ride? He's not even supposed to be here.

Rebekah spots me. "Hey." She's wearing a long, light-blue button-up with a belt around it and tight black jeans. She gives me a side hug.

Asher leans a little, his hands in his pockets. "How's it hangin'?" he says in a snarky voice.

"Alright."

"Just alright? It looks pretty crazy in there."

"It's not that crazy."

Then there's a silence like a physical presence, a fourth person standing between the three of us.

"I'm gonna check it out," Asher says. He turns to Rebekah and puts a finger to his mouth. "Shhh. Don't tell Mark I'm here. I'm not *invited*." As he walks by me, he swats my shoulder. "Right?"

Anger burns through me. I wait to hear the door open and close.

"Did you invite him?" I say to Rebekah quietly. The smokers are still there by the door.

Her mouth drops open. "Are you serious?"

"Yes."

"No!"

"Then how does he know?"

She scoffs. "It's such a private party, I don't know who could have told him."

I shake my head, try to think straight. We need to just sit and talk.

Two canvas tailgating chairs are set up in the corner. "Can we?"

"Okay."

The chairs' joints creak as we settle in.

"Sorry I freaked out, but it's kind of awkward to see my girl-friend walking in with another guy."

She winces. "He's your *friend.*"

Is he? We still eat lunch together, but nowadays we usually talk to the other people at the table. And I haven't been over to his place or even chatted with him since that night at Waffle House.

"He's been a total ass lately. And he's obviously drunk tonight."

"He is?" Rebekah pulls the webbed netting of the cup holder up through the armrest and pushes it down again. "I didn't know. He called me this afternoon and asked if I needed a ride tonight. His friend Ben picked us up."

"Ben Hasting?"

"Yeah, I think so. He dropped us off. He wanted to park far away in case the police came."

Rebekah didn't lie to me. She didn't tell Asher about the party. She didn't come alone with him. They weren't hanging out together. And I've suspected him before and been totally wrong.

So.

"What's going on?" I say.

When she looks straight at me, the light coming in from the driveway paints half of her face pale. The green of her eye gleams.

She knows what I mean.

"It's just a lot right now," she says.

The smokers glance our way and then look off, pretending they aren't listening.

I scoot my chair closer to Rebekah and whisper. "What is?"

She looks like she's sizing up how much of a hit I can take.

244

And backing down.

"Rebekah," says a lanky, sheepish figure waving away cigarette smoke.

It's Ben Hasting. He walks over. "Hey, Phillip," he says.

"Hi."

"I parked, like, practically in the next school district."

The door to the kitchen bursts open. Three or four different voices yell over each other and the music.

And a body slaps onto the concrete.

Asher.

The smokers both go, "Oh!" Rebekah bolts out of her chair and crouches beside him, but he waves her off, pushing himself up.

Mark and Dan stand in the doorway, and people crowd behind them trying to see what happened. I stand up, but can't bring myself to walk over.

Mark holds the side of his face with one hand and gestures wildly at Asher with the other. "Get the fuck out of here!"

"I told you, you faggot!" Dan yells.

Ben rushes to join Rebekah. With two quick shakes, Asher brushes them off.

"I'm fine!" he says, and he storms out of the garage.

"Asher!" Rebekah calls.

Ben runs after him.

Dan yells some more. Mark steps down into the garage. He breathes heavily.

"What happened?" I ask him.

"Fucker hit me."

"He started it?"

"*Yeah*, he fucking started it." He glares at me.

"He wouldn't do that," Rebekah says.

Mark snorts. "Oh, he wouldn't? He just *did*."

"I don't believe you," she says.

"I don't even *know* you," Mark says.

"Rebekah," I say. "Come on."

"'Come on'? I can't believe you just abandoned your best friend like that. You didn't do *anything*."

"What was I supposed to do?"

"Dude," Mark says, "is this your girlfriend?"

She stares me down.

Then she runs out of the garage and down the driveway.

"Shit," I say. I go to the garage door. "Rebekah!"

"Dude!" Mark says. "Shut up. Neighbors! Just let that shit go, man."

I start to yell after her again, but her name catches in my throat. She reaches Ben and Asher and puts her hand on Asher's shoulder. The street is long, and I can see all the way down. I watch them walk to the corner, and then they turn, and I lose sight of her.

JUNE

Two hundred plastic jugs of water.

Stacked on shelves and bunched into a rectangle on the floor, battling for space with batteries and books, candles and creamed corn.

"Do you think this is enough?" I said, poking a jug with my toe. Mom and I had just finished bringing the supplies down from the truck.

"It's hard to say."

"We can get more if you want."

"Mmm, thanks."

Her voice was monotone and her eyes were blank, like the real mom was hidden away somewhere inside herself. This had been happening more and more.

"Mom," I said.

She snapped to. "Yes?"

"You weren't paying attention."

Her hand flew to her chest. "Oh, I'm sorry," she said, looking disappointed in herself. "I'm distracted."

"By what?"

She shook her head. "Nothing."

"Nothing" never means "nothing." It means "something I don't want to talk about." Any kid knows that.

"What's going to happen, Mom?"

"Phil, this is all just in case something—"

"You don't have to tell Chris, but you have to tell me."

She smiled, and her eyes looked tired. "I'm doing it again. Treating you like you're too young."

I nodded.

"I don't know what's going to happen. I don't know if anything's going to happen. Most likely, nothing will happen. But if it does, I want to make sure that you and Chris are okay."

"And you and Dad."

"Yes."

"But what do you think might happen?"

"Things can change quickly, Phil. The world can change—just like that."

"The world's going to change?"

She looked down at her feet. "Phil, maybe you do need to be a little older for this. I'm not trying to scare you."

I looked at her, waiting for her to finish. But she didn't.

"I just want to know what's going to happen," I said.

Mom started to cry. Then she came over and hugged me. "I'm sorry. I shouldn't have involved you and Chris. This is too much for you. You don't need to worry. We'll be okay."

She told me to go upstairs, that she'd finish up down there. Later the door to my parents' bedroom was closed, and I heard them having a conversation, though I couldn't tell what they were saying.

Afterward Chris and I were banned from the basement.

FORTY-THREE

"Okay, let's give it another shot," Dad says. He stands in the parking lot, his baggy teal Windbreaker and Falcons cap on, waving me back. I lean out the window. Check my mirrors again. I'm going to do it this time. I have parallel parked before. I can do it again, even with a hangover.

I reverse.

"Goooood," Dad says. "Gooood."

I turn sharply.

And feel the orange cone crunch beneath the back tire.

"Shit!" I pound the armrest. "Shit shit shit!"

I have tried to do this thirteen times in a row, and I'm only getting worse. I can't believe you have to do this to pass a driving test. Who parallel parks? Everywhere has regular parking. *Perpendicular goddamn parking.*

Dad walks up to the window, worry lines on his forehead. He puts his hand on the side mirror and leans down.

But he doesn't say anything.

He's afraid to ask.

Because I've made him afraid.

But he's the dad. He should ask anyway.

I stare ahead, gripping the steering wheel. My head hurts so bad.

Ask me.

Ask me.

Ask me.

"Phillip, I really don't mean to pry. But this isn't about the parking, is it?"

I don't even look at him.

"I don't want to talk about it," I say.

He stands back up straight, buries his hands in his Windbreaker pockets. "Well, what do you say we call it a day, then? Sometimes when you're having trouble, it's best—"

"No. I want to keep going."

I can tell he's looking at me, wondering what's wrong with me, what's wrong with him. What's wrong with us.

"Sure," he says. "Drive up a little and I'll see what's left of that cone."

FORTY-FOUR

Asher wasn't at lunch today. Which means he probably wasn't at school. Which means his five-year perfect attendance record is finished.

Which means maybe he was hurt worse than I thought.

At night I find him online, supposedly available to chat.

u werent at lunch

My words sit in the chat box by themselves. For a minute. Two minutes. Three.

Then he sends a webcam photo of himself. His room is dark, but in the dim light from his desk, I see a purple bruise swelling on his left cheek. His eyes look floaty and red, like they've popped out of his head and been pressed back in a few times.

shit, I write.

thx 4 ur concern

does it hurt?

no it feels gr8

sry didnt know it was that bad

yeah obvsly

I'm trying to reconcile, and he's being an ass. Why is it always like this now?

well thats y u dont get drunk n start fights

wtf? u rly think that?

u were drunk

1. no i wasnt 2. i didnt start it

1. i can tell when ur drunk 2. mark said u did

oh well if mark said it then I must have imagined the part when dan shoved my head against a wall and then mark pushed me onto his garage floor

so u didnt do anything to start it

NO

I stare at my words. Try to figure out if I really meant it.

I start to write something else. Maybe step back a little.

But he speaks first.

u have become such a dick ever since ur "conversion"

u really cant get over that

i dont like when my "friends" lie to me

i dont like when my "friends" keep trying to get with my gf

Deny it. You better deny it.

not my fault she isnt into u

No. Not true.

mark was right. u think ur better than everybody else. u really do think u can do whatever u want. well thats fucked up.

haha ok pope phillip ii tell me my sins

pope phillip? seriously? good joke very funny

oh wait i forgot to show u my broken finger

He sends me a webcam photo flicking me off.

ur a shitty friend, I write.

And then he blocks my chat.

A few minutes later I call Rebekah, but it goes straight to voice mail again.

FORTY-FIVE

Two minutes until we start CORE.

"She's supposed to be here," I say. I look back at the youth center doors, willing them to open. They don't.

Amanda nips at her thumbnail. "Well, she's really busy these days."

I wonder what Amanda knows. Would she tell even a white lie, though?

After what happened at Mark's, I decided to give Rebekah some space. Or, I guess we both did. I didn't call or text her on Friday night, which, three beers later, felt like one of the hardest things I've ever had to do. I didn't call or text on Saturday. And I didn't even go to church on Sunday.

When she wouldn't take my calls after that, I had to do something. So I actually went to her locker yesterday. That didn't go super well.

I mean, she said she'd see me tonight. But that's pretty much all she said before she hurried off with her varsity friend to practice.

I just want her to tell me what I did wrong. Because I really don't understand.

Maybe she'll be here later.

Please, God, let her be here later.

Tim one-claps. "Ladies and gentlemen! How are you tonight?"

"Good," other people say.

"Wonderful. Let's jump right into it. We're having a special workshop tonight, put together by Randy here. For those of you going to the Summit, this will count toward your service hours, but it should be beneficial for everybody. This is one of Randy's areas of expertise. So, take it away."

A workshop? I've done some service hours with Ferret over the past few days and he didn't mention anything about this. Of course, I didn't mention anything about me and Rebekah after his marriage tangent, but this is different.

And, as much as I have actually, disturbingly come to kind of almost respect Ferret, it's potentially disastrous.

"Thanks, Tim," he says, looking over the dozen or so of us. "Not everybody from the Summit group is here tonight, but that's okay."

I glance at the doors again. Nothing.

I don't know if I can deal with this right now.

"This is one of those things that we talk about doing but rarely follow through on," Ferret says. "The highfalutin word for it is 'evangelism.' You can call it spreading the Word, witnessing, or just plain telling people about Jesus. It's about sharing your personal experience with God. How it's shaped your life, changed your life. And I can tell you that there is nothing like the thrill, the outright *joy*, of bringing someone to Christ. Absolutely nothing. And it's something each and every one of you can do."

He pauses. And paces. And stops. "But it can be scary to put yourself out there like that. To share something so close to your heart with a perfect stranger. And if you're witnessing to a friend or family member? That can be even more challenging. Believe me, I'd rather witness to Satan himself than my uncle Gary."

He gets a few chuckles. It's a corny joke, but not as bad as I expected from him.

"Some of you are old hands at this, so you might feel like I'm wasting your time, but everybody can use practice. This is a lifelong endeavor, and truly one of the most important things you can do as a Christian, so you should strengthen your God muscle whenever you can. And there are people here tonight who haven't ever witnessed before, so your experience can help them."

Ferret's eyes graze me. My heart is beating like I just ran a race.

"Anyway," Ferret says. "I've jabbered enough. Hopefully I can pass on some tips tonight that'll help you. I have worked personally with Kirk Cameron, so you guys are in good hands."

It's not clear if that's a joke or not, and I don't even know who that is, so we're all quiet.

"Amanda. Why don't you get on up here?"

"Me?" she says.

"No, the other Amanda. Come on down! Give her a round of applause, y'all."

She gets a few whoops and some appreciative clapping. She's taking one for all of us right now. Though, to be fair, this isn't a disaster. So far.

She stands across from Ferret and smiles shyly. Ferret makes this gesture as if he's "presenting" her. "Now, Amanda's one of those old hands I was talking about. I've personally seen her witness to two different people at a gas station while in the middle of a snack run. Convinced a guy to buy a twelve-pack of Diet Coke instead of Bud Light."

Some real laughter for that one.

"Turning beer into soda pop! That was a fun trip. But anyway, that's what I'm talking about. Sharing the truth in real life. So, Amanda, if you don't mind, let's do a little role-playing game here. I'll be the guy buying beer. You be you. Okay?"

"Okay."

Ferret puts an over-the-top scowl on his face and hunches over like he's looking at a refrigerator case of beer. Amanda looks like she doesn't quite want to do this, but she bucks up and approaches him slowly.

"Good evening, sir," she says.

Ferret grunts. He dangles his arms, looking more like a hunchback than a real person.

"Hard to choose sometimes, isn't it?" she says.

"Mmhmm."

"You know what kind I like? Sprite."

"Sprite ain't beer." He sounds like a caveman.

"True. But tomorrow's Sunday, so you probably shouldn't drink tonight if you want to wake up early enough to get to church."

"I don't go to church."

"So you pray at home, then?"

"No. God ain't real. He's made up."

"Well, now, He'd say otherwise."

Ferret turns to her and glares. "What is this?"

258

She looks startled, but keeps her cool. "A conversation."

He tries to stare her down, but she is still. Finally he slumps. "I don't like Sprite. I like Mountain Dew." He walks past her to the soda case, I guess.

"Don't stay up too late," Amanda calls after him. People laugh.

Ferret drops his act and claps. "Give her another round of applause, y'all. Well done." He gestures for her to have a seat. I give her a thumbs-up. That was impressive, even though I'm not totally sure what just happened.

"Couple things from that," Ferret says. "First, respect. Did you all notice she called me 'sir' even though I was just some drunk at a gas station?" A few murmurs of yeah. "Respect is crucial. You're both sinners here. It's just that one of you's heard the Truth, okay? Important.

"Two, no fear. Amanda did not back down. Obviously, this wasn't real life, and if you ever feel truly threatened, then you should run or protect yourself, but most people just act scary. Until you show them you ain't scared. That's how *you* earn *their* respect.

"And a bonus three: Work God into it in a natural way. Try to connect to what you can see in this person, what they're interested in."

My heart has slowed. Amanda was great at that, and she wasn't even expecting it. And Ferret is still his awkward self, but he really does know this stuff. A couple of people take notebooks out and start writing down what he said. Even Tim looks impressed.

"Thank you, Amanda," Ferret says. "Now let's get some fresh meat up here." He hunkers down, scans the crowd.

No. Please.

"Phillip. Come on up. I won't bite. Maybe."

I walk to the front, my mind screaming, *No no no*. I feel everyone's eyes on me.

259

Ferret puts his hand on my shoulder. "Phillip here is relatively new to the faith, so he's got a lot of courage coming up here. Give him a hand." They give me a hand. Amanda whoops for me. "Now, Phillip, keeping those three points in mind, let's do the same thing. This time we'll be at a bus stop."

A bus stop? I've never been at a bus stop in my life.

Ferret holds his hands out like he's reading a newspaper.

I would never interrupt a random guy reading his newspaper at a bus stop.

This isn't real life.

Ferret clears his throat, turns a page.

Whatever. I can do this.

Fear is the mind-killer.

I walk up to him. "Excuse me, sir."

Ferret doesn't look up. "I'm reading."

A few people laugh.

"Sorry. I know. I just—" Bring God into it naturally. "What are you reading?"

"The newspaper." A few more laughs.

"What story?"

"It's about China."

"What about it?"

"They're taking over everything."

"What religion are they?"

"The Chinese? Heck if I know. Communist?"

"I don't think so. I bet they're not Christian, though."

He closes his newspaper. "So what?"

I swallow. "Well, it'd be better if they were."

"Why?"

260

"Just . . . because then we'd finally make this a Christian country."

He narrows his eyes. "Are you out of your mind? That's how it is with you crazy Christians? You want to conquer America?"

"No."

"Why do you even believe that crap, anyway?"

"It's—"

"Well?"

My mind is blank.

Why do I believe?

Why?

"It's complicated."

"Complicated? You're trying to sell me on this nonsense and you don't even know why? Forget it. Here's the bus, anyway. Don't sit next to me."

A few laughs. Ferret drops his scowl and reaches over to grab my shoulder again. "Give it up for Phillip, y'all. That was a brave effort."

I don't even hear their applause. I don't want Amanda's reassuring hair tousle.

"So," Ferret says, "let's go over what the strong points were there and what needed work."

I sit down, hug my knees to my chest, and wait for it to be over.

"Love your brothers and sisters in Christ," Tim says.

Amanda and I stand up and stretch. I rub my eyes and blink away the smudginess in them. I feel like I could sleep for a month. Maybe I should.

Rebekah never showed up.

261

"You okay?" Amanda says. Her smile tells me she knows I'm not.

"Just tired."

"I always feel so much better when I actually get some rest." She rubs my back in a motherly way. "See you soon, okay?"

Amanda walks off to be really nice to somebody else. I look around, make myself dizzy searching for Ferret. I should be mad at him. He used me as an example of how not to witness and then dissected me in front of everybody.

Not that I was the only one. But I was the worst.

The truth, though, is that he was right. I didn't know what to say.

I couldn't even answer the most basic question about what I supposedly believe:

Why?

I don't see Ferret anywhere, which is strange since he usually lurks around afterward. I decide I'd rather leave, so I walk outside and look for my dad's car in the idling line of parents. He isn't there, so I sit down on one of the benches by the volleyball court.

At first I think I see words drawn in the sand, but of course they're only random lines from where people have stepped or dragged their feet.

I know I'm only making myself feel worse by sitting here, but I want to.

Because Asher was right.

I'm a fraud.

I became a Christian because it was easier that way. Because I wanted to piss off Dad. Because I wanted to be with Rebekah.

All this going to church and CORE and racking up service hours and reading the Bible is about proving to myself that I'm not lying.

But I am. To everybody else. To myself.

I can't answer the question because I don't have an answer.

And everyone knows that now.

My phone vibrates. Probably Dad telling me he's running late. Awesome.

I look at the screen.

I let it ring. And ring. And ring.

I pick up.

"We should talk," Rebekah says. "In person."

FORTY-SIX

There was a boy who sat on a bench waiting to get dumped.

In person.

And he deserved it.

He had something really good.

But then he completely fucked it up.

And now he doesn't even have any friends.

So ends the Book of Phillip.

I mash my face with my hands, listening to the youth group stragglers walk behind me out to the emptying parking lot. I feel their glances like pinpricks on my scalp.

She could have done this over the phone. Saved herself and her mom a late-night trip to church. Saved me this parade of shame.

But this is the "nice" way to do it.

A three-minute phone call would have been the actual nice way to do it.

I could just call Dad back, tell him to turn around *again*, leave here, and never come back.

"Phillip?"

Rebekah's wearing a gray hoodie, with the hood up and pulled tight, framing her eyes and round cheeks. Little spirals of hair stick out along the edges. It's fucking cute.

"Are you crying?" she says gently.

"No." I show her my eyes as proof, but I'm blinking a lot, and they're probably red, so I don't know if she believes me.

"Can I sit down?"

I point to the empty spot next to me. She sits down. There is a good three and a half feet between us.

"How was CORE?" she says.

I laugh. "Awesome."

"Really?"

"No."

A couple of younger girls walk behind us, promising to text each other.

"Can we go somewhere more private?" Rebekah says.

Just end it. Please.

"Sure," I say.

She gets up and starts walking toward the main church building. "Come on."

I sigh, pick myself up, and follow her lead. We walk beside each other across the lawn, in the dark. The swish of our shoes through the grass is the only sound. We go past the church entrance, the word "FAITH" lit from beneath so the letters' shadows stretch up the wall.

And we sit on the Sittin' Stone. The granite looks phosphorescent.

"Am I keeping you up late?" she says. "Do you have homework to do?"

"I would have done it on the ride to school tomorrow anyway."

She laughs, but it's not that funny. "Well, sorry. For not being available."

"It's fine."

"It's not, but okay."

The silence swells, and I can feel it coming.

The end.

Do it.

Finally.

There's a crinkling sound, and then she holds out a piece of notebook paper.

"This is great," Rebekah says.

It's the drawing I gave her.

When I was browsing my Bible, I found this little book Song of Songs. It's much shorter than most books in the Bible, and a lot different. It's basically a love poem, and not even one to Jesus or God but between two people. It's really nice.

And then there's this one part that's kind of funny.

It starts, "How beautiful you are, my darling! Oh, how beautiful!" After that the Lover compares different facial features of his Beloved to other things, trying to describe how gorgeous she is.

But some of them are kind of strange. "Your hair is like a flock of goats," he says. "Your teeth are like a flock of sheep just shorn." I thought a drawing of all the comparisons, with the poem next to it, might make Rebekah laugh.

She hits my leg. "I can't believe you drew that." She points to the part where the Lover describes the Beloved's breasts as "like two fawns."

"It's in the Bible!"

"Still!"

I look at her.

She's smiling at me.

She liked my drawing.

But she's just handing me a flagon of water before she exiles me to the desert.

"So, what did you want to talk about?" I say.

"Mark's party, for one thing." She puts the drawing back in her pocket. I wait for her to explain what I did wrong, recite the Book of Phillip. But she looks at me and says, "So?"

I've been wanting to talk for days now. I explained myself to her over and over again in my head. I had a whole monologue basically memorized.

But now, with her next to me, everything seems a lot simpler.

"I should have run after you guys," I say. "I should have made sure you were okay."

She clears her throat. "Yeah, you should have."

"Yeah." And that's all I've got. I already apologized for thinking she lied and all that. I know there's more, but I want her to say it.

"Okay," she says. "My turn. I'm sorry I didn't look at your drawing until tonight."

"You just looked at it *tonight*?"

"*Well.*" She taps the toes of her shoes together. "We've been moving so fast lately. You more than me. Coming to church, meeting my mom, going to CORE."

There it is. I close my eyes, taking my punches, each one self-inflicted.

"And then you called me your girlfriend, which you never did before, and that was a lot to think about. We never talked about whether we were officially going together."

Going together. It sounds so old-fashioned. Like I have to give her a ring or something.

"I didn't know," I say.

"You didn't ask."

"You didn't tell me."

"I know."

I open myself for another shot.

"Is that the real reason we aren't going to homecoming?" I say.

"Part of it."

I barely feel it.

"So your dad really doesn't want you to go?"

She sniffles and I see a shine in her eye. "I think so."

"I thought you said—"

"We haven't spoken in over a year."

"Wait. So, the letters?"

She shakes her head.

Those times she said she couldn't do something because of him, because of what he said.

"You lied to me," I say.

She's really crying now. "I didn't mean to. I knew what he'd say, what he'd think. I could hear him telling me, but I didn't want to tell you that I was just imagining it, like I was crazy. Or stuck-up."

"I wouldn't have thought that."

"Yes, you would. That's what any normal person would do."

"I'm not normal."

Rebekah looks at me and laughs—a whimpering sound. "I know."

Then she takes my hand. It's like a static shock.

I squeeze back.

"Why don't you talk to him?" I say.

She wipes her eye. "Because he's on the other side of the world, and he thinks he can just stay there and not take care of his family even when they have to move into somebody else's house just to have a place to live that they can afford."

"That's a pretty good reason."

"We got into a fight last year when he said he wasn't coming back for Thanksgiving or Christmas. He'd already been gone for almost a year by then. We used to write to each other, but when I told him I wouldn't write him if he didn't come home, he wrote back and said I was being selfish and not setting a good example for Christ. I haven't talked to him since."

"Wow."

"Yeah. I keep checking the mail, waiting for him to write again. But he hasn't."

So when I met her, that's what . . .

I squeeze again, harder.

My dad is lame sometimes. A lot of the time. But he's not like that.

"I try so hard to be like him," she says. "And I am. I'm so busy that I hurt the people in my life."

"Why do you still listen to him, then?"

"Because he's my *dad*."

"He doesn't really act like it."

She lets go. "Hey."

"I'm just saying. You shouldn't do something just because somebody else tells you to. Or *not* do something."

"I know that. But don't you ever do something because you think your mom would want you to?"

I shake my head before I even start speaking. "No."

We both look straight ahead, out across Wesley Road, away from here.

"Do you think I believe in God?" I say.

"Why would you ask me that?"

"Because I want to know the answer."

"Why?" It comes out as a whisper.

"Because I don't think you do. Because I don't think you think I should go to the Summit. Because it seems like maybe that's another part of why we aren't going to homecoming together."

Because I still don't know if I'm being broken up with or not.

"Phillip, look at me."

It hurts, but I do.

"I believe you believe, if you believe you believe."

But that's the problem, I want to say.

Then, with a sound like a clipped fingernail, all the lights at the youth center turn off at once.

Rebekah yelps and puts her hand over her heart.

"I totally planned that," I say. I feel for her hand. Her fingers touch mine.

Beneath us the stone glows brighter. In the parking lot a lone white SUV waits with its interior lights on.

Rebekah's phone vibrates and shines like a lamp. "Crap," she says. "That's my mom texting me. And now she can totally see where I am."

"You should probably go, then."

"Yeah," she says. But she doesn't go.

I want to kiss her so badly.

"So are we . . . going together?" I say.

"Well, we're not *not* going together."

"Do you want to not not go together to homecoming?"

"Yeah," she says, punching my leg.

Then she kisses me on the cheek, jumps off the stone, and runs toward the parking lot.

I sit alone in the dark, undumped.

FORTY-SEVEN

Dad drops me off at the Publix on Saturday afternoon. I walk across the parking lot, some three-day-old swagger still in my step. Ferret waits for me on a bench near the entrance, in the shade. There's a cardboard box next to him.

"My apprentice," he says. "Have a seat."

I do.

"You crushed it this morning," he says, talking about the meet. "Blam! Pushed right past that Nivens Mill guy at the finish line."

"I did fine."

"Your humility is inspiring." He puts his hand over his heart. "Alright, then. First thing on the agenda." He takes off his sunglasses and puts them in his denim shirt pocket. "I want to make sure you know I didn't set out to embarrass you the other night."

"You sure?"

"Yes. You shouldn't *feel* embarrassed either."

"I know." But my cheeks are burning with the memory.

"How did it make you feel?"

"Like a fraud."

He leans his head against the brick wall. "Well, now I feel pretty fraudulent myself. I meant it as practice, not as a test. I left you alone afterward so you could have some time to think about it, come to your own conclusions. I didn't mean for you to—"

"It doesn't matter. I'm fine now."

"Yeah?"

"I'm here, right?"

And that's exactly it. That's what I realized, sitting there on the stone by myself. I was there. I wouldn't have been there if I didn't believe. I wouldn't have cared about being a fraud if I didn't believe. Rebekah wouldn't believe me if I didn't believe.

I wouldn't be here if I didn't believe.

"Second item on the agenda, then," Ferret says. "Spreading God's Word."

I feel my gut twist. Evangelism again? Already?

He opens the box. Inside are two stacks of pamphlets. One pamphlet has pictures of a cave and a cross on the front with the words "The Best News You've Ever Heard" at the top. The other is full black, with even darker black lettering that reads, "Your First Day in Hell."

"Pretty smart-looking, huh?" Ferret says.

"Well," I say.

"Figured this might be more your style. Tracts are old-school, but they still work. Especially when they look so dang good."

"So we're giving these to people?"

"Yessir."

I take a hell pamphlet from the pile. This is the kind of thing that, if I saw somebody else giving it away in front of a grocery store, would make me think there was something wrong with that person. And I'm about to *be* that person?

"Some people say why bother in a place like this, where so many folks go to church on the regular?" Ferret says, slipping his shades back on. "I say, just because a person goes to church doesn't mean they're saved."

Oh.

I open the pamphlet to the first page. Above a lake of fire that's probably from a stock photo of a volcano, it says, "Welcome to hell. The final, eternal destination of all who do not believe in the divinity of Jesus Christ."

I close the pamphlet.

Wait. Wait wait wait.

"Everybody who isn't a Christian goes to hell when they die?"

Ferret cocks his head, grins. "Are we role-playing right now?"

"No. I'm serious."

His grin melts away. "You're not pulling my leg?"

"No."

He whistles. "Hoo, boy. Were you not aware of that?"

Was I not aware of that? I knew there was a hell. I thought it was for *bad people*. Not just non-Christians. Not Chris. Not Dad. Not Mr. V.

Does Rebekah think that?

Ferret takes his glasses off again. He looks like he's trying to do calculus in his head. "Haven't you been reading your Bible?"

"Some of it. Genesis. Revelation. Matthew."

"You didn't catch the parts about salvation and damnation and such? Nobody told you about it?"

I slap the pamphlet back on the stack. "I guess not."

He leans forward, rubs his temples. "I should've seen this."

"What?"

"When we were talking about *Dune*. You said it was 'cool.'"

"So what? So did you."

"Just as the deeper meanings of *Dune* escaped you, so have the crucial aspects of the Bible."

"Uh, I think I understand most of it. *Dune*, too."

"Sure, sure, you're a smart kid. But we should've been talking about this stuff from day one. Didn't this come up on Wednesday nights?"

"Not exactly like that." Tim talked about being saved, but not really about the consequences of not being saved.

"Didn't you and Rebekah discuss this?"

"A little." Not at all.

Ferret shakes his head. "I thought you were a little more curious than that, Phillip. I thought you were looking for the Truth."

I thought I was too. But now I feel emptied of all the self-assurance and swagger I had. How did I miss this?

"Don't worry," Ferret says. "This is my fault. I'm your mentor, and your knowledge is my responsibility. We're going to have to set up some extracurricular sessions. Then we'll be all good, okay?"

"It's only two weeks until the Summit."

The Summit is the Olympics of knowing stuff about Christianity, and I didn't even know why people go to hell.

"Don't worry about that, Phillip. The most important thing is, you believe in Christ. That's the only thing you absolutely need to know. The rest of it is important, and we can get to that, but you're already good."

He slaps the box. "So, let's get to it. Onward, Christian soldier."

Ferret grabs a handful each of the two pamphlets and gives "Best News" to me.

"But," I say, "how can I do this?"

"You can do it because you already believe the things on these pages, Phillip." Ferret puts on his shades. "You just don't know it yet."

Two hours later we're at the opposite end of the shopping center, having been shooed away from seven different stores. We sit on a bench, fanning ourselves. My brain hurts.

"You crushed it again, man," Ferret says.

"Shut up."

The only thing that got crushed out there was what was left of my self-esteem. I didn't rescue a single soul.

"I'm serious," he says. "For a first-timer that was good. Especially toward the end there, you started engaging with people. Half of it's just getting them to notice that you're there."

"I don't think I did that, either."

"You did," he says. He wipes his hand across his brow. "And at the very least you're a couple of hours closer to the Summit. You'll be ready in no time."

No. I'm not ready now, and I won't be then.

"Maybe I shouldn't go," I say.

Ferret grabs my shoulder, points his finger at me. "Ah-ah-ah. No, you don't."

"I'm going to look like a faker."

"It's not an inquisition, Phillip. It's a learning experience. For everybody. We're all equal in God's eyes. And if you seek Him out, I promise He will reveal His plan to you."

"But I *do* seek Him out." I'm flat-out yelling now and I don't care. "I work hard. I go to youth group and CORE and church and I read the Bible. So why don't I understand it?"

Ferret lets out a long, slow breath. "Those are all important. But what's more important is building a relationship with God. Trusting in Him. Trusting that for all this"—he waves his arm, showing me the parking lot, the people, the world—"there are answers. Some of them may be uncomfortable at first. But if you give Him your trust, and patience, and self, you will understand." He shrugs. "And if you just show up and check off boxes . . . you won't understand as much."

Oh.

Shit.

Oh, shit.

I've been doing it wrong. This whole time.

I've just been showing up, checking off boxes, doing what I thought I was supposed to, and expecting answers to flow into me and fill me like a praise song. And even when I looked for answers, I got them from Mom, from *It'll All Be Over Soon*, from Dad, from Asher, from Ferret. From Rebekah.

I thought they had them. And maybe they do have some, or parts.

But God has all of them.

Of course He does. He's God.

"You can't be afraid to seek Him out," Ferret says.

But I am afraid. I am scared. I won't pretend I'm not anymore.

I want answers, though.

I want to seek Him out.

"Okay," I say.

"Okay what?"

"I'll go."

Ferret's laugh starts as a rumble and caps off with a wheeze. He shakes his head. "You're a trip, boy."

I shrug. "You're not going, are you?"

"Nope. Got a marathon that weekend. Plus, older folks from our church are only going as chaperones. The Summit staff is from other churches or elsewhere in the country."

I can't believe I'm sad Ferret isn't going. But it's a fact: I wish I could bring my spiritual adviser.

"Rebekah's still on track, right?" I say.

Ferret coughs, looks away. "Sorry?"

"She's pretty close to fifty hours?"

"Tell you the truth, I'm a little worried about that."

My hand starts to shake.

"She just has a lot of stuff to do," I say. "It's not her fault."

"You're a busy man yourself, but you seem to find the time."

"Not as busy as her. And she can't be that many hours short. You said she was fine."

"She was then. I thought she'd show up every once in a while for a service project. Now I don't know."

I stand up. "You're going to keep her from going to the Summit?"

He stands up too. "*I'm* not keeping her from anything. She has to get her fifty hours just like everybody else."

"What if she doesn't?"

"Then she ain't going."

"I'll do the hours for her," I say.

"No way, Jose. No way."

"Why not? She saved me."

"Hmm?"

I've never thought about it like that before. But it's true.

"She saved me. She brought me to church. She gave me her Bible."

"Well, that's fantastic, but—"

"How is that different from what we've done? You helping me. Training me. Talking to me. You counted those as hours for me, so why don't they count for her?"

Ferret scoffs. And snorts. And shakes his head.

"You'd still go if she didn't go, right?"

I nod. I say, "Yeah." I nod again.

I'm a terrible liar.

JULY

"She's gone," Chris said, his nose still pressed against the window.

I took off down the hall and opened the basement door. My steps sounded like hammer blows as I ran down the wooden stairs. Then I made a sharp turn, ran through the finished room, and went into the back part of the basement.

Dad was away again on another weekend conference. Mom had just left for the post office, barely a mile away.

I had five minutes to find what had been hidden from us.

Chris and I had mostly stopped fighting and become junior detectives in our own house. We had been too scared of being caught to venture into the basement before, so we mostly just hovered around our parents' room. We didn't find anything or hear anything, but we could pretend that it was all an adventure. And that what we needed to do to break the case was break the rule.

Stepping into the dim back room, I was so nervous I had to pee. I felt *stupid for feeling scared. I'd been down there hundreds of times before. And it was the middle of the freaking afternoon.*

But the weather was cloudy and rumbly, and the shades were drawn, and the house was quiet enough to hear it groan.

I flicked on the light.

There it was. The same cluster of stuff, just bigger.

And that was it.

What did I think I would find? Government agents? Aliens? The real Mom, tied to a chair?

I looked for them. For something.

Then I heard Chris's call from upstairs, and I ran out of the basement and up the stairs and closed the door and stomped up the next flight to my room.

"Did you find anything?" Chris called after me.

"No," I said.

At the top of the stairs I looked into my parents' room, which was wide open, as usual, because there wasn't anything in there, either. It was all in my mom's head.

But I checked again anyway. Everything was the same. Her two pink pillows. Her bathrobe draped over her chair. Her heating pad hanging on the closet doorknob.

Her Bible on the bedside table.

I heard the door open downstairs, and I went to my room.

FORTY-EIGHT

Thank you, God.

Thank you for the wind flicking my hair.

Thank you for the bright blue dome above our heads.

Thank you for the heat of the sun on my skin.

Thank you for "More Than a Feeling" on the radio at the exact right moment.

Thank you for this.

I open my eyes, my prayer finished.

"Catching some shut-eye?" Dad says.

"Naw," I say.

"You must be tuckered out, though."

My leg muscles burn, but it feels good. "Not really."

He laughs. "To be fifteen again." He looks at me, raises an eye. "Almost sixteen."

I swear he picks up speed after that. We are driving up I-85 back home from a meet in deep south Georgia, where I crushed it for real this time. Nineteen minutes flat for a 5K—a new personal record and one of the best times on the JV squad.

Dad promised me "parkway driving" when we got back to Baxter—as in Emerson Parkway, a double-lane road that connects I-85 with Baxter and is almost like a highway but not as fast. It's not Steven Pillory, but I'll take it.

I have spent the past week remembering how much I used to love learning stuff, before school became boring and pointless. Between small service projects, Ferret has taught me about the history of Christianity, the meaning of salvation, the function of prayer. I am finally beginning to understand His plan.

And tonight I am going to homecoming with a beautiful girl who thinks my drawings are funny. (Though I had to make sure "not not going" meant "going.")

Thank you, God, for this.

A few minutes later I wake to the sound of the turn signal. We are exiting the highway at an exit that is not even close to our exit.

"Not tuckered out at all, huh?" Dad says.

I rub my eyes. "Where are we going?"

"You'll see. It's really close."

I am too content to be annoyed, so I close my eyes and drift off again.

I am jostled awake. My head bobbles when the seat belt catches my body.

"Sorry about that," Dad says. "Hole in the road. I don't know if you can call it a pothole if it's dirt."

I look around and realize, with a touch of fear, where we are.

The Land.

"Recognize it?" Dad says.

I remember he said he wanted to come back here with me and Chris, but I figured he'd forgotten about that after the running away incident. Why are we here? Now?

We emerge from the tree-lined road and the view opens up, revealing a wild meadow. As we drive up, a rabbit flees into the tall grass. Dad stops the car on a dirt patch and looks like the happiest man ever to be reunited with some weeds.

"Let's get out," he says, not waiting for me. He walks up ahead of the car and observes his property. I join him.

"I forgot how beautiful it is," Dad says.

It *is* nice, though it's not as big as I remember. Back then, in the dark, the field had no edges. It just faded to black. Now I can see the tree line a quarter mile away. It curves around and encloses the meadow, and us.

"I don't think I ever apologized for that night we spent out here," he says.

"It's okay."

"Not really, it isn't. That was pure stupidity." He reaches down, plucks a long, pale yellow stalk of grass, and twists it.

"It's fine, Dad."

"Well, thanks. That was a confusing time. Neither I nor your mother was thinking too straight." He turns to me, drops the grass stalk. "I'm sorry."

We hug, pat each other's backs.

"No big deal," I say, surprised at how it already isn't.

He picks another stalk. "Your mother had big plans for this place."

Of course. Of course he'd bring up Mom.

But I keep my eyes from rolling.

I'm being forgiving.

"Talked about building a house down here, stocking it up. Buying seed and agricultural equipment in case things got bad. As if we knew how to use that stuff."

I never heard her talk about that. This must have been toward the end.

"She even got a couple of shotguns and some ammunition from her uncle. Stored them in the basement for a week without even telling me. You or Chris could have—"

He stops himself, wraps the stalk around his finger.

I must have missed them. Or maybe they were there later, after I'd given up.

I don't know. I don't care.

"I'm not saying it's all her fault," Dad says. "I'm not saying it's anyone's fault. I just want to make sure you're not going where she did."

"What?"

Dad takes some papers from his jacket pocket and unfolds them.

It's the hell pamphlet.

"Where did you get that?" I say.

"Your older friend handed it to me when I went to Target. I didn't want to interrupt."

So you spied on me instead, I want to say.

But no. I'm not letting this get to me.

"What's the problem?" I say.

"There's some pretty extreme stuff in here, Phillip. You were handing these out?"

"I was handing out different ones."

"Well, that's better, but if yours were anything like this one . . . I mean, this is talking about eternal damnation, Phillip."

"I know."

"And there's stuff in here about gay people being abominations."

I didn't know that. I just nod.

"Is this what you believe now?" he says.

Dad drove me out here to ambush me. Just like he made us go to Jimmies and got us stuck in traffic.

So is that what I believe now?

I think of what Ferret said. I believe it, but I don't know it yet.

Dad would never understand that.

"Why does it matter? I thought you were letting me believe what I want."

"I want you to have the freedom to explore, but I want you to be careful, too. And when I see this stuff, which is exactly the kind of thing your mother was mixed up in—"

"No," I say.

It's harsh and angry, and I pull back instantly. I'm tired of fighting him. I know what I believe is right. That's enough.

"Mom was wrong," I say, slowly and carefully. "All her plans, all that stuff in the basement—a real Christian wouldn't have done that."

Dad squints. "A 'real' Christian?"

"Somebody who actually tries to understand God's Word and doesn't just use it to justify whatever they want to believe and ignore the rest of it."

He realizes the grass stalk is still on his finger, and he shakes it off. "You're saying your mother did that?"

Deep breath.

"Yes. She just used it to run away from us."

She was scared and she ran away, into herself.

"It *was* her fault, Dad. Okay? So let's stop talking about this."

Dad looks stunned. "How long have you thought that?"

"A while."

I wait for him to say something, but he doesn't.

"I have to get back, Dad," I say. "Let's go." I walk back to the car.

"Phillip, hold on. You don't have it as figured out as you think you do."

"Dad," I say, turning around, the anger spilling out. "This isn't some fad or something. This is what I believe."

"I'm not talking about religion. I'm talking about your mom and I. There's more to it than what you've decided there is."

"Like what?"

"Like I cheated on her."

Everything in me just stops.

Dad looks at the ground, shakes his head. "This is what I've been trying to work up to. I didn't mean for it to come out this way, but hearing you say that—"

"You cheated on her?"

I can only hear that, only think that.

"It was a fling. A one-night thing at a conference. Before she ever went to church. Our relationship had become very tense and distant, and I made the worst mistake of my entire life." He groans. "It was my fault, Phillip. Just as much my fault."

My dad cheated on my mom with some woman at a conference.

And then, everything else.

One mistake.

One huge mistake.

"I'm sorry," Dad says. "I didn't even want to bring that up yet. *Shit.*" He spins himself around and kicks the dirt. A rock skips off and rattles the grass.

I want to scream at him.

I want to run at him and knock him down.

But I can't.

I don't want this to ruin tonight. I don't want this to ruin anything. This was years ago.

I won't run away. I can't push him back.

"I forgive you," I say.

Dad looks at me, tears in his eyes. "What?"

"I forgive you. It's fine."

"No, you can't just—"

"I want to. And I need to get back."

"We should talk about this, Son."

"No. It's over."

I get in the car. After a while Dad wipes his eyes on his shirt, slips the pamphlet back in his pocket, gets behind the wheel, and starts the car.

He looks at me. "Phillip, I know you're angry at me, and you deserve to be, but please reconsider this youth conference thing. I don't think it's healthy for you."

"I need. To get. Back."

On the way home neither of us says a word, even when I'm driving down Emerson Parkway for the first time ever.

FORTY-NINE

It all fits in the frame. The generator. The canned goods. The fuel. The rope. The batteries. Two hundred gallons. Months of work. Three years' time.

All of it fits in a two-inch-by-three-inch camera window.

I take the picture. Check the image. Looks fine. I take another just to be sure.

I go upstairs. I grab a large trash bag from beneath the kitchen sink.

On the computer I look for a folder called "Survival Kit," or something like it. And there it is in the Documents folder. All the stuff listed and counted.

I log in to Dad's account on the site. I upload the photos. I copy and paste the list. I start things off at $150, click the seven-day auction option, and fill out some forms.

"Survival Kit—everything you need to survive the Apocalypse."

And that's it.

I go to my room, whip open the trash bag. I take it into my closet and start filling it with curled printouts and worn-out books.

Human Extinction.

Sweatbox.

Worldwide Conflagration.

The Water Problem.

Disintegration.

The Long Crisis.

Nuclear Catastrophe.

And more. In less than a minute the shelf is empty and the bag is nearly full.

I pull it closed and start to take it downstairs.

But there on my desk is one last book. Next to *Dune*. And the Bible.

It'll All Be Over Soon.

I pick it up. It's so old and beaten, it droops in my hand like a wilted flower. The mushroom cloud heart on the cover blooms in orange and red.

I remember when it was brand-new. I walked into the bookstore with Dad, and the big block letters and the black-and-white cover transfixed me. And then I saw the title. And the mushroom cloud heart. And the letters inside. I had to have it.

I flip through it, and the words pass under my fingers again.

I open up the bag, toss it in, and tie it up quickly. I take the bag down to the garage and drop it in the big plastic garbage can. On the kitchen counter I see the crumpled pamphlet. I take it and walk upstairs.

My favorite way the world could end was supercollider accident. Around the world there are huge underground tubes where scientists fire particles at other particles to test hypotheses about physics. Some people say there's a chance one of these collisions could create a black hole that basically ends up swallowing the universe.

I liked that one because it would be over so quickly. And *everything* would be over. No one would suffer. No one would feel pain.

No one would live. Or die. Ever again.

I preferred that.

What a dick.

Upstairs Chris's door is open. He's on his laptop, leaning back in his chair. I knock on the door frame. I startle him, and he nearly falls back.

"What's up?" I say.

"Nothing. What's up with you?"

"Getting ready for homecoming."

"Oh, yeah. You going with somebody?"

"*Yeah*, I'm going with somebody. My girlfriend."

He looks like he thinks she's either ugly or imaginary. "Sorry, I didn't know you had one."

"Yeah. I'll show you her picture online," I say, walking into his room.

"Uh, that's okay. I believe you."

No, he doesn't. But that's fine.

"Here," I say, handing him the pamphlet.

He laughs. "What is this?"

"Something to read."

"Alright. Thanks." He puts it on his desk, goes back to his computer.

"I'm serious. I care about what happens to you."

He flips his hair out of his face. "*Alright*. I'll read it later."

I want to say something else. A lot else.

I did all I can do for now.

I go get dressed for my homecoming date.

Matthew 24:42 says, "Therefore keep watch, because you do not know on what day your Lord will come."

If you read it in context, instead of plucking it out to fit what you want to think, this isn't about fear. Jesus describes the signs we'll see at the end of days, but even so, nobody will know when he's really coming back.

Matthew 24:40–41 says, "Two men will be in the field; one will be taken and the other left. Two women will be grinding with a hand mill; one will be taken and the other left."

So "keep watch" doesn't mean stop what you're doing, stock up on supplies, and wait. It means that He could come back at any second, and those who believe will be saved. It means *don't* live in fear. It means trust in God.

Trust.

FIFTY

"Let's get one over here," Mrs. Joseph says.

"Here?" Rebekah says, standing in front of a tall bush that's turning dark red with the fall.

"Yes. Perfect."

I slide in next to Rebekah and smooth the front of my suit jacket, as if that's going to help anything. This is my dad's suit, and it's too bulky. This is my dad's tie, and it's too cubicle worker-y. My flat, combed hair is my own fault.

Rebekah, of course, looks amazing. Her dress is like a waterfall, with blue and cream-colored streams running together down her body, foaming at the bow on her waist. Her hair is pulled back in an intricate knot. Her freckles, even frecklier after a season of cross-country, might just kill me.

"You okay?" she whispers, pulling at my sleeve.

I'm not bringing all that here. It's done.

"Yeah. Why?"

"Just checking."

She takes my hand.

"Smile!" Mrs. Joseph says. We do, and she snaps a few more pictures and puts the camera down. "The best of the bunch. What a great choice for this, Rebekah."

The hidden area behind the library. It's beautiful.

"It's really too bad your dad couldn't make it, Phillip."

"He wanted to," I say, "but he didn't want to get anybody else sick."

Mrs. Joseph doesn't know me well enough to detect when I'm lying.

"Well, I'll make sure to send these along."

"Okay, Mom, I think that's good," Rebekah says.

"You guys want to hit the restaurant?" Mrs. Joseph says. She seems surprisingly happy I'm the guy who's taking her daughter to homecoming. It makes me think Rebekah's said good things about me. Which makes me wish Mr. V was driving us. It seems wrong that he's not.

But Asher probably has a date with some former low-level crush of mine.

"Can Phillip and I have just a minute, Mom?" Rebekah says.

"Oh, sure! I'll be in the car. Let's not make you late for your reservation, though."

She leaves. We sit on our bench and wait until we hear the car door open and close.

"This was a good choice," I say. "Even though it didn't go so great last time."

"We're here now."

"True."

"And I got a good book out of it."

"What?"

"*It'll All Be Over Soon?* Ever heard of it?"

"Oh, yeah. I forgot."

"Is that still your favorite book?"

"I'm not sure." I cross my legs and sit back. A breeze sends a brown leaf skipping across the grass.

"Are you sure you're okay?"

I need to snap back into it. I need to be here.

I take her hand. "Yes."

She looks down, swallows. "Okay, well. You know how I owe you a song?"

"Yeah."

"Now I don't."

She takes her hand away and sits facing me. She closes her eyes and breathes deeply. The hairs on my arms stand up.

In a quiet, cutting voice, she sings.

> *"In the secret, in the quiet place,*
> *In the stillness, you are there."*

I've heard this song before. At youth group. Many times.

But this is different.

I feel like I understand it. Here. For the first time.

She lifts her chin to sing the chorus.

> *"I want to know you,*
> *I want to hear your voice,*
> *I want to know you more."*

I close my eyes too. I feel every breath.

I am only here.

When the song is over, Rebekah and I open our eyes at the same time, as if waking from the same dream.

Not yet.

I close my eyes again. Lean in. Pray.

And we kiss.

The administrators are confiscating Asher's smoke machine. He's gotten away with the secretly explicit DJ name he's had posted by his table all night, and a few not-so-secretly explicit tracks, but using a personal smoke machine in the Baxter High School cafeteria was too bold. A small crowd of students around him boos as the vice principal unplugs it.

I join them.

Because, why not? I won. He lost.

Plus, his song choices actually have me dancing—or bobbing my head and shuffling from side to side.

DJ Brown Star is pretty good.

I lean in so Rebekah can hear me. "This is fun."

"Yeah." Rebekah smiles and shakes her hands like she's holding maracas.

I flap my tie around to make her laugh.

Thank God we are equally hopeless dancers.

Thank God we are both weirdos.

Thank God for all of this.

The song ends, and Mark and his date walk over. He's wearing a bright green tie.

"Hey, dude."

"Sup," I say.

He extends his hand to Rebekah. "Hi, I'm Mark. Sorry about what happened at the party. Things got a little crazy."

She takes it. "Thanks. That's nice of you."

"I'm a nice guy. Really." He gives her a big goofy Mark smile. "This is Bianca," he says, introducing Bianca Banks, who sat next to me in health class last year but acts like she's never seen me before. Whatever.

"You want to get some drinks?" he asks me.

"Uh, yeah." I look at Rebekah. "You want something?"

"Water would be good."

"You ladies have a nice chat," Mark says. "We'll be right back."

I try to apologize to Rebekah with my eyes. I don't know if she notices.

Halfway to the refreshments tables, Mark slaps me on the back. "So that *is* your girlfriend."

Well.

We still haven't officially said so.

But she sang for me. And at dinner, when I told her how I made up her remaining service hours, she was so happy she teared up.

And—oh yeah—*I kissed her.*

"Yes," I say, smiling.

He slaps me on the back again. "Dude, well done. She's hot."

Unconventionally hot, actually.

We go to the drinks table. I get some waters. Mark gulps down a Coke. He picks one of the few remaining chicken nuggets from the tray nearby and tosses it in his mouth. He whispers to me, "I've got a flask if you want some."

"Naw, I'm good."

"No worries. I get it." He wipes his nuggety hand on his pants. "Hey, I'm sorry, again, about what happened at the party. But, you know, it had to be done."

"Did it?"

"He took a swing at my *face*."

"I thought you said he hit you."

"He *did*, basically, but he would have hit me more if I hadn't dodged it. I was just trying to hold him back, and he lunged at me. Dude's not cool anymore."

I gulp down a water, pick up another one. "I don't know. Maybe we should all just get over this shit."

Mark doesn't seem to hear me. He's staring off somewhere.

I speak up. "Maybe we should just—"

He taps my chest and points to the dance floor. "Dude. This is what I'm saying."

I look where he's pointing.

Asher. Talking to Rebekah.

He touches her arm. She nods.

"See?" Mark says.

Asher waves to her and jogs back to his table. Rebekah watches him go.

"You see?"

"Yeah. Shut up."

It could be anything. It's nothing.

We kissed.

"I'm gonna go find Bianca," Mark says. "Don't worry, dude, you've got it in the bag." He walks off.

I grab a Coke, swallow it all at once, and belch. I bring a couple of waters with me back to the dance floor, where Rebekah sways alone.

I want to kiss her again, right here on the dance floor.

I stand in front of her. She looks up at me and smiles.

And I go for it.

It's very quick and a little sloppy, and I spill some water on the floor. People back away.

Rebekah glares at me. Hands on her hips.

"Sorry," I say. "You just looked . . . really pretty." I hold the cup of water out.

She takes it. And kicks me. "Uh-huh."

We dance slowly and sip our waters. When the song ends, I take her hand. "Hey, do you want to head out?"

"I thought you were having fun."

"I am. I just thought we could get to the church, help set things up. I know Amanda was going to show up a little early."

Rebekah looks across the dance floor. At Asher's table.

"Don't you want to stay a little longer?" she says.

"Not really. I'm kind of sweaty."

She bites her lip.

"We can dance at the lock-in," I say. I shake my tie.

She doesn't laugh this time.

We roll up in front of the youth center in Mrs. Joseph's SUV. Rebekah and I unbuckle our seat belts and grab our bags full of regular clothes to change into.

"I'll be here at six a.m. sharp," Mrs. Joseph tells Rebekah. She looks at me in the rearview mirror. "Am I picking you up too, Phillip?"

"If that's okay."

"Of course! Your father needs to get his rest, I'm sure." She turns to Rebekah. "Now, hon, you'll be okay to go to services in the morning? I can come get you a little early."

"I'll be fine."

Mrs. Joseph smiles. "Okay, hon. You two have fun. Be safe."

We get out of the car. The air is crisp and smells like burning leaves.

"You're going to church in the morning?" I say.

"It's important to my mom."

Rebekah still seems a little upset that we left.

"Maybe I'll go too," I say.

A foldout table is set up by the walkway, which is the only way to get in, since everything, including the volleyball and basketball courts, has been enclosed with bright orange barriers, like at a construction site. This way, people can go outside but still be "locked in." The parent chaperones welcome us and check our names off the list and remind us we can't come back in once we leave. We know. We thank them.

"This is better, right?" I say as Rebekah and I walk up the stairs.

"Yeah," she says quietly.

"This'll be fun." I reach to open the door.

"Phillip, wait. I need to tell you something."

She's wearing a dark green coat over her dress now. Still, I can tell she's cold.

I rub her arm. "Let's go in."

"No. I need to tell you before we go in."

Her face is expressionless.

"It doesn't look like a good thing."

She shrugs. "It's not a good thing or a bad thing. It's just a thing."

"What is it?"

"I'm not doing this for the Summit."

I let go of the door handle. "But we were counting these hours in your total. When are you—"

I stop myself. I can see it right in front of me. I should have seen it a long time ago.

"You're not going," I say.

"I'm not." She reaches out to touch my arm.

I watch myself pull away.

"But you said you were."

"I know I did. I'm sorry. But I never really *wanted* to go."

"And you're just telling me this now?"

"You were so excited about it at dinner, I didn't want to say anything then. And I only decided a few days ago."

She wasn't crying because she was excited to go with me.

She was crying because she felt sorry for me.

I shake my head, try to think.

"But, why not go? I mean, what else are you doing?"

"There's an academic team tournament that weekend."

"Can't you skip it?"

"I don't *want* to skip it. That's what I'm trying to tell you."

"But this is important. This is only once every three years. You can to go a tournament any weekend."

"Phillip," she says. She reaches for my hand again.

I pull back again.

She groans. "Why do you want me to go so badly?"

"Because."

Why?

"Because you're my girlfriend! I *think*. I don't know. Maybe we still need to figure out if we're 'going together' or not."

"That's mean."

"*You're* being mean." I drop my bag on the ground. "This is what I've been working for. All this stuff. Going to CORE, meeting with Ferret—"

"You can still go."

"But I want you to go too."

"So you did all this just for me?"

"No. I mean, some of it. But some of it *you* did for *me.*"

"What?"

"The time we spent together. When you brought me here and gave me your Bible and we talked about things. That was service. That's why Ferret counted it."

Rebekah looks kind of stunned. "I didn't ask you or him to do that, Phillip. And I wasn't doing that to get service hours, so it's actually a little insulting that you would tally it up and ask Ferret to write it down so you could get what you wanted."

"I thought it was what *you* wanted."

"But you didn't even ask me."

I tap my foot. Adjust my tie. Think of a million things to say, but I don't.

Then: "You're right."

"I *know.*"

We're quiet. Bubbly Christian pop music vibrates the walls of the youth center. Parent chaperones smooth the volleyball sand with rakes.

All of this is still hers. So much more than mine.

"Maybe you should go anyway," I say.

"I 'should' go?"

"It's not just me that wants you to go—it's everybody. They gave you a scholarship."

"And I can give it back."

"Tim will be disappointed."

"Then Tim will be disappointed."

"What about your dad?"

"What *about* my dad?"

"Wouldn't he want you to go?"

She steps back, shaking her head. She turns and walks to the edge of the porch, leans against the brick wall.

I wait. Then I walk over, slowly, and stand next to her.

She won't look at me.

"I didn't ever tell you why my dad named me Rebekah."

It's not a question.

"It's from Genesis," she says.

"I know."

"Be quiet."

She takes a deep breath.

"He told me that Rebekah makes two important choices. When she's young, Abraham's servant comes to take her as Isaac's wife. She's humble, and she gets water for the servant and for his camels. And when the servant asks her parents to give her away to Isaac, she accepts. She does what she's supposed to, and she honors God."

She sounds like she's reciting something she memorized.

"When she's older, and her two boys are grown, they fight for Isaac's blessing. Esau is the older brother, so he has the right to the blessing. But Rebekah loves Jacob more. So she gets Jacob to pretend he's Esau and trick Isaac into giving Jacob the blessing. She tricks her old, blind husband because of what she wants. But

303

because of what happens, Jacob goes on to become a great ruler and a great follower of God."

She stops there. I feel like I should get her point, but I don't. She sees it.

"So no matter what or why she was doing something, she was always doing God's will."

"When did he tell you this?"

"That's what he's always told me."

"Since you were a kid?"

"Yeah."

"Wow."

"Exactly. So maybe you can see why it upsets me that you'd say that, and act like this. After what you said about doing what I wanted to do and not what he wanted me to do." She looks at me. "Or were you just trying to convince me to go to homecoming?"

"No," I say. "I meant it."

I reach for her hand. She pulls away.

"Then why don't you mean it now?" she says.

"I *do*. I just—" I stick my hands in my pockets. "I don't want to be by myself when you're off with Asher somewhere else."

She looks down, shakes her head. "I knew it. I knew that's why we were leaving. You saw him talking to me."

"I saw *you* talking to *him*, too."

"He's my friend. He's also *your* friend, remember? He wanted to—"

"Rebekah, you may think he's just your friend, but he likes you."

"I *know*."

"Then why do you hang out with him? He's just trying to get with you."

"No, he's not."

"He is! He told me he is."

"He's not. He knows I don't like him like that. I told him."

"When?"

She sighs. "After Mark's party."

Wait.

"Did he ask you out?"

"Yes."

I bring my fist down on the wall, and it hurts so bad but I hold it in and just shake my hand and try to breathe.

The son of a bitch.

"And you're still friends with him?" I say. "You don't care what I think? You don't bother to tell me?"

My voice is too loud. The chaperones look over.

I lean back against the brick, my hand still burning.

"How did this happen?" I say.

"Maybe we just don't know what we're doing." She wraps her arms around herself, shivers. "Maybe my dad *was* right."

"About what?"

"About not having a boyfriend until I'm eighteen."

"That's crazy."

"This is kind of crazy too. It *hurts*."

A tear wells up in the corner of her eye and falls across her cheek. I reach to catch it, but she jumps, startled. She wipes her face with her coat sleeve.

"You can't let your dad do this to you," I say. "You can't let this guy who hasn't even spoken to you in a year tell you what to do or what not to do."

"Hold on," she says. "I'm not clear: Should I do what my dad wants me to do or shouldn't I? Or does it just depend whether it's what *you* want me to do?"

I swallow. "No, you're right, I'm—"

She smacks her hand on the wall. "And why the hell do you think you can give me advice about my dad? Especially when you can't talk about your mom *at all*."

She looks away right as she says it.

"I'm sorry," she says. "But it's true."

I bite my lip. I feel like something vital inside me has ruptured. I try to pull her gaze back toward me. If I do that, we can fix this. But I can't. She still won't look at me.

"You know, you don't have to stay tonight," I say. "You can leave."

"Why?"

I shrug. "I'm staying because I'm going to the Summit. But since we're not pretending that you're going anymore, why would you stay?"

Now she can stare me down. "Because being a Christian isn't about racking up points, Phillip."

"I know that."

"You're not acting like you know it."

"Well, you're not acting like someone who's really seeking God."

"So you're buddies with Ferret now and suddenly you're 'seeking God.'"

"I'm just as Christian as you are, Rebekah."

"It's not a contest!"

She throws her hands up and then grabs her bag and walks back to the doors.

I follow.

"You treated it like one," I say. "You said you didn't know if you could be with me unless I was a Christian, but then when I was one, you started to back off. You didn't want to talk about the Bible anymore or help me at all. I mean, I had to find out about salvation from *Ferret*."

She turns quick. A hair clip springs off. "I wanted you to find your own way."

"I thought you wanted to 'know me more.' What about that?"

She laughs. "That song wasn't about you, Phillip. It's about God."

Rebekah laughed at me. *At* me.

"I still can't pass your test," I say. "You don't *want* me to believe."

She pinches her nose. Composes herself. "You know what? I don't. Not if you've been coming here to impress me or yourself or Ferret or God or somebody else."

"I'm *not*," I say.

"Well, good for you," Rebekah says. "Neither am I. So I'm staying."

"So am I."

We walk in, side by side, and don't say another word to each other until around three thirty in the morning, when I tell her my dad will pick me up instead, and she nods and turns back to the girl she was talking to.

FIFTY-ONE

The stove clock numbers float.

10:18.

No.

10:16.

Whatever. Plenty of time.

"Phillip," Dad says, his cup stopped halfway to his mouth. "What's going on?"

"Coffee," I say, shuffling into the kitchen, heading toward the cup cabinet.

"Coffee? You need sleep. Go back to bed."

"No."

"You've been up all night."

"I slept."

"For what, three hours?"

One at most. I woke up shaking.

"I'm fine."

My eyes are droopy. My head feels mushy. My thoughts come one at a time and slowly.

Coffee will make it okay.

I grab a black mug.

"You don't even drink coffee," Dad says.

"Now I do."

I pull out the pot. Steam rises from the top. I pour the coffee into the mug. The color of the mug makes it hard to see the coffee, and I spill.

"Come on, Phillip," Dad says, putting down his mug and snatching two paper towels from the roll.

I bring the coffee to my mouth. It warms my face and smells awesome. Why did I think it tasted bad before?

I drink it. It scalds my lips and tastes disgusting. I force it down my throat and feel my insides shiver.

"See?" Dad says. He wipes up the spill. "If you want to start drinking coffee, we can talk about that, but you shouldn't start right now. Go back to bed."

"I'm going to church."

I take another sip. Swallow it. Feel its heat trickle through me.

"You were just there. Surely you can miss one Sunday. You've done it before."

I gulp it down, burning my throat.

Focusing my brain.

Opening my eyes.

"Jesus, Phillip, that's enough," Dad says. He takes the mug from me, puts it on the counter. "What's gotten into you?"

I start to walk out of the kitchen.

"Wait," Dad says. "I'm not driving you to church."

"Yes, you are. I'm going upstairs to take a shower. I want to leave by ten forty-five."

My eyes bore into his.

He looks away.

I win.

"Two minutes!" the usher calls.

The remaining crowd in the lobby hustles toward the sanctuary, grabbing sermon outlines as they go. I crane my neck, stand on my toes, rub my thumb across the initials on the Bible.

She's supposed to be here.

I go to the plate glass window overlooking the parking lot. A few stragglers here and there. None of them her. Or her mom.

I check the sanctuary again.

She's not here. She's not coming.

I crush the outline in my fist. The usher looks at me disapprovingly, and I scowl back at him. He's so shocked he nearly drops the rest of the outlines. I sit in the back pew by myself, the Bible and the crumpled outline next to me.

Services begin.

I can't follow them. I have my own scattered thoughts swirling in my sleepless head to pin down and examine in the light of day and coffee.

One, she lied to me. *Again.* She pretended like she was going to the Summit because she was too scared to tell herself or Tim or Amanda or me or her imaginary evil dad that she wasn't. Then she acted like I should be happy about it, or at least cool with it, even though she didn't say anything until last night and even though I repaid her saving me and worked extra hours to get her in at the last second because I stupidly still thought she wanted to go.

Two, she admitted, finally, that she doesn't believe I believe. Even though I ran through the rain and prayed with her at YouthLife. Even though I read her Bible. Even though I'm going to the Summit and she's not. Even though I believe.

Three, Asher. He betrayed me. For real this time.

Four.

I'll skip four.

Five, she openly talked about breaking up.

On the night of our first kiss and second kiss she talked about ending things.

I don't want that to happen.

And I don't think she wants that to happen.

It shouldn't happen.

I mean, I was unfair about the dad thing. And I overreacted when she told me she wasn't going to the Summit. And at the end there we were both trying to hurt each other.

Which makes me sick. It makes me so *sick*.

I smack my hand against my forehead. People turn around and look at me. I look down.

Breathe. Focus.

We can work this out. We're good at that. I think about drawing in the sand. I think about the Sittin' Stone, after church. I think about her song. Our first kiss.

It makes me smile.

I wish she were here.

We could get past every one of those things.

I'll call her. I'll make her laugh. I'll draw a hundred weird portraits of her.

Finally the service ends. I start to get up, but I realize no one else is. The assistant pastor comes to the mic. He carefully clears his throat.

"We begin the ceremony of Communion, our remembrance of Jesus Christ."

And the usher is standing right by my pew, holding out the tray of little pieces of bread like he's daring me to take one. I do. He moves up a pew.

The assistant pastor says, "The ceremony of Communion is for all those who know and acknowledge Jesus Christ as our Lord and Savior. First Corinthians Chapter 11, Verse 27, reminds us, 'Therefore, whoever eats the bread or drinks the cup of the Lord in an unworthy manner will be guilty of sinning against the body and blood of the Lord.' If you have not acknowledged Christ, we ask you to please let the tray pass you by."

I have acknowledged Him. I hold my piece between my thumb and forefinger.

The assistant pastor reads, "The Lord Jesus, on the night he was betrayed, took bread, and when he had given thanks, he broke it and said, 'This is my body, which is for you; do this in remembrance of me.'"

And we eat. After, I take my tiny plastic cup of wine. Light shimmers on its surface.

"In the same way, after supper he took the cup, saying, 'This cup is the new covenant in my blood; do this, whenever you drink it, in remembrance of me.'"

And we drink.

I believe. I believe in Jesus Christ. I believe He has the answers. I'll go to the Summit by myself.

After a final hymn it's time to go. Time to call. Time to save this.

I grab the Bible, hit the lobby, head outside.

"Phillip," someone says.

I stop. It's Tim, looking a little bleary-eyed. His smile is still at full wattage.

"Didn't expect to see *you* here," he says.

"Me neither."

He laughs. "Well, thanks for staying up with us. It was a big help."

Not really. I was mostly either playing terrible volleyball or sitting alone.

"No problem," I say.

"I can't believe you've only been coming here for, what, a couple of months now? You're already pretty crucial, Phillip."

"Thanks." I mean it. And any other time I would probably be supergrateful. But seriously, I need to go call Rebekah. What is this?

"If you've got a second, do you mind if we talk?" He looks around. "Maybe outside?"

I say sure and follow him out front. A strong wind whips across my face, unsettles the delicate brain balance I have going on. We walk around the corner and stand in the shadow of the building, out of the wind. On the lawn the Sittin' Stone shines blindingly white in the noon sun.

I rub my eyes.

"Well, look," Tim says, "I just wanted to ask you a couple of quick questions here. No big deal. Just wanted to get your thoughts on something."

He looks away, clasps his hands together, searches for words. "You probably know this, but last night Rebekah told me she's not going to the Summit. We went back and forth a little, but at the end of it I could tell she knew this was the right choice for her, you know?"

"Sure."

"Here's what had me confused. Rebekah told me that she hadn't been able to complete the service hours requirement, but when I went to retrieve her paperwork, it was filled out as though she had."

"Huh."

"I spoke to her about it, showed her the sheet, and she said that a bunch of the hours at the top of the list were from service projects she had worked on before the Summit application process, so those shouldn't have counted, and that a lot of the hours at the bottom of the list were from work she said *you* had actually done with Randy."

My stomach churns.

"Uh-huh."

"So, and I'm not pointing fingers here at all, do you have any sense of what was happening there?"

Shit.

Shit shit shit.

Why did she do that? Why did Ferret already fill them in?

"I was just working for *my* Summit application when I did that stuff. So I—"

"I'm sorry?"

"I was getting service hours. For me. Maybe he wrote them on the wrong form?"

Tim bows his head. He rubs his hands together.

He knows I'm lying.

"Are you going through a separate church?" Tim says.

What?

"No," I say.

"I hadn't heard anything about you wanting to go."

"Ferret didn't tell you?" I say, my voice going up an octave.

"Who?"

"Randy."

"No, I'm afraid not."

"Well, I completed the hours already. I can get the money. No big deal."

Tim clears his throat. "Well, Phillip," he says, "I don't quite know how to say this, but the final application deadline was a few weeks back. I knew you were taking part in some service projects, but Randy hadn't told me they were Summit-related."

Ferret never told Tim?

Ferret never told Tim?

"But I can still go, right? There's still a few days until it starts. We can talk to somebody or—"

Tim one-claps so softly I can barely hear it. "I'm sorry, Phillip. I don't know exactly what happened here, but it sounds like Randy either made a mistake or, well, I don't want to think about the other option quite yet. But either way, maybe it's actually better that you wait.

"You know how they say you should learn to walk before you learn to run? I think that might apply here. Keep that energy. Keep that enthusiasm. Keep learning. Then, next time, you'll be ready for the Summit."

He pats my shoulder.

"So I can't go," I say.

Tim cringes, then tries to hide it.

"Let's give it a little more time."

I nod. My brain sloshes back and forth.

"Great," Tim says. "So, just to make sure, you weren't aware of the business with Rebekah's hours sheet."

"No," I say.

And, for once, it's so easy to lie.

"Okay, thanks, Phillip. Let's talk again soon." He backs away. Smiles. "Get home and get some rest, alright?"

He turns the corner.

I feel the anger again, burning deep in my stomach, like a ball of magma.

I'm not going.

I never was.

I shouldn't.

I can't.

The wind kicks up and wraps around the corner and whistles past my ear. I shudder as if startled awake. I blink. Look around. And see Ferret, emerging from the side door, scurrying to his old red pickup parked on the newly resurfaced lot.

I run. The wind pushes me. Just as he starts to roll back, I tap the driver's side window. He brakes and rolls down the window, just an inch.

Ferret talks up at the window crack. He looks like a dog gulping for air. "I can't talk right now, Phillip. I've gotta—"

"Tell me what's going on."

"I got places to be, son, so let's just—"

Son?

I kick the tire. "Let me in."

"Alright." He rolls up the window and unlocks the passenger

door. I get inside. The cab smells sour and dank. Lukewarmth flows out of the vents.

My voice is steady. "You lied to me."

"No, sir. No, I did not. About what?"

"That you could get me to the Summit."

"Now, I realize I'm a little late on the paperwork, but—"

"You never told Tim."

"What? That you wanted to go? Sure I did."

"You're lying to me *right now.*"

Ferret flicks the rubber Yosemite Sam key chain that dangles from the ignition. It comes back, and he flicks it again. And again.

"I intended to," he says. "I wanted to make sure you'd done the work first, because I knew it would be a hard sell. We can still make this happen. All I need to do is—"

"No. It's over. Tim doesn't want me to go."

He smacks the armrest. "That's crazy. He told you that? He cannot—"

My anger is burning hotter, growing. I try to control it.

But so much of this is his fault.

"You told me I could go," I say, my voice even, my muscles tense. "You made it seem like a sure thing, but it was never going to happen. All that work was for nothing."

"Not nothing," Ferret says, sounding like a child. He flicks the key chain again.

Suddenly I get it. What all of this has been about.

"It's not that I was special, or that you really wanted me to go to the Summit. That's why it was easy to fudge the hours, because they didn't actually count. You were just bribing me to hang out with you."

He didn't want to help me. He just wanted a friend.

"Come on, now. That's nonsense." He flicks the key chain harder, so it slaps against the dash. "We've got a good thing going."

"You screwed it up. Again."

He rubs his hand across his face. "I know. But we can make this right."

He'd just do it again. And again. Like he always does.

He holds the key chain by the feet and stares at it. "Story of my life, Phillip. Screwing up. Alienating people. Why? What the hell is wrong with me?"

Why?

I think about what Asher told Dan the night of Mark's party. What Dan said about Ferret. What Ferret said about the shower. The tracts.

"Maybe you're gay."

Yosemite Sam hits his poised finger and stops.

Slowly Ferret turns to me. "The hell'd you just say?"

"Maybe that's why you're so lonely. Maybe that's why you act like you do. You know you're gay but you know it's wrong. That's it."

I can see how guilty he is, how the self-loathing gurgles up inside of him and spills over into rage. His jaw is rigid with it.

"You're trying to hurt me," he says.

"I'm trying to help you."

"That is bull. That is such *bull*." He shifts into reverse. "Get out of my truck."

"You should get help."

"Get *out*."

I open the door, and the wind rushes in. I step out of the truck.

He stares at me. "You came up with that nickname, didn't you?"

"What?"

He spits it out of his mouth. "Ferret."

I don't say anything. I don't owe him anything.

"Close the damn door!"

I slam it. He barely even looks back before he pulls out of the spot. Then he shifts into drive and squeals out of the parking lot.

I watch him go, then I walk back toward the church. Families gather outside. Kids chase each other on the lawn. The usher walks with his wife down the sidewalk, spinning his keys on his finger.

All these people in each other's lives. Who do I have?

My assistant pastor and cross-country coach is a closeted homosexual who made my life hell and then tricked me into being his friend.

My pastor pretends to respect me.

My friend Mark is an asshole.

My ex-friend Asher betrayed me.

My brother thinks I'm crazy.

My dad is an adulterer.

And my mom is dead.

Who do I have?

I take my phone out. Call.

It rings.

And rings.

And rings.

And rings.

Answer. Please answer.

It rings.

It goes to voice mail. The automated voice asks me to leave a message.

319

So who do I have?

No one.

Beep.

The wind rushes into the microphone. I turn away.

"Sorry," I say. "I'm outside church. You're not here."

I swallow.

"But you know that. I guess what I wanted to say is . . ."

I look at the cover of the Bible. Those initials. Hers. His.

Not mine.

"I'm tired of not feeling good enough."

The phone beeps. I look at the screen, and there's an incoming call from Rebekah. I watch her name flash three times.

"So I'm breaking up with you."

I hang up on both calls.

I look for dad's car. There he is. I walk through the crowd, tap on his window.

He rolls it down. "You look beat," he says. "Ready to get back?"

"No," I say. "I need to go to Asher's. I'm driving."

FIFTY-TWO

I come to a quick stop in the half-circle driveway. Asher's family's huge house looks quiet.

"Phillip, why are we here?"

"I just need to talk to him."

"You couldn't do that over the phone?"

I grab the Bible from between the seats. I remember that Dad keeps a pocketknife in the glove compartment. "Hand me the knife."

He laughs nervously. "You boys are having a knife fight?"

I hold my hand out. The anger roils in my gut. "No, Dad."

He sighs, gets the knife, and drops it on my open palm. "So what's going on?"

I place the Bible in my lap and pull out the blade. I point the tip of the knife right in the middle of the *R* and drag it along the *F* and the *J*. Then, above it, I carve my initials: PDF.

And then I cross those out too.

I flip the knife closed and hand it to Dad. His eyes look fearful.

"Please tell me what this is all about," he says.

"I'll be back in a couple of minutes." I get out and walk to the door. The front of my brain is throbbing, and I feel dizzy.

Only a little farther to go.

Just a few seconds after I ring the doorbell, Mr. V answers. His face lights up.

"Phillip! What a pleasant surprise. How are you doing?"

"Fine. Is Asher here?"

"He's in his room. Do you want me to fetch him? He may still be sleeping, the lazybones."

"No, I'll go up."

He steps aside. "Be my guest. Wake him up. And is that your father?"

"Yeah." I walk past him, up the stairs. The plush carpeting and laundry-scented air and the dozens of framed pictures of the Venkataraman family and their relatives—they're things I used to know.

Asher's door is closed. I suck in a breath, clutch the Bible, and open the door.

The blinds are shut so tightly that only a sliver of sunlight sneaks in, throwing itself against the wall just over his bed. Asher is a lump under a comforter.

"Sleeping, Dad," he says, annoyed.

I close the door. "Get up."

He peeks his head over the covers and then sits up, rubbing his eyes.

"Phillip?" He can't see me. He searches for his glasses on the beside table. Puts them on. "What's up?"

He looks so weak.

I throw the Bible at him, spine first. It twists and flaps and just misses his shoulder before it falls behind the bed. He only gets his hands up after it's over.

"What the *fuck*?"

"Give that back to her. She's yours now."

"What are you talking about?"

"Rebekah. What else?"

"You broke up?"

"Yeah, you finally got what you want. Maybe she'll say yes this time."

"Yes to what?"

I walk over to him. He sits up, scowling.

"Say yes to you asking her out, you dick."

He opens his mouth, but all that comes out are sputters.

"Oh, you didn't ask her out?" I say. "Just like you didn't start that fight with Mark? Just like you weren't drunk that night? Just like you didn't try to sabotage me and Rebekah?"

He throws the covers off, puts his feet on the ground. "I did *not* start that fight. And I wasn't trying to sabotage you."

"Bullshit."

He shakes his head. "I know I wasn't acting right. I tried to apologize last night, but you guys left so quickly."

"I don't care if you're sorry."

"That's fair. That's completely fair." He starts to stand up. "But maybe it's better this way."

And all my anger finally empties out.

I punch him in the stomach, and he makes an almost comical *oof* sound and falls right back down, groaning.

"It's not," I say, backing away.

Asher looks at me like there's something wrong with my face. I walk out and slam the door behind me. My vision is blurry. My hand stings. My foot slips on the stairs and I almost hit my head on the corner of a step, but I catch myself on the banister.

"Hello?" Mrs. V says from somewhere in the house.

I run out the front door and hurry to the car. Mr. V is talking to my dad.

"Going already?" Mr. V says.

"Yeah," I say. "Sorry." I get in and start the car.

"You'll have to stay longer next time."

I look over, and he sees my face and looks startled. But he just says bye, and Dad says bye, and I get out of there.

"You're crying," Dad says.

I look in the mirror. He's right. I wipe the tears on my sleeve.

I wait for him to ask why.

All through Asher's neighborhood.

Ask me.

Turning onto the main road.

Ask.

But he doesn't.

We come over a hill. Up ahead is an overpass for Steven Pillory Memorial Highway.

I drive beneath it and put on my left turn signal.

"Phillip, don't," Dad says.

I pull into the turn lane.

"You're not in a good state for this."

I keep going. Out of the corner of my eye, I see Dad clutch the door handle.

324

"You're upset, Phillip. Let's come back later, okay? You're not ready for this."

"Yes, I am."

I turn onto the on-ramp.

"Jesus, Phillip."

I drive up to meet the highway. The tears have dried on my cheeks and in the corners of my eyes. I grip the wheel at ten and two. Sit up straight. In the side mirror the road comes into view.

And so do the cars, coming fast behind me, in a solid block in the right-hand lane. I ease up on the gas, wait for an opening. The front wave of cars catches up with me, but there are more behind them, driving just as fast.

My lane starts to merge. Still there's no opening.

I press the brake. I put the turn signal on. Cars whoosh past, right on each other's tails, not giving me any room.

I honk the horn. Crane my neck.

The lane is almost done. There's nowhere else to go.

I poke the nose in.

A dude in a van backs off.

And I merge like a champion.

I fist pump.

Dad is silent.

I coast for a while, realizing how easy this is. How amazing it feels. We might as well be flying.

After a few minutes we reach the exit that's closest to our house. I take it. At the bottom of the off-ramp, we're stuck at a red light. I look over. Dad is still clutching the handle and the armrest, staring right ahead.

"I had to," I say.

He doesn't speak.

"I was ready."

Doesn't acknowledge me at all.

"I did it. It's okay now."

Nothing.

"Dad?"

"Go." He points ahead. The light has turned green and the car in front is long gone.

I hit the gas.

"Go *straight* home," he says.

Where else am I going to go?

AUGUST

"I love you, Phillip," Mom said. "You know that, right?"

I looked away.

"I love you," she said again.

I looked away, harder.

FIFTY-THREE

It's 8:34 p.m. on Wednesday, and I am not at Wesley Road Faith Church. I am lying in bed, holding my phone above my face, staring at Rebekah's last words to me.

i didnt say u werent good enough. u did.

I found the text after I drove back from Steven Pillory, and I've been staring at it for three days now, getting myself angry again and again.

Because it's total bullshit. Maybe she didn't technically speak the words "You aren't good enough." But she said them anyway. When she didn't tell her mom about me even after we'd been going out for a month, she said them. When she didn't look at my drawing for a whole week, she said them. When she lied to me, she said them.

But right now the words she didn't say bother me more.

No *i m sry.* No *lets tlk abt this.*

Not even *fine i m brkng up w u 2.* Or *we were alrdy brkn up.*

Like it was a given that we were over. Like she didn't do anything wrong. Like all she had for me, after all that, was pity.

It's 8:35 p.m. Youth group has probably ended. Or maybe they're on the last song and—

I need a distraction. But I can't draw anything. I've tried. So I keep lying here, pressing buttons every time the phone screen dims, just so I can look at her message in full light and get angry again.

Maybe I deserve to be pitied.

The phone buzzes in my hand, and I freak out and drop it. My heart starts pounding. I pick the phone up, check the name. But it's just a number. No one I know.

I answer anyway.

"Phillip?" A girl's voice. Not Rebekah's. "It's Amanda."

Rebekah must have told her what happened. I'm finally going to see her aggressive side again.

"Oh, hey."

"You sound very excited to hear from me."

"Sorry. I'm just kind of—"

"I know, I know. Let me ask you something."

Here it comes.

"Do you still want to go to the Summit?"

I try to comprehend what she just said.

"Hello?" she says.

"Wait. How?"

"Don't worry about that right now. Just, if you could go, would you?"

"Well."

"You'd have to take Friday off from school. And get permission to ride in my car."

"Um."

329

"Phillip, say something."

"Let me check, okay? Hold on."

I put the phone down and sit up.

I can still go. If I want to.

If I can.

I get up and go to the computer room. I knock on the door and push it open. Dad is dead still, reading some website.

"Dad?"

"Unbelievable."

"What?"

"Absolutely unbelievable."

"Dad, I have to ask you something."

He swivels the chair around to face me. His face is red. "Really? Why would you ask *me*, Phillip?"

"Well, I need permission to take Friday off. And ride with a friend. So I can go to that conference in Atlanta."

"Why not just do whatever the hell you want?"

"I'm not trying to."

"You are, Phillip." He turns back to the computer, scrolls up the screen, and reads. "'Survival Kit—everything you need to survive the Apocalypse.' Did you think I wouldn't find out about this?"

"I don't know."

"You just did it. Without thinking about the consequences."

"Kind of like you."

He just shakes his head. "People go to jail for this."

"What are you talking about?"

Dad clicks on one of the photos and enlarges it. I step closer to see what he's looking at. He points at a couple of bags slouching in the corner of the picture.

"And?" I say.

"That's fertilizer. Several bags of fertilizer."

"So?"

"So you don't sell large amounts of fertilizer to anonymous people on the internet, Phillip! For Christ's sake. I checked to see if it was listed in the contents, and fortunately it's not, but who knows what these people think they're getting?"

"Dad, come on. Nobody—"

He slams his hand down on the desk. "I am so tired of this. The way you've been behaving goes way beyond the usual teenager stuff. You just outright and openly don't give a shit what I think or say. I'm sorry if something bad happened to you this weekend, but this is so far over the line, I just don't know what to do."

He picks up a pen, brings it to his mouth, then flings it back onto the desk.

"Dad, I didn't mean—"

"What you meant is irrelevant." He turns back to the screen, starts clicking. "I'm tired of talking about this. I'm canceling this auction."

"Well, I'm still going to the conference. Right?"

"Do whatever you want."

I just stand there. The only sound is his livid clicking. Finally I slink back to my room and pick up the phone.

"Amanda?" I say.

"I'm still here," she says.

FIFTY-FOUR

Amanda turns off the road, following the big green arrow into the parking garage under the hotel. The sign outside says WELCOME, YOUTH LEADERS.

I'm here. I'm actually here.

We follow the sloping, rectangular spiral downward. Two levels below, sunlight disappears and the motor's hum is trapped in concrete, reverberating off every surface. Finally, toward the bottom, we see other Summit-goers. Teens, and even some who look like college students, with bags slumped over their shoulders, wearing long-sleeved T-shirts with names of bands I've never heard of and slogans of mission trips to Caribbean countries. I know these mostly because Amanda points them out to me.

"You okay?" she says. "You're being kind of quiet."

"I'm just looking."

I'm still not sure how I'm here. Amanda said she talked to Tim, and he agreed to approve the funding as long as Amanda acted as my mentor for the weekend. That doesn't explain how I got in after the deadline passed, or who I'm staying with, or why he changed his mind about me, but I didn't want to push it.

I don't feel like pushing anything right now.

We find a spot, one of the last ones on the lowest level. Amanda and I grab our stuff from the trunk and take the elevator, which is filled to capacity by the second floor, when a pudgy, bearded man wearing an Atlanta Hawks cap backs into the elevator. "Beep, beep, beep," he says, getting a few laughs. "Wide load!"

He and the lanky kid he's with barely fit. As we go up the Hawks cap guy makes a joke about the weight capacity of the elevator that has everybody laughing nervously.

After a tight minute we spill out into the lobby, which is swarming with people. Amanda tells me to wait while she goes to check us in.

A few minutes later I recognize some people from our church on the other side of the lobby. They're people I know—sort of. I think about going over, saying hi. But I can already see the puzzled looks on their faces.

I take my phone out. Dad told me to text him when I got here. He also said that if I want to leave at any time, to call him and he'll come get me.

I text him and turn off my phone. Then I slip the battery out just to be sure.

Amanda walks up and holds out a blue plastic key card. "Take this."

I take it.

"Now you go to your room and drop your stuff off, and then you meet the rest of us in the"—she looks at a slightly crumpled sheet of paper—"Atlanta Convention Hall. Which is down that way."

She hooks her hair behind her ears and smiles. "Any questions?"

A thousand, actually.

"Who am I staying with?"

"A couple of guys from another church. They were nice enough to offer up their room, so you should get along fine."

"You talked to them?"

"No."

"Then who did?"

Her smile falters. She reaches into her bag, takes out a sealed envelope with my name scrawled on it, and hands it to me.

"Mr. Farragut."

I knew it. I knew he had something to do with this. He's trying to unscrew things that are permanently screwed. It's too late.

I reluctantly take the envelope and stash it in my bag. I'm not looking at that right now. Maybe never.

I look around the lobby, at all the youth leaders and their chaperones, and I have a flashback to Asher's and my first visit to Wesley Road Faith Church. Everyone seems excited, experienced, ready. Like they already have the answers.

Amanda hugs me—crushes me—and growls. She lets go.

"Had to be quick," she says. "PDA is not cool here, I'm sure."

"What?"

"You'll be fine. That's all I'm gonna say."

I nod. "Thanks."

She smiles, walks away. "See you in a minute."

I take another packed, chatty elevator to the twelfth floor. I find my room and open the door, preparing myself for whatever strange roommates I'll have, but they're not here yet. The beds are crisply made, and the plastic wrappers are still on the cups. I put my bag down on the far bed and open the blinds. Twelve floors up, the city looks different than I've ever seen it. It's not just a jumble of winding roads and mismatched buildings with a highway cut through it like a scar. From here it looks whole.

The door slams open.

"He beat us to it!" somebody says.

It's pudgy, bearded Hawks cap guy, with the lanky kid. Hawks cap guy throws his bag on the other bed and extends his hand.

"Phillip, I assume. My name's Bob Yoder." We shake. "But you can call me whatever you want—except 'fat.' This is my son, Devin."

Devin stands with his bag over his shoulder, not making eye contact. Though there's obviously a big size difference between them, I see the relation in the rusty red color of their hair and the thrust of their jawlines. Devin looks about my age.

"Sup," I say.

Devin's eyes tick over me, and he mumbles something that sounds like "Hey."

"So you're a friend of Randy's," Bob Yoder says.

"Sorry?"

"Randy Farragut. You go to Wesley Road Faith, right?"

"Oh, yeah."

"Great guy. One of the best. We went to seminary together, so we go way back."

Great guy? One of the *best*?

"Well, thanks for letting me stay here."

"My pleasure, absolutely. He called right out of the blue the other day. Hadn't heard from him in a couple years, I'm afraid. So he said can you help this kid out, and I said of course, anything for old Randy, anything for a young Christian soldier, my pleasure. We didn't get to catch up too much, but sounds like he's doing great, of course."

Of course. I can see why Bob Yoder and Ferret are friends.

"Well, let's get down to brass tacks, gentlemen," he says. "To put it politely, I am a tub of lard, so I was thinking you two skins and bones would share a bunk."

From the size of Devin's eyes, I'd bet Bob didn't tell his son about this plan.

"No, that's okay," I say. "I'll just call down and get a cot."

"Phillip, that's honorable of you, but Devin can deal, right?"

He looks at Devin. Devin looks at the floor.

"Devin can deal," Bob says.

Devin huffs as he walks past me. He tosses his bag at the foot of the bed.

Bob checks his watch. "We better get a move on, boys. I'll christen the john."

Bob zips into the bathroom. Devin is messing around on his phone, his bag untouched since he threw it. The top section is unzipped, and some of the contents have spilled out. As I reach into my bag for my new NIV Bible and a pen, I peek inside his.

The Late Great Planet Earth.

No way. I used to have that book. Way back when I first started reading about the end of the world, I got that. But I decided it was too religious and I threw it away.

"Do you like that book?" I say.

"Huh?" Devin says, not looking up.

"The book in your bag. Do you like it?"

He glances at the bag. "Yeah, I like it."

336

"Are you into that stuff?"

"What stuff?"

"I don't know." After all this time how do I not have a word for it? Other than "Apocalypse section." "End of days stuff."

"Yeah, I guess."

"You should read this book *It'll All Be Over Soon*. It's pretty funny."

"What's so funny about it?"

"Just . . . I don't know. The writing."

"You don't know a lot." He smiles to himself, keeps on texting.

I hold tight to my Bible.

I'll be fine.

I head for the door without saying another word.

Bob pops out of the bathroom just as I'm passing.

"Heading out?" he says. "Okey-doke. See you late—"

The door closes on his last word, and I head down the hall to the elevators.

"*You* are an inspiration," says Hank Umberland, jabbing a finger at all of us. According to the official packet, Mr. Umberland is the founder of the Summit. He's supposed to speak until nine forty-five, when Pastor Dave Cruz takes over the Weekend Warm-Up, which features the Ninnies ("all the way from Austin, Texas") and lasts until ten fifteen.

After that come the "break-out groups" at ten thirty. I'm in Group 9/10D and Amanda is in Group 11/12A, so I think the numbers are grade levels. Later tonight is the Fellowship Dinner, followed by either Movie Night (*The Passion of the Christ*) or Mix and Mingle ("Chaperones will be present").

I'm a little skeptical. I'm a little scared.

"*You* are the young people who are going to make this country come alive for Christ again," says Mr. Umberland.

But I'm also a little excited.

I look over at Amanda and smile. She writes on her program, "See?"

Hank Umberland leaves to thunderous applause as Pastor Dave Cruz jogs to the stage. "Who's feeling that fire today?" he says, and from the response, I'd say just about everybody is feeling that fire today. He tells us to "turn the heat up" several times, and then reviews all the stuff we're going to do today. Then the Ninnies come on, and Amanda just about loses it.

They look like standard hipsters, and I'm afraid I'm not going to like them, but then they launch into really solid versions of songs from youth group, and everybody joins in. As they play I realize that I know the lyrics.

I start to sing.

So of course not only do I end up in the same break-out group as Devin, but also the only remaining empty seat is right next to him. I take a water from the table, sit down, and gulp half the bottle. Then I realize we're crossing our legs the same way, and I uncross mine. Then I cross them back. Devin's not going to determine which way I cross my legs.

There are twelve kids in the semicircle, and some of them talk to each other. A bunch of them are wearing Christian gear of some kind, while I'm just wearing a plain navy blue polo shirt. I think about the part in Matthew when Jesus says you shouldn't brag on how good or how faithful you are.

And then I think about how I'm bragging to myself.

A woman enters the room and closes the door. She's in her twenties, has long blond hair and elfin ears, and I'm already smitten.

She's unconventionally smoking hot.

"Sorry I'm late," she says, sitting down in the chair that faces the semicircle. "I'm Andrea. I'll be your break-out session leader for the next couple of days." She leans forward and smiles in a way that's simultaneously warm and commanding.

"Looks like some of you have already introduced yourselves, but let's go around the room and get a sense of where we're all coming from, okay? So we'll start over here and just say your name, something interesting about you, and what you think is the most important issue facing our country today."

Holy crap. What? The third thing is not at all like the other two things. We're just supposed to *know* what the most important issue is, off the top of our heads?

The first guy is Lee, and he plays water polo, and he thinks the most important issue facing our country today is abortion.

Catherine; she makes jewelry; abortion.

Veronica; um um um she went to Sydney, Australia, this summer; abortion.

Okay. Fine. This is easy enough.

Darrell; can do a split; abortion and too much government in our lives.

Kelsey; just met Tyler from the Ninnies; abortion.

And now:

"I'm Devin," he says in his rumbly, stiff voice. Andrea smiles for him, and I want her to take it back. "I do a lot of online animation, though people don't always think that's interesting." Correct.

"Abortion is an important issue, but it's part of something bigger. I don't think we're doing enough to make His voice heard, not just in this country but everywhere. We don't have a lot of time, and I think the more people who know Jesus, the more people we save and the fewer abortions we have. So it's all connected."

Such BS.

"Interesting," Andrea says, nodding seriously. She didn't do that for anybody else.

"You said we don't have a lot of time," she says. "So you believe Jesus is coming back soon."

"Probably."

"Thank you," Andrea says. Then she looks at me and smiles.

"Phillip," I say.

And I realize I was so worried about my issue that I don't have anything interesting about me.

I *um* for time.

Oh, hell.

"I've only been a Christian for a couple of months."

"Huh," Andrea says. She tilts her head and folds her hands and is clearly intrigued. "That's very cool."

Yes, it is. Eat it, Devin.

"And," I say, "I think something that's important right now is that in Matthew how it talks about, how Jesus talks about that no one knows when He's returning. So maybe we shouldn't, as a country, or as Christians, act like we know what His plans are. Specifically."

Andrea wrinkles her forehead. She's trying to figure out what I just said.

So am I.

340

"Hmm," she says. "So you think we're doing that now? As a country?"

"Well. Yes. Some of us. Are overreacting."

"How?"

I shift in my seat. Panic seizes me. I feel like there's a floodlight inside my head, blinding my brain.

Devin clears his throat. "I don't mean to interrupt, but in Matthew, Jesus also describes signs that will appear in the times before His return. He talks about specific things that will happen that we can see happening today. He says that he wants us to keep watch for these signs."

"But you don't know when it's going to happen," I say.

"Not the exact hour, but in Matthew 24, Verses 43 and 44, He compares it to a rich man who stays home because he finds out a thief is coming. We are the rich man, and the thief is Armageddon."

"That's not what it says," I say.

"Yes, it is," Veronica pipes up.

"It is," Lee says.

"Well, I didn't mean that it didn't say that. I meant—"

"What *did* you mean?" Devin says.

We finally make eye contact.

"Hey, hey, hey," Andrea says, putting her hands out. "These are complex verses. We can talk about them later when we've cooled down a little, okay? Phillip's new to the faith, so let's welcome him and respect his ideas."

Silence.

Andrea smiles. "I can tell we have a spirited group. That's a good thing. So let's keep it moving."

Erin; does an impression of Kermit the Frog; abortion.

FIFTY-FIVE

When it's over, I get out of there as fast as I can. Which is not very fast, because the hallway is just like school between classes—everyone crushed into one another, pushing to get where they need to go. Except I don't know where I'm going. There are five workshops to choose from, and I can't even figure out what some of them are. I need one called "Answers," but it's not on here.

Veronica jostles past me, and I swear she swings her bag into my stomach on purpose. I scoot into an alcove with an open door and see Amanda sitting by herself in a conference room.

Thank God.

"Hey," she says. "I was hoping you'd come to this one. I didn't want to pressure you, though."

"Thanks." I lay my face on the cool surface of the conference table and shut my eyes.

So I didn't remember a couple of verses from one section of

Matthew. Why did they have to pounce on me like that? And what the *hell* is Devin's problem?

I thought good Christians were supposed to be nice—like Amanda.

"Are you okay?"

I lift my face up. "Yeah. Just—"

"Overwhelmed?"

"Yeah."

"You'll be fine," she says, patting my hand.

As we wait, and other people come in, I look at my program again. Based on the room number, we're in "Apologetics in Action" led by Jeremy Snider. I don't know what "apologetics" means, and there's no description anywhere.

I know I can trust Amanda.

"This is about apologizing?" I whisper. A few more people have come in.

She laughs, but she doesn't answer.

"I'm serious," I say.

"I thought you chose this."

"Honestly, I just saw you in here and came in."

"Phillip, you should go to the workshop you want to go to."

"I thought you were my mentor."

She looks at me sideways. "I'm *being* your mentor."

"Sorry. I know. So what is this?"

"Witnessing."

Shit.

"Like Ferr—I mean, Randy's thing at CORE that time?"

"Yes, but we're going to Centennial park and doing it in real life."

I should leave. I should go to "The Seminary Experience." Or "Musical Devotion," with Tyler from the Ninnies. Or back to the room to take a nap.

"You don't have to do this, Phillip," Amanda says. "I just thought you might want to try it again."

Try embarrassing myself again? Try proving just how right everyone is that I shouldn't be here?

i didnt say u werent good enough. u did.

Amanda puts her hand on my arm. "Witnessing is one of the scariest things you can do as a Christian."

Devin walks in and sits in the corner of the room.

I shift my arm away from Amanda. "I'll do it."

She looks at me as if I just had a complete change of heart. Strange.

"Why don't we team up?" she says. "That'll be fun."

"No, it's alright. I can do it."

"Phillip—"

"Hello hello hello," says a guy walking into the room wearing a gray and navy blue jersey shirt and a bottleful of hair gel on his head. That must be Jeremy Snider. "Awesome turnout. You guys ready to get out there?"

"Gorgeous!" Jeremy says, smiling up at the sun.

It is. The temperature is mild and the sky is a show-offy blue. Kids dance in the jumping fountains, businesspeople in suits have lunch, and tourists amble across the lawn, from the silver wedge of the aquarium to the brown hulk of the CNN Center.

And we're here to save them.

"Don't worry about silly things like ruining these people's day,"

Jeremy told us back in the conference room. "Most of them will forget you instantly. But one person might be truly, eternally grateful."

His presentation was a lot like Ferret's, actually, except without the purposeful humiliation of anyone in the room.

"You guys ready?" he says.

I'm not ready. I'm afraid.

But I don't need pamphlets. I don't need a teammate.

I just need to trust Him.

"Yeah," I say.

This *is* Answers.

"Awesome," Jeremy says. "Fan out, gang. And remember, try to talk in-depth with at least three individuals or groups. We'll meet back here at one o'clock."

I start off for the far corner of the park, near the World of Coca-Cola, fast enough that I build up a sweat.

I see Rebekah laughing. At me.

I walk faster.

I don't need her. I only need God.

"Excuse me," I say, remembering to smile.

A thirtyish hipster-y couple stops.

"I know this is kind of a weird question," I say, remembering to be genuine, "but have you guys thought about where you're going when you die?"

The guy looks at me witheringly. "No," he says. And they keep walking.

"Okay, have a nice day," I say, remembering to be kind to people who aren't kind to me.

Most of them are going to be like that, I remind myself. It's not your fault.

Trust.

Three friends, stylish women in their forties, walking down the path and laughing.

Why do they remind me of Asher, Mark, and me? Because one of them is Asian?

No. It's just the way they are with each other. How we used to be.

Maybe that's a sign.

"Excuse me, do you know Jesus Christ?"

One woman looks at the other two, then at me. "Not *personally*." They bust up laughing, but I was expecting that.

"Well, He wants to—"

But they're already walking away.

Okay. Fine. I was reading too much into that one. Just keep trying.

Lone stout dude with a mustache. Looks friendly. Here we go.

"Excuse me—"

"No."

And that's it.

I just want a chance. I can do it if somebody just gives me more than five seconds.

Right there. A "stationary target." Late-twenties woman with dreadlocks, sitting on a bench, sipping on a ginger ale, and reading a gossip magazine. She looks bored.

Thank you, God. This is perfect.

I sit down next to her. "Hi," I say.

She lifts her sunglasses, looks at me, puts them back down. "Hi."

"Nice day."

"Mmhmm."

"I'm sorry to bother you. Really. But I was wondering if you've thought at all about where you're going when you die."

Slowly she places the magazine on her lap. "Not lately. But yes."

Yes yes yes.

"Where do you think you're going?"

She laughs. "I think I'm going a lot of places. I'm an organ donor."

"But what about, you know, *you*?"

"I'll go wherever I was before I was here."

"So do you believe in Jesus Christ?"

"Some of him."

"I think you need all of Him to go to heaven."

She takes a long sip. "Well, I wouldn't be so sure."

Is she playing with me? It's hard to tell.

"I just think you need to believe that Jesus died for your sins and that He was resurrected."

"What if I don't?"

I swallow. "Well, then, I think you could go to hell."

She lifts her sunglasses on top of her head. "What about my grandmother?"

"I'm sorry?"

She puts the ginger ale can down on the bench. "She doesn't believe that Jesus Christ died for her sins. She's a Muslim. So is my grandmother going to hell?"

I don't want to say yes. But I have to.

Some answers are uncomfortable.

"If she doesn't convert—yes. I'm sorry."

Very uncomfortable.

"No, you're not," she says.

"I am."

She takes her sunglasses off her head, folds them up. Rolls her magazine and points it at me. Raises her voice. "Look, I'm aware you're just fifteen, sixteen, and you know everything there is to know, but maybe *you* need to think about where you're going *right now* and stop telling people their grandmothers are going to hell."

She stands up, grabs her ginger ale, and stomps off. People around us pretend not to stare.

I didn't mean it like that. I was trying to help her.

Why is this so hard, God?

"Need some help?"

It's Devin, standing in front of me, smiling.

He had the entire park to creep through, and he chose this distant corner.

"No."

"That's not what it looks like."

He actually sits down next to me.

"Why are you here?" he says.

"Why are *you* here? You're supposed to be witnessing."

"Exactly," he says, straight-faced.

He thinks he's witnessing to *me*.

"I'm a Christian. You know that. Leave me alone."

"Actually, I don't know you're a Christian. Just because you're here doesn't mean you're a Christian. You don't seem to have a very good understanding of the Bible, and that's normal since you've only considered yourself a Christian for two months, right?"

"It's not a contest."

Devin's eyes light up. "But it is a contest. And the losers go to hell. You should know that."

"Losers like me?"

"Have you accepted Jesus Christ as your personal savior and acknowledged that he was and is the embodiment of God on earth and that he—"

"*Yes.*"

"Have you been baptized?"

I'm speechless. Ferret was wrong. This *is* an inquisition.

"You know, when they dunk you in the water?"

"No, but so what?"

"So you're not going to heaven."

I feel light-headed. "I've never heard that. You're making it up."

He snickers. "How are you supposed to save these people if you aren't saved?"

"I *am.*"

"Do you believe Jesus was both fully God and fully man?"

"What?"

"It's a simple answer. Yes or no."

"I just . . . I'm not sure."

"God said he will spit the lukewarm from his mouth."

"I'm not lukewarm."

"Then what do you believe?"

"I don't know!"

I yell it. I yell it in his stupid face.

People passing by stare at us. I'm used to it.

Devin has so much anger in his eyes, but his face is as still as a photograph. He sits so upright it must hurt him.

"Why do you care?" I say.

"Because you don't belong here," he says, and he gets up and leaves.

I wait. I feel it build up inside me. But I wait.

And then when I can't take it anymore, I raise my face to the sky and yell.

"Ahhhhhhhhhhhhhhhhhhhh!"

Again, people stare. Some look genuinely concerned. I hold my hands up and mouth, "I'm fine."

But I'm not, am I?

Because as much of a dick as Devin is, he's right, and Tim's right, and Rebekah's right, and Amanda's wrong.

I'm not fine.

I don't belong here.

I don't have any answers.

And until I can find somebody to baptize me, I'm going to hell.

I lose.

And now I have forty-five minutes—no, a whole weekend—no, an entire miserable existence—to kill, and all I have is this Bible and this pen and this program.

But I suck at drawing. All my medieval letters and mushroom-cloud hearts were just copies. Those hands I drew for Rebekah were ugly. Even that Lovers thing was lame.

I lose at everything.

I lean my head back again and close my eyes and feel the sun braising my face. I wonder if this is even close to what hell feels like.

And something opens up.

I turn the program over to the blank side, use the Bible as a flat surface, and poise the pen just above the paper. The pen starts to move. In a straight line. Then a corner. Then a square. Then another square behind it. Then the lines to complete it: a cube. With a stick figure slouching inside it.

It's not what I expected. But it looks right. Hell isn't a blaze. It's a box.

I shade the area outside the box, all around it. Me inside, trapped with my thoughts, and nothing outside. Exactly right.

Why do I feel this good imagining my endless torment?

And then I understand: It's because I'm not.

If there were a Hell, this would be it.

But I don't believe in it.

If hell is full of Muslim grandmothers and gay people and little brothers and atheist dads and very confused sixteen-year-olds who didn't realize they had to be dunked in some water to qualify for eternal bliss, but *Devin* gets to go to heaven, then I don't believe in hell. In fact, I don't believe in hell at all. I refuse.

I fucking refuse.

I look off at the skyline and shake my head. And I start to laugh.

Because Devin was right. Devin was *right*.

But only sort of.

"I don't know," I say.

I laugh even harder.

"I don't know."

I laugh my ass off.

Everybody around must think I'm crazy, and they are completely right.

I am going to hell, and I'm crying laughing about it.

Or I'm not going to hell and I'm crying laughing about it.

I don't know.

I don't know.

I. Don't. Know.

I have to tell somebody. I take out my phone and text Amanda.

i dont know, I write. Then I finish shading in hell.

In less than three minutes Amanda sits down next to me.

"That was quick," I say.

"I was nearby." She shows me my text on her phone. "What does this mean?"

"That I don't belong here. I'm sorry."

She looks at the text again, and back at me. "I don't get it."

"That's the thing, neither do I. I don't know what I believe. I don't know if I'm going to hell or heaven or whether Jesus was a man or not."

"What?"

"I don't know. Devin said it."

"Oh, the red-haired kid? There's something kind of off about him."

"Well, there's something off about me, too."

Amanda furrows her brow. "Are you saying you have doubts?"

"Yes! A lot of doubts."

"So do I, Phillip."

I look at her funny. She might as well have said the sky is orange.

"No, you don't," I say.

She laughs. "Yes, I do."

"About what?"

"About a lot of things. Doubt is a huge part of faith."

"What? That doesn't make sense."

"It doesn't sound like it makes sense. But think about it. Don't you understand something better if you read about it and think about it and question it and listen to different opinions on it?"

"Not always."

"No, not always, but it's better than just listening to one person, whether it's somebody else or yourself, and deciding that they know everything and you'll believe whatever they tell you. That's just lazy and ignorant."

"But Jesus is one person."

"Jesus is one person. And Matthew is one person. And Mark. And Luke. And John. And Paul. And Solomon. And Moses. I'm not saying they're the same as Jesus, but obviously God wants us to listen to many voices to understand Him. He wants us to ask questions."

I think about what Devin said, what Ferret said. What Rebekah said to me, forever ago, about the end of the world. "But what if you get different answers? How do you know what the real one is?"

"Sometimes you'll know. A lot of the time you probably won't. And you have to live with that. It's called humility, Phillip."

Humility. Doubt.

It's like I've never heard these words before.

"Why didn't anybody tell me this?" I say.

"People don't like to admit when they don't know something. So they pretend they do."

"I know that."

Damn, do I know that.

"I guarantee you," she says, "that nobody in our group, nobody at the Summit, knows exactly what God wants."

"Is it true you have to get baptized to go to heaven?"

"Some people think so. I don't. Did Devin tell you that?"

"Yeah."

"Well, Devin isn't God's representative on earth. Probably."

I grin and page through my Bible. "How are you so wise?"

She laughs. "I'm not. In fact, you probably shouldn't listen to me."

"I think I will anyway."

For a while we watch people go by. I tap out a slow beat on the folded-up drawing of hell in my pocket. The air smells a little sweet—but I think that's just how air smells when you pay attention.

I feel so *calm*. It's weird.

"When I went on that refreshments run with you and Rebekah," I say, "why were you interrogating me?"

"To see if you were a good guy. Good enough for her."

"And?"

Amanda bites her lip. "You were."

"Past tense?"

"Still are."

I let out a long breath. "Does Rebekah hate me?"

"Honestly, she and I haven't talked much about what happened. But she doesn't hate you."

"I wouldn't blame her."

"Don't be so hard on yourself, Phillip." Amanda thumps the back of my head and stands up. "I'm going to talk to people about Jesus's love and all that crap. You want to come? We'd make a good team."

"That's okay. I've already talked to three people in-depth."

"You're *ahead* of me?"

"The mentee becomes the mentor?"

"Watch it," she says. And then she goes to save somebody else.

FIFTY-SIX

When we get back to the hotel, it's officially lunchtime, and everybody heads down the hall to the Piedmont Dining Room. I hang back to make sure Devin is going with them, and then I take the elevator up. In the mirrored walls, the six of me smile.

I need to read Ferret's note while I still feel invincible.

The room is cool and quiet. I slip the envelope out of my bag, sit on the edge of the bed, and rip it open so quickly that I tear the paper. I hold the loose corner up to the rest of it and read:

> Phillip,
>
> I forgive you, and I hope you forgive me. Mine was the graver error.
> I have tried to atone for my mistakes by helping you get to the Summit. As I told you, I know some of the folks involved with the organization.

Furthermore, Pastor Tim was gracious in listening to my appeals on your behalf. Amanda should be a much more helpful mentor than I have been.

Remember: You're not a faker. You're the real deal. This has the potential to be an eye-opening experience for you, so let your eyes be opened.

Sincerely,
Randall T. Farragut

Wow, I suck.

Did I actually convince myself that being gay is wrong? Did I really *accuse* Ferret of being gay and then act like I was trying to *help* him?

Yes, I did. And seeing his name written out like that, I realize what he must have been called all through childhood. It actually makes "Ferret" seem kind of nice.

I thought I had this perfect, God-endorsed answer to his situation, when really I was just being a total dick.

And he turned around and not only forgave me but helped me. *Wow*, I suck.

I put the pieces of the note down and rub my forehead.

I have some things I need to take care of.

I pick up my phone and find his name. I hesitate to press call, but he's probably in class right now anyway, so maybe I can just leave a message.

It rings. And rings.

"Hey," Asher says.

"Oh, hey."

A short pause.

"Sorry for punching you," I say.

A longer pause.

"Good," he says.

A medium pause.

"Sorry for being a shitty friend," he says.

"I was kind of shitty too."

"Yeah, you were."

"Shut up, DJ Brown Star."

"You know that was good."

"Yeah. But I knew you when you were just DJ A-Hole. I *made* you."

And just like that, we're back. He says he's going to sixth period but he can be a little late. I try to tell him what happened here today, but it's too confusing and I'd rather save the stories for when we hang out.

Then Rebekah comes up.

"I was going to play 'Let's Stay Together' and dedicate it to you guys," he says.

"I don't know that song."

"What? Al *Green*, son."

"Whatever. Did you, uh, give her that Bible back?"

"Yeah."

What he doesn't say says everything. She must have been furious.

"Damn," I say.

"Well," he says, "you never know."

We make plans for the weekend. I stop him before we hang up.

"I'm glad we're, you know, friends again."

"Yeah. Me too."

We hang up. I exhale. I take one more look at the city.

And I start to pack my things.

I told Amanda: I'll get a job and repay the church for the fee. Or I'll be Ferret's manservant for a month. Two months. I don't care.

It's time for me to leave the Summit. I didn't find what I came for.

I found something better.

No answers. But a million questions. Scary, big, small, stupid, impolite, humble, absolutely vital questions.

Starting with one.

"Dad," I say when he picks up, "when you get off work, can you come get me?"

FIFTY-SEVEN

That night I step out of the car into a pool of light from the streetlamp.

"Good luck," Dad says, reaching over and holding his hand up for a high five. I have to laugh—he looks so awkward.

"Thanks." I slap him five.

We still have a lot to talk about, but for now we're good.

I shut the door, and he drives away. I take my phone out, walk over to Rebekah's fortress of a mailbox, and call her.

"Phillip," she says.

She still has my name in her phone.

"Hey," I say. "What's up?"

"You're leaning against my mailbox. At eight thirty on a Friday night. When you're supposed to be somewhere else, pretty far away."

"Oh. Yeah, I am."

"You know that's kind of stalker-y, right?"

"My dad said it was romantic." I look up, trying to find her window.

"Top right," she says. And I see her—or her eye and nose and maybe ear—as she peeks through the slats of her shades. "Your dad is a freak."

"That's where I get it from."

She doesn't laugh. "So, what's this about?"

"It's about me being an idiot. And wanting to talk to you, if you're not too creeped out."

"We're talking right now."

"Yeah, but."

Her sigh is like a gust of wind. "Hold on."

Her eye disappears, and the light in her room goes out. A minute later the door in the garage opens and I see the outline of her in the dark before she closes it. She stands at the edge of her garage, looking like she might decide to go right back inside. Then she sticks her hands in the pockets of her sweatpants and idles down toward me, her flip-flops smacking on the driveway.

She stops about ten feet away.

"First of all," she says, "don't apologize. I'm tired of the sorries. From me and from you."

"I don't know what we're going to talk about, then."

She crosses her arms.

"Sorry," I say. "I mean, not sorry. I can do that."

"You sure?"

"Yes."

And then here we are in silence again, figuring out what to do with it.

"Do you want to walk?" I say, nodding toward the street. "We can just walk around the cul-de-sac."

Rebekah looks at her house and then looks at the cul-de-sac, like she's contemplating the relationship between the two of them for the first time.

"Yeah, okay," she says. "Let's walk."

So we cross to the other side of the street and walk. The neighborhood is so quiet, I can hear the echoes of our steps from the surrounding houses.

"You're not supposed to be here," she says.

"Yeah. I didn't leave just to come here, though."

She looks really skeptical.

"I swear," I say. "I had this . . . revelation."

"I thought it was revela*tions*."

"Whoa. Old-school."

She smiles, and I die.

"I'm being serious, though," I say.

"What was your revelation?"

I kick a pebble, and it skitters across the asphalt. "That I don't know."

"You don't know what?"

"I don't know what I believe."

Rebekah scrunches up her forehead. "At all?"

I stop. The streetlamp shrinks our shadows into stumpy versions of us.

"All I used to think about was the end of the world," I say. "But then you just, like, *appeared*. And you were so smart and you had these beliefs and you seemed so sure about them. And I wanted that too. And I thought you wanted me to want that.

"And then I thought I *had* it. That night when you sang, I felt like I understood what it was about. And we started going out and it was awesome. But after that it didn't feel the same, so I thought if I went to CORE enough or read enough of the Bible or hung out with Ferret enough or went to the Summit with you, then I'd believe again. I'd impress you again."

I did say I wasn't good enough. I said it so many times.

"I knew that," she says. "The last part, anyway."

"I know."

"But you're saying you're confused about God? That's normal, Phillip."

"I just figured that out today."

She makes this face like a rabbit chewing. "Come on," she says, and we start walking again. "I'm not going to apologize, because I said I wasn't going to. But I could have helped you more."

"You said you wanted me to find my own way."

"I did, but there was something else."

"What?"

"Church has always been my thing. Sometimes I feel like it's been my whole life. So when you started coming to youth group and then Sunday services and then CORE and all that, it was like *my* thing was suddenly *our* thing. And then when Ferret came up to me and practically begged me to do service projects so I could go to the Summit—"

"He did that? When?"

"It was right around Mark's party."

Right around when she started to pull away from me.

But no. It's not his fault. That was one thing. The rest was me.

And Rebekah.

She looks down at her feet. "Anyway, I started to . . . withdraw."

"I knew that. The last part."

She smiles a little. "I never meant to make you feel unworthy. I just didn't know what I wanted. From you or from us."

"Is that why you were hanging out with Asher all the time?"

"Phillip, no. I hang out with Asher because he's my friend and we're on academic team together. And I don't regret that or think I did something wrong by hanging out with him. Maybe I should have been clearer that I didn't like him. But you're being unfair."

"You're right. I won't say I'm sorry. But. You know."

We complete the curve and head back toward her house. But she holds her arm out and stops me. "You're not giving up, right?"

"On us?"

"On God. On figuring out what you believe."

"I don't know."

"I'm not joking, Phillip."

"I'm not either. Sometimes I feel like I believe and sometimes I feel like I don't. And I don't even know which version to believe. Like, do you think people who don't believe in Jesus are going to hell?"

She starts to say something, then stops. Then starts. And stops again. Finally she says, "That's a tough one."

"I *know*. And I know I'm not supposed to understand *everything*, but I think I'm supposed to understand *some* things. I mean, gay people aren't 'abominations.' Right?"

She looks like she might stop herself again. But she says, "Right."

"But obviously some Christians think that. So how do you figure out what to believe?"

She's still for a moment. "*Who* do you believe in?" she says.

I can't say her. That's too much. The next one that comes to mind, though . . .

"Amanda," I say.

"And?"

"My dad."

"And?"

"And Asher. My brother. Ferret. God, sometimes. Or something like God."

"Okay. So now, what do you believe in?"

"Not being a dick? Forgiveness—*real* forgiveness. Helping people, especially when it's hard. Doubt. That's a big one." I swallow. "And being here. With you. Right now."

She doesn't move, barely even blinks. "When it feels like that, then you believe."

"But what do you call that?"

She shrugs. "A start? I don't know. Come on."

We walk again, side by side. A breeze bends just the tops of the trees. I want us to keep walking and talking and not talking, in a loop, forever. We could do that.

But Rebekah stops at the edge of her driveway. I look at the patch of grass I was standing on earlier, that small stretch of lawn where we met. Where Rebekah rescued me.

Now's the time.

I take out my phone. Cycle through a couple of menus.

"Rebekah," I say. "If I could sing, I'd sing this."

I hit the button, and the Reverend Al Green's sweet voice pours out of the speakers, softly suggesting we stay together.

"What is this?"

"This is what Asher was going to play for us at homecoming."

She looks down, tries to hide her smile. But she can't.

"That's nice," she says.

"And these." I take a stack of uncrumpled, reflattened, folded pieces of notebook paper from my pocket. I unfold all seven of them and hold the phone over them so she can see. "I drew these when I met you. I was rusty, so they're kind of embarrassing."

"They're so wrinkled," she says.

After I ran to see Rebekah sing, I salvaged the drawings from my trash can and stored them in my closet.

"See, the oatmeal raisins are at war with the—"

"I get it."

The song ends, and the phone's light goes dim.

"These are great," she says. "Really."

And then she hands them back to me. "But they're yours."

"No, I'm giving them to you."

"I know. I'm giving them back."

The phone's light turns off.

"Why?"

Rebekah runs her hands through her hair and closes her eyes. A tear falls down her cheek.

"*You* broke up with *me*, Phillip."

I take a step toward her. "And that was really stupid of me."

"You defaced my Bible."

Another half step closer. "I know. I didn't mean it like that. I thought—"

"You thought after that you could win me back with some drawings."

I step back. "It's not just drawings."

She shakes her head. "We hurt each other too much."

"But we don't have to. It's different now. We're different now."

"Are we?" She points at the drawings. "You're still giving me things."

"I thought you liked them."

She sighs. "I still feel like you need me to fill some hole in you, Phillip. And I can't do that. Nobody can do that."

I look down at the drawings.

Fold them back up, stick them back in my pocket in a big wad. Shit.

"But I know that now," I say. "*We* know that now. So we don't have to hurt each other. We can still be together."

I take the tip of her pinkie finger and squeeze it.

"Team Weird, right?"

She squeezes back.

And lets go.

"I'm sorry," she says, and she leaves me at the bottom of her driveway.

SEPTEMBER

The two of them, seated several feet apart on the couch opposite from me and Chris, kept saying it was "nobody's fault." As if I hadn't heard that line just a few months before, when it was also bullshit.

It was Mom's fault.

It was Dad's fault.

And this time it was my fault too. I'd shattered a basement window with a can of green beans. I'd said no when she asked if I wanted to study the Bible at home with her. I'd looked away and refused to tell her I loved her.

I'd made her leave. This time for good.

FIFTY-EIGHT

Three sharp knocks on the door. I hide the shot glasses under Asher's bed. Asher rushes to the door. Ben keeps scrolling through Rock Band songs for us to play.

"You guys are having fun in there?" Asher's dad says.

"Dad," Asher says. "Please."

"I just want to say hello. Then I'll leave you alone for the night." Asher sighs and opens the door a crack.

"Let me come in, Asher," Mr. V says. He steps into the room and smiles wide at us. Asher never told him what happened when I came over here that Sunday, just that we had an argument over a girl. I don't think I could bear the look on Mr. V's face if he ever found out what really happened.

"What are you boys up to?" he says.

"Nothing," Asher says.

Mr. V sweeps his eyes across the room with a goofy look on his face, pretending to snoop for incriminating evidence. Like a bottle of vodka, for example.

"I see," he says. "'Nothing' sounds like fun. I'm always doing *something*."

The room is silent as Mr. V sweeps his eyes across the room a few more times. He's not trying to catch us doing anything wrong. It's more like he's memorizing the scene. *This is my son's life.*

"Dad," Asher says.

"Okay, okay," Mr. V says. "Nice to see you again, Phillip. And you, Ben. Make yourselves at home."

"Thanks," we say in stilted unison.

The door clicks shut, and Asher locks it. He shakes his head and helps us retrieve the contraband. "My dad's pretty sad sometimes."

"He's harmless," I say.

"Maybe to *you*."

"Fight, fight, fight," Ben chants under his breath.

We both look at him.

"Please?" he says. "Just until first blood."

And we crack up.

As it turns out, Ben Hasting is kind of awesome. When I came over to Asher's two weekends ago—the Saturday night after *it* happened—and he told me Ben would be hanging out too, I was pissed. I wanted to take my mind off of *it*. I wanted to take my mind off of everything. I wanted to just drink and have fun with my friend without some quiet kid awkwarding things up.

And he *is* quiet and awkward, but he's also funny. He keeps trying to get us to fight, and complaining that Asher "never gets beat up anymore." He's a weirdly good fit with the two of us, and we've hung out each weekend since *it*, drinking and having fun.

We get back to the game. I play drums poorly, Asher plays guitar mediocrely, and Ben basically owns the microphone. He comes out of what's left of his shell and hits every note with the right inflection, adding the occasional mic pump for showmanship.

Halfway into a particularly hard song, my phone vibrates on the floor. The phone flashes "Mark" as it rumbles silently over the carpet.

He and I haven't spoken since homecoming, but I know he ran into Asher at school and they reached a truce, basically. Maybe he wants to get together now that we're all on speaking terms again. It'd be kind of cool.

I pause the game. "Hold up."

"Maaaan," Asher says, looking so disappointed. Ben freezes in mid-mic-pump.

"Sorry," I say, and then I open up the phone. "Hey."

"Hey, dude," Mark says. "What's up?"

"I'm at Asher's."

"Oh, cool. What're you guys doing?" I'm pretty sure I hear Brad yell something in the background.

"Rock Band," I say. "What are you doing?"

"Just chilling. You guys drinking?"

"Yeah, a little."

"Oh, awesome. What do you guys have?"

"Uh, just some vodka."

Asher gives me a *Wtf* look.

"Hey, dude, you don't have any to spare for a dumbass who forgot to secure his weekend hookup, do you?"

Ah. So that's why he's calling me.

Still. We're friends. I want to hang out with him. We could be us again. For tonight, anyway.

"Hold on," I tell Mark, and then I hold my hand over the phone mic. "Ben, you have another one at home, right?"

"Who is that?" Asher says.

"It's Mark."

Asher's face turns to stone. "He wants our liquor."

"Well, he asked about that, but I think he wants to hang out."

"*You* want him to hang out?"

"I mean, yeah, you know."

Asher scratches his ear again. "You already told him we have it. And now he's been waiting so long, he knows that we're talking about this. So do what you want."

He shrugs. Ben just looks at the screen, all his passion drained.

If things are fun with the three of us here, wouldn't they be even more fun with Mark, too?

I want to hang out with him again. I don't want everything to be different now.

It would help me not think about *it*.

I watch the seconds on the phone conversation timer tick away. The quiet of the room runs through me. I look at Asher. I look at Ben.

No.

We're not the same. A bottle of vodka can't change that. I can't change that.

I take my hand away from the phone. "Mark," I say.

"Hey, dude. So what's the—"

"I thought we had some extra, but we don't. Sorry."

Half a second of silence. "Yeah. No problem. I was just checking."

We say we'll hang out sometime, then we hang up. I put my phone in my pocket and look up at Ben and Asher. They're ready.

"Let's do this," I say.

We rock.

FIFTY-NINE

Ferret's door is closed.

He must be even more depressed than I thought.

He hasn't been at cross-country practice since the Summit, and when I asked Amanda earlier this week if he was okay, she said he was but that I might want to visit him soon. That's all she would give me.

But I know the rest. I'm the reason this door is closed. So I should open it.

Or, at least, knock.

I raise my fist to knock.

"Mother Mary and Joseph!" he shouts inside his office. "That was incredible! Goodness gracious!"

He keeps hollering, and I keep standing there, my knuckles poised, wondering what the hell is going on.

Ferret flings the door open and starts to run out, but he sees me, yells, and catches himself on the door frame.

"Jesus Christ, Flowers!" he says, holding his hand over his heart. "You've got me taking the Lord's name in vain. What are you doing?"

I see the state of his office, and I'm speechless. Except for a few cardboard boxes on the floor, sealed with masking tape, it's empty.

"What are *you* doing?"

"I'm nailing the unnailable shot, Phillip. Did I just call you Flowers a second ago? Apologies. Old habits die hard."

"What?"

"'Old habits die hard.' It's a saying, Phillip. It means—"

"I know. I mean the shot."

He smacks himself on the forehead. "Duh. Duh duh duh. Come on in."

We step inside. It's strange.

"When I was packing up, I found that basket in a drawer somewhere. And this ball." He grabs a faded purple and orange foam ball on his desk. "I've been reliving my glory days at seminary, making all these trick shots, but there was this one over here"— he stands in the far corner behind a filing cabinet—"that I just couldn't make."

He holds the ball like he's going to try it again. But he doesn't.

"Anyway. As you saw, I got a little excited."

He puts the ball on the desk, and it rolls slowly until it hits his computer monitor.

Ferret's supposed to be depressed. And not moving out of his office.

"Why was your door closed?" I say.

He laughs. "I didn't want anybody to know I was wasting my last day shooting a tiny basketball by myself, okay?"

"Your last day? You're leaving?"

"Yeah," he says. Then he looks at me, and his eyes go wide. "You didn't hear."

I'm speechless. Again.

"You think this is your fault, don't you?" Ferret says.

I nod.

"Well," he says, squaring his shoulders, looking at me dead-on. "It is."

I want to tell him how sorry I am. But it wouldn't be enough.

He stares into my eyes, finding them again as I look away, locking on to them.

Then the corner of his mouth curls up. And he laughs a wheezy laugh.

"I got you good," he says, slapping his leg. "Hoo, boy."

I dash over and grab the ball and throw it at his chest. It bounces off and rolls under his desk. I'm laughing too. "I can't believe I fell for that."

"Shoulda been a movie star, like Momma always said." He rubs his chin. "Too handsome, though. Wouldn't be believable."

Then he sits down in his chair and I sit down in mine.

"Where are you going?" I say.

"For now, back home. Momma's pretty excited. I am too, though that may sound odd coming from a thirty-year-old man. But it'll give me time to think."

"Why are you leaving?"

He puts his feet up on the desk. His navy blue socks are ratty and linty.

"Not because of you," he says. "Not because of what happened."

"You weren't fired?"

"I might have been, but I resigned before Tim could even bring it up. And I would have deserved it if he had. I've done a lot of screwing up lately. More so than usual."

"Why?"

"I was bitter. I was lonely. I see that now." He leans all the way back in his chair, looks right up at the ceiling. "I felt thwarted. And it came out as, well, *Ferret*ness."

I cringe. "Sorry about that. It wasn't—"

"Say no more. I earned it." He sighs. "I just haven't been doing what I want to do. I've been doing what I thought I was *supposed* to do. Turns out that's, ironically, kind of an arrogant way to live. Self-destructive. Heck, just plain destructive."

"But doing what you want to do can be destructive too."

Ferret smiles. "I knew you were a smart one."

"Then how do you know what to do?"

"Asking the big questions. I like it. Though you might be asking the wrong fella." He looks down like he's looking into himself. "I think it's just about making sure what you want and what you should do are lining up." He throws his hands up. "Or maybe that's a load of horse crap. I'm not such a great spiritual trainer these days."

"You helped me."

"Well." He clears his throat. "Thanks."

I reach into my pocket and get the check, made out to Wesley Road Faith Church for six hundred dollars. The funds come from the recent sale of the Flowers family survival kit.

Ferret looks at it, then up at me. "I heard you left on Friday," he says.

"Yeah."

"Was it worth your while?"

"Yeah."

He nods. Then he rips the check in half. And quarters. And eighths. And smaller.

"Sorry. That may have been a tad melodramatic." He smiles. "Anyway, I appreciate it, and so does Wesley Road Faith Church, but you earned your time there, so don't worry about the money. The Lord provides."

I watch him scoop the scraps into the trash. "Are you sure?"

"Couldn't be surer. By the way, Bob Yoder sends his regards. And apologies for his son's behavior, if that's what—"

"That's not why I left." I smile. "I mean, it sort of was, but in a good way."

We sit across from each other in silence.

Finally he says, "I have no idea what you're talking about." He laughs. "But I'm happy for you. I truly am. Maybe you can regale me over email, but in the meantime I gotta get the heck out of Dodge. Mind helping me bring these boxes out?"

Ferret's leaving. This is so weird. In an I'm-not-sure-what kind of way.

"Okay," I say.

He rubs his hands together. Then he stops. "I should give you something."

"I don't need any more service hours."

"Very funny. No, I mean as a souvenir. A token of our . . . time together." He grabs his *Dune* and holds it out to me. "Here."

"I already have one."

He puts that back, takes his Bible. "Here."

"Again. Already have one."

He puts it back, holds his hands on his hips.

"Really," I say. "You don't have to. There's nothing—"

His eyes light up. He turns around, yanks the little basketball net from the top of his cabinet door, grabs the ball, and tosses them on his desk.

"There," he says. "I bet you don't have one of these."

"No. I don't."

He points his finger at me. "Don't ever tell nobody I never gave you nothing."

"I won't," I say.

And we get him the heck out of Dodge.

SIXTY

It's more of an absence than a place. All that remains is some empty shelves, a few stacks of books, and a bare concrete floor.

I walk to the basement window and watch the rain. I think about the families leaving church right now, huddling under umbrellas as they flee to the parking lot. Rebekah, outrunning all of them.

I look down at the windowsill. Right at the edge, partially hidden under chips of concrete, is a tiny shard of glass. I press my finger against the flat side and lift it up. It's shaped like a sail.

"Hey."

I jump.

It's Chris. Holding his soccer ball.

"Jesus," I say. I wipe the dust and glass on my pant leg.

"Sorry. I didn't know you were down here."

"No, I'm going up. You can stay." I walk past him.

"What were you doing?"

"Just . . . looking at it."

"Yeah." He flips his hair back, lets the ball drop, and traps it under his foot. Then he kicks it hard against the wall. When it comes back, he traps it perfectly.

"You're a lot better than I was," I say.

He shrugs. Kicks the ball again.

"But I sucked."

I see him smile.

He kicks the ball and traps it, kicks the ball and traps it. Then he stops and looks at me.

"I can't concentrate when you're staring at me."

"Sorry." I start to go, but I hold back. "Sorry about that thing I gave you. The pamphlet thing."

He shrugs again and passes the ball to me. I stop it with the inside of my foot.

"Do you really believe that stuff?" he says.

"I thought I did."

"But not anymore?"

"No."

I roll the ball under my foot. Back and forth.

"Do you remember when I broke that window?" I point with my chin.

He laughs. "Yeah."

"That was crazy."

He shrugs. "Everything was crazy."

"Yeah."

I kick the ball, but it glances off my toe and skitters away from Chris. He chases it and tells me I suck.

"I know. I'm really leaving this time."

I head for the door. The ball hits my heel and spins off into a corner. I turn around, and Chris grins at me.

"I'm glad we got rid of all that stuff," he says.

I look around.

"Yeah," I say.

OCTOBER, NOVEMBER, AND DECEMBER

It wasn't the end of the world.

Mom got an apartment about twenty-five minutes away, and Dad dropped us off on weekends. We'd watch movies and eat pizza on Friday night, and do soccer or whatever on Saturday, and Mom would take us home on Sunday.

Life kept going. It felt almost normal.

Then Mom finally took us to church.

Dad had dropped us off at her apartment. We'd said hi to Mom with quick hugs. Then we'd gone to our room, dropped our stuff off, and pretended to take swords off the awesome hand-drawn sword poster on the wall and fight each other with them.

We'd started to walk out of the room, when we heard the two of them still talking. That hadn't happened before. We stopped short of the door and listened.

"You should come too," Mom said.

"Thanks, but you three should go."

There was a pause. Chris and I looked at each other, wondering if they'd heard us. But Mom just said okay, and Dad said alright, and they both said goodbye.

At dinner Mom asked us if we wanted to go to church to see a Christmas concert.

"Yeah," I said.

"Okay," Chris said.

Later, as we walked to the car, we fumbled with the heavy gloves and coats Mom had made sure we wore. As we drove, the air from the heater stung my face, and Sweet 103.5 played constant Christmas music. Twenty minutes later we pulled into the parking lot of Crossroads Bible Church.

"Wow," Chris said.

The church and the trees were covered in light. Fat multicolored bulbs shone all over, crisscrossing and rising and swooping on the strings. It looked like an enormous, happy spider's web had fallen onto the church.

We got out of the car. As we walked up to the front doors of the church Mom pointed at the lights. "They're trying to catch reindeer in those nets," she said.

Chris squeaked in disbelief, and I laughed a little.

Mom smiled and rubbed the back of my coat. "I know. It's not a very good joke. I just heard one of the church ladies say it one time, and I laughed really hard."

We walked into the lobby, which was walled in shiny brown wood and smelled warm and sugary. A few different women said, "Diane!" Mom shuttled us around and introduced us, and Chris and I stood quietly or poked each other while they talked.

I felt more like his age—everything then was this new.

Mom eventually led us into the worship hall, and we sat near the back on a slick, solid wooden pew that was the same color as the wood in the lobby. Chris's feet didn't touch the floor, and he kept kicking the red tattered hymnal in the pocket in front of us, and Mom kept telling him quietly to stop.

The room wasn't full, but it was pretty close to full. The echoey sounds of conversations faded quickly as the choir walked solemnly onto the stage. Mom handed down two programs, one for each of us.

Someone was scooting toward our end, and when I looked over and saw Dad, I just said "Dad!" without even thinking about it. Chris said it too, and people around us started to look. Dad just smiled and nodded his head at them. He sat next to Mom and waved at us. We waved back.

The concert began. I wanted to sing with them during each song. When finally the choir leader told us that this one was for everybody to sing, Chris and I held our programs open with both hands and breathed carefully as if we were the ones onstage. And we belted out "Silent Night" so hard that our throats hurt.

After the concert ended, we left quickly. Mom told us to get in the car, that she had to talk to Dad. We hugged him and slowly walked over to the car and got in.

We watched them talk. Chris said he could read lips, and he made up things they were saying to each other. "Phillip smells like a butt," Mom said. "Yeah, and his face looks like a butt," Dad said.

Finally they hugged each other goodbye. Dad waved at us, and Mom came back to the car. As soon as she turned the key, the radio came on, and "Sleigh Ride" played. Mom pulled out of the space and down the lane to drive to the exit. The trees surrounding the church were cast in pale blends of color.

How could a place like that make Mom so sad? So crazy?

"Is it usually like that?" I said.

"Church? No."

"How is it different?"

She thought about that. "Well, there's usually a man who gets up and talks about God, or a story in the Bible."

"But there was a man." He had stood up at the beginning and talked about "the reason for the season," Jesus.

"I guess you're right. It wasn't that different—there was just more singing tonight than usual. It was a little more . . . celebratory."

She smiled when she said that. I realized, when I looked into her eyes, I saw her. There with us. She was back—this time for real.

When "Silent Night" came on, we all sang it again until my voice broke. Mom and Chris laughed and made fun of the honking sound that had erupted from my throat instead of the word "holy." I did it again.

The song ended, and there was a second of dead air.

"Are you and Dad getting back together?" Chris said.

Mom's smile wobbled. She didn't say anything for a few seconds. Then she looked at Chris, looked at me, and then back at the road.

"I'm sorry, guys. We're not."

I held my hands up to the heater. "That's okay," I said.

"Yeah," Chris said. "That's okay."

We listened and sang and honked all the way back.

About a month later the world finally ended.

SIXTY-ONE

Stone Mountain is huge. I had forgotten that.

"How far up are we now?" Dad breathes to Chris, who leads the way.

"Half a mile," Chris says, reading the trail sign.

"That's halfway, right?"

"Almost!" Chris yells up into the pine canopy.

The full trail is 1.3 semi-steep miles. I'm a little worried about Dad. He's breathing heavily and slumping a bit.

Maybe we should go back down. Maybe we shouldn't be here at all.

A couple of weeks ago, Amanda called me. She said she missed me and that the youth group was still going to the Christmas laser show on the nineteenth. Did I want to go?

No, I said.

Rebekah would be there, I didn't say. I've seen her, of course— a glimpse in the hallway after school, a shot of the varsity girls on the morning announcements. But I avoided her at the few remaining meets of the season, and I never went anywhere near the hall where her locker is. And I haven't drawn anything Rebekah-related—only wizards and robots and non-Rebekah-related versions of hell.

No sorceresses. No unconventionally hot androids. No me stuck eternally in the moment she walked away.

I was proud of myself. So when Amanda told me to let her know if I changed my mind, I told her I wouldn't. Sorry.

Then I did. One slow-driving afternoon three days later, I realized Amanda had given me the perfect opportunity to make it up to Dad for being such a punk-ass of a son. Me and Dad and Chris could do what we used to do as a family in the summer: walk up the mountain, go to the touristy town stuff, and watch the laser show and the fireworks. After, I could drop by and see Amanda.

And if that meant I had to be in close vicinity to Rebekah, maybe even make eye contact or hear her voice, I could handle it.

So I told Amanda I'd be there. It bothered me a little that she didn't seem surprised. It still kind of does.

I walk up beside Dad. "We can turn around," I say quietly.

"What?" he says. "No, no." His words rise on three puffs of breath.

We keep following the bright yellow line painted on the rock. Eventually the trail becomes bumpier and the granite becomes slicker. Dad doesn't speak. Chris plunges ahead, sometimes so far that we can't see him. Then he waits for us, impatiently.

Near the mile marker the path grows steeper, but there are handrails. I was thinking Dad would immediately grab them, but he hasn't yet. He walks right beside them, rubbing his hands together to keep them warm while his forehead shines with sweat. Chris and I exchange looks, and he stays closer.

We should stop.

I start to say so, but then I hear something slip off the rock and then a slap as Dad's hands hit the granite. "Ah!" he yells.

Chris and I stop and kneel down. People nearby stop too.

Dad closes his eyes and curses quietly. He rubs his knee. "Dammit," he says.

"Dad, are you okay?" I say.

"No, I'm not okay. I hit my damn knee." He cradles his leg just beneath his kneecap, and he rocks back and forth. A woman pulls out her cell phone and offers to help, but he stops rocking and waves her away. He looks at us and grimaces. "You two looked like you needed a break anyway."

We sit and wait. Chris and I look at each other, not really knowing what to do. Why didn't Dad just stop for a second? Does this mean we have to leave early? Why does he always have to be so damn stubborn?

I pick up a corner of spongy moss that grows on the rock, and then press it back down with my finger. I do it again, and again, and again.

Get up, Dad.

Finally, he stands and walks around, and I feel this wave of relief.

But it's followed by a stomachful of guilt. Yes, I'm relieved that Dad's okay. But I'm more relieved that we don't have to go home.

Because I want to see Rebekah.

I told myself this trip was for Dad and Chris and me. But it was mostly for me.

So when Dad announces he's ready to "get this over with," I spring to my feet. We start climbing again, and I walk behind Dad for a few steps before he glances back and gives me a *Don't insult me* look. So I walk up ahead, try to get away from the guilt.

Finally we reach the bald top of the mountain. Sheets of wind push against us and whip around our faces. Hands in our jacket pockets, we walk in a huddle toward the lookout. It's a clear view for miles, and even if a lot of it is neighborhoods and strip malls and highways, most of it is sky.

We stand silently for a while, as other families and couples and groups of kids linger and shuffle and watch around us. Someone behind us calls Chris's name. It's a friend from school, and Chris dips away.

Dad turns to me, raising his voice over the wind. "I'm glad you made us come out here. Even if I did almost have to go to the hospital."

I almost sigh with guilt. He has no idea.

Dad steps closer. "I remember the last time we came here."

So do I, of course. It was that April, when Mom came back and we played the car game and got ice cream and walked up here and stood together and I felt like we all knew we would be okay.

I let the moment pass.

But Dad pulls it back. "Do you remember? With the—"

"Yeah."

Obviously I'm not the only one who had another reason for being here today. I start to move away, acting like I'm getting a different view.

"Say something," Dad says.

I stop. "Say something?"

"You know what I mean, Phillip. Say something. Anything."

"Dad, no, I'm not doing this."

"I thought you were ready to talk about her."

"I don't need to."

He grabs my shoulder. "Do you miss your mother?"

"What?"

"Do you miss—"

"*Yes.*"

Okay, now I'm *really* not doing this. What a fucked-up question. I turn away from him again.

"I'm not apologizing," Dad says, following me.

I freeze.

"I know you're angry at me for asking that," he says, "but I'm not sorry. I needed you to say something."

I turn around. "Why?"

"Because we can't keep pretending that not talking about it means we've gotten over it."

"I'm sorry if you haven't, but I have."

He smiles like it's painful. "I know when you're lying. And even if I didn't, I still wouldn't believe what you just said. You're telling me that all your books had nothing to do with Mom? Your church activities? Putting the gear in the basement up for sale?"

The wind kicks up and scours my eyes. I hold my hand up to block it out, along with Dad.

"You keep doing this," I say. "Why can't you leave it alone?"

Dad holds my arm. "Because I need your help."

"Why?"

He laughs, wipes a tear from his eye. "Because I'm an old man

390

who thinks he can climb a mountain. Because I'm trying to be a good dad, but sometimes I feel like I have no clue what I'm doing. Case in point, I wanted to sell that stuff in the basement because I thought it would help us move on, but I never said that, did I? I'm supposed to be an example for you boys, but all I did was reinforce our silence. That's why I've been trying to get you to talk about her. Even though I know you miss her, I wanted to hear you say it. Because I miss her too."

He looks down at the ground and shakes his head.

"I lost my wife. *Twice.*"

"It wasn't your fault," I say.

"Please don't blame it on her—"

"I'm not."

I look behind us, searching for Chris. He's still with his friend.

"It was my fault too," I say.

"Phillip—"

"I made her leave."

"It's not—"

"If I hadn't made her leave, she would've never moved out and she wouldn't have been driving there and she wouldn't have died."

"No," Dad says, holding both of my shoulders. Squeezing them.

"It's true."

"None of it's true. None of what you just said is true."

"I broke the window. I didn't want to read the Bible with her. I didn't tell her I loved her. It's my fault."

Dad places his hands on my head and holds me against his chest. I close my eyes. I can hear his heartbeat.

Tears build behind my eyelids, and I blink them out.

"Your mother was depressed, Phillip," Dad says. "Deeply depressed. That's why she moved out—or one of the reasons, anyway. Don't you remember how happy she was once she got her own place?"

I lift my head up, wipe away the tears. "Yeah."

"It wasn't because she was happy to leave you guys with me. She missed you terribly, couldn't wait to see you on the weekends."

"But why was she depressed?"

"It wasn't because you broke a window or didn't read the Bible with her. Or even because you didn't tell her you loved her. I wish I'd known you thought that all these years."

He pinches the bridge of his nose. "The truth is I don't know why. She didn't know why. I mean, I fucked up in a major way. But there was more to it than that. At the time all she knew was that moving out was the right thing for her and for us. And it was going as well as it could have until . . ." He coughs into his fist. "Until the accident happened. Which was pure blind chance and not anybody's fault."

"Except the other guy's," I say.

"Well, yes. Right."

The wind has dried my tear tracks. Dad and I stand silently, looking around, our breaths colliding now and then.

"I just hope I'm not a total failure as a father," Dad says.

Sometimes I like Dad. Sometimes I don't like Dad.

But I guess I always basically love him.

"Not a total failure." I try to keep a straight face, but I can't.

He slaps me on the back. "You're one of my few success stories."

"That's pretty sad."

"It's not," he says, but not quite to me. He looks around. "Where's my other one?"

"There he is."

We scream across the mountaintop and embarrass the hell out of Chris.

SIXTY-TWO

My mom died on January 12. She was working from her new apartment, but she had gone out for lunch. On the highway some guy was driving too fast and hit her. He survived. She died instantly, so there wasn't any pain.

I miss her.

SIXTY-THREE

"To the top!" Dad says. He ambles forth, leading us up the much-less-steep slope of the Great Lawn. It rises away from the foot of the mountain, where the show is projected, and Dad wants us to watch from there so we'll be ahead of the postshow rush to the parking lot.

I hang back. There isn't much daylight left, and people are rapidly claiming vacant spots on the lawn with their blankets. All along the half-mile stretch, neon whisks shake and neon snakes writhe. The crowd's breath is like a fog.

Somewhere in there is the youth group.

But I won't be joining them.

I get out my phone and call Amanda.

"I was wondering where you were," she says. "You're here now?"

"I am, yeah. But."

"But?"

"I'm here with my family, actually. So I kind of have to watch it with them."

"Can you come and say hi?"

Dad dodges a family running downhill, arms full of pretzels and hot chocolate. Chris and I whip to the side, following him like ducklings.

"Phillip?"

"Yeah, sorry. I think we're trying to find a spot right now. It may take a while, so—"

"Rebekah's not with us."

I stop. A woman slips by me and gives me a grumbly face. I catch up with Chris.

"If that's what you were worried about," Amanda says.

"Well. Sort of."

"You can tell me the truth, Phillip."

"I know. Or, I forgot. For a second." I look over at the crowd. "Why didn't she come?"

"She's here. But she's with her family somewhere. Her dad's here."

I stop again. "What?"

A guy speed-walks past me, mumbling, "You can't just *stop*." I apologize and keep moving.

"He's back from Indonesia," Amanda says.

"For good?"

"You should ask Rebekah."

"That'd be awkward."

"Why?"

"You know what happened."

"I do. But it's not like you can't ever speak to each other again."

"It isn't?"

Amanda's silent for a second. "It's up to you, Phillip. But am *I* ever going to see you again?"

"Yes. Definitely."

"I'll hold you to that, mentee."

"I know you will, mentor."

We say bye. As I run to catch up, my mind races.

Rebekah's dad is back. When did that happen? *How* did that happen?

"Over here," Dad calls back to us. He slings our duffel bag onto a small rectangle of grass on the edge of the lawn. We lay the old gray blanket on the ground and sit down.

From here we can see the whole crowd. Knowing she's out there is torture. I imagine her laughing at her dad's jokes, having forgiven everything. I imagine her sitting there with her arms crossed, having forgiven nothing.

I imagine going over there, spitting on the ground in front of him, and walking away.

Ugh.

This isn't helping. We need to leave soon so I can go back to pretending she doesn't exist.

I feel my phone vibrate in my pocket. I take it out.

No way.

It's her. Why is she calling me?

What should I do?

What do I want to do?

Dammit.

"Hey," I say, turning away from Dad and Chris to answer it.

"Amanda told me you were here," she says.

It's her voice. It sounds exactly the same. I know how to do this. I think.

"Amanda told me *you* were here," I say.

"She told me she told you."

"She didn't tell me she told you."

"Well."

"Yeah."

Neither of us knows what to say after that.

I wait for her to try first.

Eventually she says, "Where are you?"

"Way up at the top."

"Oh, so are we." A beat passes. "Do you mind meeting up for a second? I have something for you."

Please. No.

Why do you have to have something for me?

"Okay," I say. "Where?"

"See that big rock by the building?"

We agree to meet there. I stand up and tell Dad and Chris that I'll be right back.

"It's starting pretty soon," Dad says.

"Just a second."

And I drag myself to go meet Rebekah.

Earlier, as Dad and Chris and I rode the cable car down the side of the mountain, and the enormity of the park stretched out on each side, I had this feeling of total clarity. I knew I wasn't over Mom's death. But I was over not talking about Mom's death. I was over not talking about her life.

I knew I was done looking for answers as a way to not feel

worry. I was done hoping for a supercollider accident to obliterate all the pain in the universe.

And I knew in that instant, in a way I hadn't when I was deliberately not drawing unconventionally hot androids, that Rebekah and I were through. And trying to see her was a terrible idea. And that I just wanted to spend the rest of the night watching lasers crash into a mountain with my dad and brother.

I knew that. I thought I knew that.

But now I'm standing next to this ridiculous rock, rising up like the mountain's small toe wiggling in the air, waiting for Rebekah.

So, clearly, I was wrong. As always.

This isn't over.

Yet.

She walks over from a dark path. When she comes into the light, she waves, sheepishly. It looks strange on her.

"Hi," Rebekah says. In her dark blue track jacket she is excruciatingly cute. "Sorry if this is uncomfortable."

"What can you do?" I say, shrugging. It doesn't sound like something I've ever said or would say.

"I just wanted to give you this."

The Bible. She must have been holding it this whole time, but it seems like she conjured it from nothing. In the bottom left-hand corner are her and her father's neatly drawn initials crossed out, my scrawled initials crossed out, and, above those, two more letters, carved carefully.

TW.

"Team Weird?" I say.

She smiles, and looks at me like I should know what that means.

At one point I did. But now.

No.

"I can't . . . I don't think we should get back together, if that's what you—"

"No, that's not—I'm sorry." She hangs her head. "I'm not as good at giving things as you are."

"I'm not very good at it either, so you must suck."

"Obviously."

I can feel some of the tension drain away.

"So . . . what *did* you mean?" I say.

"I'm not sure. I just thought that we could still be Team Weird in a different way. If you want."

I have no idea what to say, and I don't want to say anything without thinking about it. I look away. The sky is mostly dark now. I follow the curve of the mountain, the way the gray rock folds into the night.

I turn back to her.

"Your dad's here?"

"Yeah. I wrote him a letter, and he called us a week later. And now he's back."

"For good?"

"For a while, at least."

"How's it going so far?"

"My parents are getting along really well."

"What about you?"

She pauses. "It's been tough. We've been arguing almost every day."

I want to reach out and take her hand.

"I'm sorry," I say.

"It's good, actually," she says, her voice suddenly a little louder.

"We have a lot to talk about. I have things I need to say." She smiles at me. "You helped me with that."

"No, I didn't."

"You did."

We let the silence settle between us.

We've always been good at that.

"Can I see it?" I say. "The Bible?"

Her eyes brighten, and she hands it to me. I take it, weigh it in my hands. It feels lighter than I remembered.

"You want to be friends?" I say, a little skeptically.

"I think we can try. If you want to."

Does it matter if I want to? People who break up don't stay friends. They break up for a reason. *We* broke up for a reason. For a lot of reasons, which won't just go away because we change what these words mean.

Maybe she knows that. Maybe she's still pitying me.

I look into her eyes.

She's not.

That makes this so much harder.

I rub my thumb across all our initials.

Team Weird doesn't mean something different just because we say it does.

It already does.

I think of her and me and Amanda, who decided I was good enough. I think of her and me and Asher, who tried to keep us together. I think of her and me and our families, who don't know each other and probably never will but are both here tonight.

Team Weird is bigger than us, bigger than our reasons.

So we might as well be bigger too.

Plus, we might actually have some classes together next semester.

"I want to," I say, cracking a smile. "But are you still weird?"

"Obviously, or I wouldn't be doing this right now, would I?"

And we both start laughing way too hard.

"LADIES AND GENTLEMEN, WELCOME TO STONE MOUNTAIN PARK."

The prerecorded male voice booms right behind us, and we cover our ears and laugh even harder. He runs down the rules and suggestions for enjoyment.

"I guess we should get back!" I yell.

"I guess so!"

I hand the Bible to her. "I think you should keep this! For now!"

She takes it, nods. "You can have it back whenever!"

I put my hand in. "Team Weird!"

She puts her hand in. "Team Weird!"

We hold our hands there, not too long.

"Break!" we say.

And let go.

In that moment it seems possible. And as I walk back toward Dad and Chris, I feel it again—calm. Like at the Summit.

But why? Why, when my clarity dissolves so easily? Why, when I just agreed to be friends with the girl who broke my heart? Why, when what I thought was definitely over, is now—

I think that's it.

Because it's *not* over.

Because things don't just end.

They change.

They change brutally and quietly. Unexpectedly and predictably. Slowly and with terrifying speed.

And if you're lucky enough to be alive, you change with them.

Or you don't.

I don't know if that's an answer. But I believe it.

Chris sees me searching in the dark and waves me over with Dad's cell phone. I step carefully between other people's blankets and drop down on ours and let out a long breath.

"Everything okay?" Dad says, patting me on the back.

"Yeah. Everything's okay."

"That the girl?"

The girl.

"Yeah, it is," I say.

"Maybe you can tell me about her sometime."

I scoot closer to Dad and Chris.

"It might take a while," I say.

Then I hug my knees and wait.

And watch.

And keep watching.

And finally a high, cheerful note blasts from the speakers.

And I see it—the first bright, shimmering green beam.

I think I do.

A tiny fraction of a second later, lasers crash into the face of the mountain.

And the sky seems to pulse with light.

ACKNOWLEDGMENTS

I would like to acknowledge the following:

That my New School MFA classmates—Maude Bond, Amalia Ellison, Morgan Matson, Zach Miller, and Lisa Preziosi—taught me a hell of a lot about writing, and I think fondly on our times together. Holla.

That my New School MFA instructors were crucial in the development of this book and my development as a writer. Tor Seidler's praise for an early version of this story encouraged me to continue it; Sarah Weeks had faith in me when I was sorely lacking it; and David Levithan, through his writing, teaching, and friendship, introduced me to the world of YA literature.

That long before I began this novel, I had exceptional English and creative writing teachers who gave me invaluable guidance and instilled in me their love of language. Thank you to Cindy

Westaway, Renee Covin, Earlene King, Jolinda Collins, Philip Lee Williams, and Molly Moran.

That Kate McKean is a kick-ass agent, which is to say she is an insightful reader, a fervent supporter, a dependable adviser, a tough negotiator, and a Southerner.

That I am tremendously fortunate to have an editor as enthusiastic, diligent, savvy, patient, perspicacious, and fun to work with as Anica Rissi. Thank you—and the whole Simon Pulse team—for seeing the potential in this story, and for your hard work in turning it into an actual (and quite attractive) book.

That my good friends Adam, Drew, Dusty, Justin, Jonathan, Katie, Kevin, and Lindsay are probably deserving of some sort of mention, even though they never once offered to help me write this thing. A-holes.

That my girlfriend, Meredith, is beautiful and awesome. Thank you for comforting me when things with the book weren't going well, celebrating with me when they were, and generally enduring having a writer for a boyfriend. I love you.

That, more than anyone, my parents made this book possible. That their love is the binding and the glue; their wisdom the paper and ink. That I am so grateful for the life they have given me. Thank you.